ALLWORLD ONLINE: PRIDE & PREJUDICE

BOOK ONE

LINDSEY SPARKS WRITING AS LINDSEY FAIRLEIGH

RUBUS PRESS

Editing by Fresh as a Daisy Editing
www.freshasadaisyediting.com

Cover by We Got You Covered
www.wegotyoucoveredbookdesign.com

9781949485189

ACKNOWLEDGMENTS

Thank you so much to my Patreon Patrons, who support my work on a monthly basis:

Teri Lindley
Allison Mayer
Aisling Ó Béara
Fred Oelrich
Carlotta Woolcock
Olivia Rodriguez
Stephanie Oaks

ALLWORLD ONLINE

AO: Pride & Prejudice

AO: The Wonderful Wizard of Oz

Vertigo

THE ENDING SERIES

The Ending Beginnings: Omnibus Edition

After The Ending

Into The Fire

Out Of The Ashes

Before The Dawn

World Before

THE ENDING LEGACY

World After

For more information on Lindsey and her books:

www.authorlindseysparks.com

Join Lindsey's mailing list to stay up to date on releases

AND to get a FREE copy of *Sacrifice of the Sinners*.

www.authorlindseysparks.com/sacrifice

To read Lindsey's books as she writes them, check her out on Patreon:

https://www.patreon.com/lindseysparks

March 6, 2026

I'm recording this one month before the launch of the Austentopia beta test. (pause)

(heavy sigh) There's a ghost in the machine. (pause) I don't know how else to describe it. It's as though the AI game controller in charge of the Pride *and* Prejudice *world is confused, altering elements of the game beyond the scope of its directives. Elements that should be static, unchangeable. Characters, setting, story— it's all being modified and revised. It doesn't make any sense. (sigh) I hesitate to use the "G" word, but it really does seem as though the AI is glitching.*

Yes, all alpha test simulations featuring an entirely NPC cast have concluded without issue and with expected results.

However, as we all know, these alpha tests are not always accurate predictors of how the game will react to and interact with live human subjects during the beta testing phase. Players are unpredictable, and they breed chaos. I do not feel as though the current rendition of this game controller will react well to player chaos.

For that reason, I'm going to recommend to the board that we postpone the beta test for all worlds within the Austentopia universe of games until my team can go through the Pride and Prejudice *game controller's code and directives with a fine-toothed comb. All we need is a few more months to rebuild the game controller and to ensure the safety of all who enter the game. I just hope the board will listen . . .*

[1]

I sat on the porch swing at my parents' house—*my* house, again, now that I had joined the growing ranks of adult children moving home—nursing a beer as I lazily pushed myself back and forth with one bare foot. If you had asked me ten years ago where I thought I would be on my thirtieth birthday, I wouldn't have said *laid off*. I wouldn't have said *evicted*. And I definitely wouldn't have said *moving back into my parents' house*.

But here I was, all the same.

At the screech of the screen door opening, I looked to my right. My tall, lanky brother, Charlie, stepped onto the porch, a wine glass filled with a generous portion of red wine in one hand, a brown beer bottle in the other.

"Want some company?" Charlie asked, pausing beside the porch swing to hold the wineglass out for me to take. "I come bearing gifts . . ."

I flashed him a weak smile and leaned forward, setting my nearly empty bottle of beer on the floor before reaching for the wineglass. I wasn't sure why I'd gone for the beer, anyway; wine was more my style.

Charlie gave me a gentle noogie. "Happy birthday, Squirt."

I swatted his hand away from my head and snorted derisively, leaning back in the porch swing once more. "Thanks, Chuckles."

Wincing, Charlie sat down beside me. "Always with the *Chuckles . . .*"

I laughed softly, grinning at him. "I could switch to *Chucky,* like Grandma. Would you prefer that?"

Charlie groaned, letting his blond head fall back. "Oh, dear God, no."

I laughed again. Charlie was doing his big brother duty and lifting me up when I was down. He was, quite possibly, my favorite human being in the whole world. He'd always been there to help me up when I stumbled and fell . . . even if he'd been the one to push me down in the first place. *Nobody picks on my kid sister but me.* That was his motto, all day, every day.

As my spark of good humor faded, I took a sip of wine.

Charlie lifted his head and raised his beer to his lips, tilting the bottle back for a long swig. He lowered the bottle, and I could sense his gaze on the side of my face. "You know, Olive, when I moved back here, I felt like the punchline of a joke. A thirty-one-year-old gamer moving into his parents' basement."

I glanced at Charlie sidelong, my heart sinking. Looked like fun time was over and a serious heart-to-heart was coming. "If this is your attempt at making me feel better, it seriously sucks," I said. "Just FYI."

Charlie chuckled. He took another swig of beer, then raised his hand to forestall any further commentary from me. "Just hear me out," he said. "I have a point, I promise."

I sent a pointed look his way, then shrugged. I brought my free hand up to my lips and mimed zipping them from one corner to the other, then turned an imaginary key to lock my mouth shut and chucked it into the rhododendron bush on the other side of the porch railing.

"Thanks," Charlie said, his tone bone dry. "You know, I

always felt like I was supposed to be setting an example for you and the others. Like I had to prove it's possible to make it out there, whatever the stats are about college grads not making it on their own. I was going to do it. To prove the stats wrong. To be independent. Strong. Capable."

I sipped my wine, dreading where this was going. I hated talking about the *dark times*. But then, I knew Charlie hated it even more. So I sat quietly, attentively, and listened to the wisdom he was offering.

Charlie laughed under his breath. "And I did it. I worked damn hard to be that strong, capable, independent millennial I thought I needed to be." Charlie glanced at me, his clear blue eyes meeting mine. "And I hated my life," he admitted. "I never had time to see my friends or to date or to even come to family dinners." He took a deep breath and shook his head. "The only people I had time for were people I didn't even like. People I had nothing in common with beyond the fact that we worked in the same office and shared a mutual apathy for the life we had worked so hard for."

I watched Charlie, my eyes stinging with tears, and I clenched my jaw in an attempt to keep my chin from trembling.

"I broke, Olive," Charlie said, his gaze dropping to the porch. "That night I called you . . ." He laughed under his breath and took another swig of beer. "I never told you this, but I'd just gotten home after sitting in traffic for two hours—two God-damned hours. And I didn't care. The traffic didn't bother me anymore," he said, "because I didn't have anything to come home to." He was quiet for a moment, but it was clear he had more to say.

I sat there beside him, studying his profile, my heart breaking for him anew even though he was talking about something that happened years ago.

"As I passed the accident causing the traffic," he finally said. "An awful accident—multiple fatalities—I remember thinking that if I was in an accident like that, if I died just like that . . ." Charlie snapped his fingers. "It would be okay."

My nostrils flared, my chin trembling despite my best efforts. I blinked, and a tear slipped free over the brim of my eyelid.

Charlie looked at me. "I wouldn't have minded dying because I didn't have anything to look forward to."

I brought my hand up to my mouth, stunned by the revelation. I had known Charlie was in a dark place, but I hadn't known it was that bad.

"I felt like I didn't have anything to live for," Charlie continued. "My future was a life I hated, surrounded by people just as miserable as me. And when I got home that evening, I got drunk to numb the thoughts, and then I called you." He reached for my knee, giving it a squeeze. "And you came over and you made me eat Top Ramen and you sat with me until I sobered up. The next day, I quit my job. A week later, I moved back here where I was surrounded by reminders of why my life mattered. Where I was happy for the first time in years."

The screen door burst open, making me jump. Wine splashed onto the back of my hand and dripped onto my jeans as Sam and Jilly ran out, the twin teen girls giggling as they raced toward a self-driving cab pulling up to the curb in front of the house. Charlie, me, and Simon—born in that order—were what my family called "round one," while Sam and Jilly came later when our parents decided they wanted one more baby. They got a twofer instead, and the family wouldn't be the same without the twins' larger-than-life, cheerful presence.

"Big double date tonight," Charlie said. When I looked at him, the corner of his mouth ticked upward.

I laughed through my nose, then sniffed and wiped my hand on my already stained jeans. "Trust me, I know. They talked about it nonstop on the ride over here."

Charlie laughed. "So *that's* why they wanted to ride in the moving truck with you. Girl talk."

I raised one shoulder. "I guess," I said. "Not sure what they thought I could bring to the conversation. I haven't been on a date since—" I laughed again and shook my head. "Since I don't know when. I honestly can't remember."

"I can," Charlie said, chuckling. "It was that guy who took you to his quote-unquote *cousin's* wedding on your first date."

A belly laugh burst out of me. "Oh, my God, you're right. When he stood during the ceremony to object on account of 'the holy edict of soul mates', I wanted to die." As soon as I realized what I'd just said, I choked on my amusement and glanced at Charlie. "Sorry."

Charlie shrugged. "No worries," he said. "I know what you meant." He glanced at me sidelong. "And for the record, I didn't *want* to die. I just didn't care if I lived. There's a difference." Charlie leaned forward, resting his elbows on his knees and letting the beer bottle dangle between his thumb and fingertips.

I could sense that the light-hearted intermission was over, and it was time to return to the heavy stuff. My whole body tensed up in anticipation, and I tried to act natural as I sipped my wine.

"Listen, Olive," Charlie said, right on cue. "The whole point of that oh-so-uplifting trip down memory lane was to tell you that there are worse things than moving in with your parents as a grown-ass adult. These are hard times. Jobs are dwindling, and there's a lot of pressure on, well, everyone. Independence isn't everything. A century ago, it wasn't even a thing, not like it is today. This whole I-can-do-it-myself mentality is all just some-thing society tells us we're supposed to strive for."

Charlie turned his head to look at me. "But it's not what's in our DNA," he said, his voice impassioned. "It's not what's natural. We evolved to be social creatures. To live in large family units. To share responsibilities and depend on one another. Somehow, we've gotten lost. And look at the world now. Our beautiful, advanced, luxurious world. Look at how miserable everyone is. This is what happens when we fight what's in our blood. What's in our bones. When we fight who we really are."

I raised my hand, balling my fingers into a fist. "Preach, brother."

Charlie chuckled. "All right," he said, "maybe I got a little carried away there."

I shrugged. "I don't know," I said. "I was moved." I took a sip of wine. "I'm just wondering when you became an armchair anthropologist. Or would it be a sociologist? Or a psychologist?"

"Shut up," Charlie muttered, the corner of his mouth twitching. He winked at me, relaxing back into the porch swing. "You'd be surprised what you can learn in *Allworld Online*. I *may* have been spending some time in *Origin* lately."

I raised my eyebrows, eyeing my brother. "Is that the Dan Brown game?"

Charlie nodded. "But it's more of a Dan Brown *experience*."

I snorted. "You make it sound like a jam band."

Charlie shrugged. "You'd like it." He leaned closer, bumping my shoulder with his. "You used to play *Uncharted* and *Tomb Raider*. It's kind of like those games, but meatier and with less shooting. Plus, it's fully immersive, so it feels like you're really there, running for your life and solving historical mysteries."

I peered at Charlie, and I couldn't help but wonder if he was using the game as a form of escapism. From everything he had told me since taking the job as a beta viewer for Rockville Soft-works—the people who sat on their couches and watched players beta test new games to help hone the streaming experience—I knew *Allworld Online* offered endless virtual experiences, and the virtual universe was ever-expanding. Charlie truly did seem happy, and way more alive than he had been since we were teens, but did life really count if it was lived in a made-up world?

"Tell me the truth, Olive," Charlie said. "Is it really so bad to be back here?"

I was quiet for a long moment, considering his question.

Finally, I shook my head. "It's not bad," I said. "It's just an adjustment. I feel this heaviness in my chest, this choking sadness, like someone died. Like I'm mourning that death."

"You *are* mourning," Charlie said. "Only it's not a person that died. It's the future you thought you'd have."

I stared up at the porch ceiling, once again fighting tears. "It's stupid, really," I said, my voice thick with emotion, "but my students were my whole life. I gave them everything. And now they're just *gone*. When the district laid me off, they didn't just take my job and my livelihood, they took my kids, too. I don't have any connection to them anymore. They can't come to visit me at their old school because I won't be there. I'm not a part of their lives anymore, and as sad as it sounds, they were the best part of mine."

A heavy silence followed my admission.

"It's not stupid," Charlie said, his words banishing the silence. "There are thousands—probably tens of thousands—of teachers spread out all across the country who feel the same, I'm sure. Who knows, maybe the school districts will start hiring again in a few years. If you just sit tight . . ."

I shook my head, a bitter laugh clawing up my throat. "Not with the virtual academies growing as fast as they are," I said. "It's a nice thought, Charlie, but I just don't see it happening."

"Well," Charlie said, "the Boomers have to retire eventually, right? Then some spots will open up."

Another bitter laugh escaped from my chest. "Boomers don't retire," I muttered. "Boomers die."

"All right, little miss sunshine," Charlie said. "Maybe it's time to consider other options. What about the virtual academies? If they're growing as fast as you say, they must be hiring—"

"No," I snapped, then flashed Charlie an apologetic smile. He was just trying to be helpful. "I mean, it's just not the same. I can't imagine there being any kind of meaningful relationship between the teacher and her students. It just seems so impersonal and—I don't know—transactional. I just—" I exhaled heavily, my shoulders drooping. "I don't know what I'm going to do. Something, obviously. I mean, I need to feel like I'm contributing in some way. I can't freeload off Mom and Dad indefinitely. My pride would die a slow death."

"Well," Charlie said, "maybe you could think about this all in a different way. Why d'you become a teacher in the first place? If teaching is no longer an option, maybe you can find something else that touches the same part of you."

I eyed him. "Way to make it sound creepy."

"That fulfills the same need," he amended.

"Honestly," I said, "that's not much better."

Charlie blew out an exasperated breath. "You're deflecting."

I sighed. "I know."

"Then answer the question," Charlie said, persistent as ever. "What drew you to teaching?"

I chewed on my lip. "I think I wanted to do something that mattered," I finally said. "To make a difference in someone's life."

I couldn't help but think back to my favorite high school teacher, Mr. Stufer. I'd always been shy, but he had gone out of his way to make me feel like my thoughts and opinions held value. He had helped me develop a sense of self-confidence that paved the way for a much happier and more fulfilling life.

Until three weeks ago, when the principal at my school called me into her office to tell me I was among the baker's dozen of teachers being laid off. English would now be taught as part of the science curriculum, along with art. Music was to be incorporated into the math curriculum. The change was district-wide, though how they were going to swing it was beyond me. High school history was being condensed to a single, year-long course Senior year that focused on civics. They'd done away with PE, too, requiring kids to keep an exercise journal instead. Because the honor system always worked so well with teens . . .

"Well," Charlie said, unaware of my wandering thoughts, "there you go. How about a school counselor or something like that? After all the changes they're making in the schools, the kids are bound to need more therapy."

"That's a whole different degree," I told him, "which would mean a second batch of student loans. And I only just finished paying off the first ones." A feat I had only managed through the state's student loan forgiveness program.

"All right," Charlie said, his not-quite-endless patience wearing thin. "How about this—why don't you spend the next year doing something just for you? Don't try to change anyone's life or *make a difference*. You know—you do you. Try to find your way back to happiness. Once you're there, you'll be in a better headspace for thinking about the future."

"But I have to work," I said. "I can't just sit around reading all day. Much as I might wish it was, reading books isn't a job."

Charlie shrugged. "So, do something else with books." He snapped his fingers, then pointed at me. "Why not work in a bookstore?"

$$[\ 2 \ ]$$

Turned out, Charlie was a genius. Physical bookstores were making a comeback despite the flourishing e-book and audio-book marketplace, and within a week, I had a job at Seattle's premier local chain bookshop.

Over the next few months, I found an easy rhythm, free of the stress and responsibilities I had been drowning under for years. I walked to work. I soaked in the smell of books and coffee all day. I walked home. Sometimes I went on dates, though those never amounted to much. Sometimes I had interviews with private schools, though those never amounted to much, either. And sometimes I caught myself smiling for no apparent reason.

Because I was happy. Not happy *about* something. Just happy.

One such happy day in mid-August, I was shelving a new shipment of paperbacks in the romance section when a title caught my eye: *Bad Boy Darcy*. Yet another Pride and Prejudice variation. Smirking, I shelved *Bad Boy Darcy* next to other books by the same author, including *Bad Boy Wentworth, Bad Boy Frankie, Bad Boy Bingley,* and *Bad Boy Knightly*.

I adored Jane Austen, but the recent trend of "sexing up" her classic tales didn't really appeal to me. In my opinion, Jane Austen's stories were perfect just as she had written them. I loved spins on her work like *Austenland* and *Lost in Austen*. Who wouldn't jump at the chance to pretend to be one of Jane's heroines for a few days, or better yet, to actually be sucked into one of her stories? But I wasn't sure how I felt about turning Jane's heroes into alpha male bad boys. It just wasn't my thing.

Curious about why these racier retellings were suddenly so popular, I pulled *Bad Boy Darcy* from the shelf and flipped to a random page, skimming from the first complete paragraph. My cheeks heated as I read, and I snapped the book shut, glancing around nervously. I started to return the book to the shelf but changed my mind, setting it on the cart instead. *Bad Boy Darcy* was coming home with me.

Maybe I had been wrong, and this was my thing. A girl deserved to have a little romance in her life, even if that romance was fictional. My brief foray into online dating hadn't been going well, but it was difficult for relationships to progress beyond the first few dates when both parties lived with their parents. And as I had quickly found out, guys my age prowling the online dating scene either lived with their parents or were married. The rare few who had achieved true independence seemed to be slaves to the job, as Charlie had been a few years ago, and they didn't have time for anything beyond a one-night stand.

A woman tapped a magenta-lacquered fingernail on the cover of *Bad Boy Darcy*. "A little light bedtime reading?" She purred, her voice music to my ears. Merina was easily my best friend, and quite possibly the most confident person I had ever met.

I glanced at her and grinned. My focus shifted past her to the oversized clock on the wall. "You get off early?" I asked, tucking a new book into its spot on the shelf below all the *Bad Boys*.

Merina nodded, her crimson lips pursing as she skimmed the

titles on the spines of the books in this section. "The teacher I was subbing for today has seventh open."

"Sweet," I said, my lack of enthusiasm for hearing about anything that had to do with teaching evident in my voice. I tended to shut down when Merina started talking about her subbing jobs. This whole "being happy" thing was easier if I pretended teaching no longer existed at all. "There's still forty minutes left in my shift," I told Merina, hoping to waylay any further mention of the details of her day at school. "Do you mind waiting?"

With a wicked grin, Merina plucked *Bad Boy Darcy* off the cart. "Not one bit," she said, winking at me before turning and sashaying away. She headed for the small seating area surrounding the in-store coffee stand.

Shaking my head and smiling to myself, I returned to shelving books. The rest of my shift passed at a slug's pace, excited anticipation slowing the passage of time. Finally, what felt like hours later, I clocked out and joined Merina at her little table.

"So," I said, pulling out the chair opposite Merina and sitting, "how is it?" I nodded to the book holding her rapt attention.

Merina glanced up from the page, then continued reading another line or two. Finally, her eyes met mine, and she started fanning herself with the book. "Mr. Darcy is a bad, *bad* boy."

I giggled. I couldn't help it. "Worth a read, then?"

"Oh yeah," Merina said, drawing the two words out for emphasis.

"Good," I said. "Because I already paid for it."

Merina shut the book, marking her place with her finger. She grinned mischievously. "Did you know they're developing a new part of Allworld Online called *Austentopia*?"

My jaw dropped, and my eyes opened wide. "What?" I

leaned forward, resting my forearms on the table. "Oh my God. No way! Tell me everything."

Merina's smile wavered. "Um . . . they're developing a new part of Allworld Online called *Austentopia*?" She shrugged. "Sorry, Liv, that's all I know. I saw a clip of Colin Firth being ambushed by a paparazzo and asked about it. It seemed to be news to him, so . . ." Again, she shrugged. "Are you done? Can we hit the road?" She smacked her lips. "Mama's thirsty."

I sat back in my chair. "Yes, please!" I told her. "I can't even tell you how badly I need this girls' night out. An evening with all my best gals, a fancy dinner, and an endless stream of wine filling my glass . . ." I laughed and shook my head. "Why are we not already in a car?"

Merina's laughter joined mine, and we quickly made our way out to the parking lot, heading for the nearest green-lit self-driving car in the lot. I pulled out my phone and opened the Ryder app to unlock the car, and we slipped into the front seats. I paused while entering the restaurant's address in the app. I could feel Merina's stare boring a hole in the side of my face.

"What?" I looked at her. "What is it?"

Merina fidgeted with the strap of her purse. Now that I was looking at her, she seemed to avoid meeting my eyes. "I got a job."

I sucked in a breath, my eyes widening. "At a school?"

"Not exactly," she said, shaking her head. "I signed on with Rockville Softworks' new virtual academy—Rockville High." She looked at me, finally, but only for the briefest moment.

I sat back in my seat and stared out the windshield. "Wow," I said. "I didn't even know Rockville was into VAs."

Merina inhaled deeply, letting the breath out in a sigh. Out of the corner of my eye, I saw her nod. "They just announced it a few weeks ago," she said. "I thought you would've heard, what with Charlie working for them and all . . ."

I waved a hand dismissively. "He's been deep in the Harry

Potter beta test." I turned toward Merina once more, my eyes locking with hers. "I thought you were going to hold out for a long-term subbing position," I said. "I didn't know you were interested in virtual teaching."

Merina shrugged, and she looked weary all of a sudden. "Honestly, Liv, I hate subbing," she confessed. "It's everything I don't like about teaching. Besides, any long-term subbing opportunities are going to get snatched up in a heartbeat. But virtual teaching is all the good and none of the bad."

I frowned. I didn't really see it that way, but I supposed everyone got into teaching for their own reasons.

"And," Merina continued, "Rockville High is going to differ from other VAs. The kids meet with their designated local teacher rep three times a week, so there's some real human interaction." She raised one shoulder. "Their rep might not be one of their actual teachers, but at least the kids aren't lost or forgotten." Her demeanor changed, excitement entering her voice. She was genuinely looking forward to the new position. "And teachers work in local teams, meeting every Tuesday and Thursday for collaborative planning and to discuss student performance."

It didn't sound all that bad. Different from the traditional teaching position, but not as isolated or cold as other virtual academies seemed.

"I think it could work for you, Liv. I think it could work really well. You should look into it." She reached for my hand, gripping it in both of hers. "They're accepting team requests. We could be the dynamic Humanities duo again . . ."

I pursed my lips, quirking my mouth to the side as I considered it.

Merina pulled my hand to her chest, jerking me closer, and hugged my forearm to her ample bosom. "Please, please, please, please, please."

I laughed, somehow managing to extract my hand without

copping a feel. "All right, Mer," I said, still laughing. "I'll look into it tomorrow." I flashed her a grin. "But first—wine."

I walked up the stairs at the front of my parents' house, my blood thrumming pleasantly with the buzz of three glasses of wine, and headed for the porch swing. With a sigh, I plopped down, reflecting on the evening's revelations.

Much to my shock, I was the only virtual academy holdout. Every teacher I knew who had lost his or her position last year had either gone back to college to switch to a more desirable educational specialty—namely, math or science—or they had signed on with a virtual academy. Some were leaning into the pajama lifestyle, choosing VAs that were entirely virtual, while a few, like Merina, had signed on with Rockville's unique program. It sounded like everyone was excited about the prospect of not having to deal with discipline or disruption issues. The virtual classroom itself handled all that, freeing teachers to focus on what we all loved: teaching.

The only problem was that after taking a break from teaching, I wasn't sure I really did love it. I was happier now than I had been in years. I made next to nothing, money-wise, working at the bookstore, but I actually had time to enjoy life. To get together with my friends. To go out on doomed dates. To watch movies and read books. To take my parents' crazy dog out on hikes. And in the grand scheme of things, what was more valuable: money or time?

But maybe virtual teaching wouldn't be as draining as being in a physical classroom. Maybe Merina was right, and it would be all the good stuff and none of the bad.

My phone buzzed in my purse, and I fished it out. The screen displayed a text message alert. It was from Merina.

Here's a link to the application. DO IT!

[3]

I sat in a packed waiting room at Rockville Softworks' sprawling Redmond campus, studying the surrounding people. The other interviewees were dressed in a surprising assortment of attire, ranging from sweats and T-shirts to traditional business casual. I'd gone for middle-of-the-road, with my fanciest dark jeans and a plum-colored silk shirt. The color tended to highlight the subtle violet tones in the blue of my irises, which I found tended to make me stand out more in people's minds. The last thing I wanted to be in an interview was forgettable.

For the umpteenth time, I glanced at the man seated in the chair beside mine, his manspreading game strong. I placed him in his mid-thirties. He was dressed in standard tough-guy fare—torn jeans, scuffed black work boots, and a worn black leather jacket. Tattoos peeked out from the neck of his T-shirt and the cuffs of his sleeves, only enhancing his strong, striking features. His dark hair was chin-length and parted down the middle, his beard short and slightly scruffy, making him look artfully unkempt. Definitely not your average teacher. Not your average *anything*.

My imagination danced with all sorts of ideas and theories

about this intriguing stranger. He had to be in the arts. Maybe music. High school, for sure. And he must have come from one of the urban school districts. The more rural and yuppy areas had policies against visible tattoos on teachers, and I couldn't imagine this guy committing to an endless wardrobe of turtlenecks. He was an enigma, and curiosity was slowly eroding my self-control.

A man in a suit emerged from the door that led back to the interview area, called out a name, and escorted a young woman in unicorn leggings through the doorway to the hall beyond.

Mr. Mysterious beside me let out a judgmental sniff. I wondered whether it was because he disapproved of the woman's attire, or because he was tired of waiting.

Sensing my opening, I cleared my throat. "There sure are a lot of us here," I said, angling my face toward him.

He glanced at me, moving only his eyes. "Uh, huh."

So, he wasn't the chatty type. Not really a shocker, I supposed. "So," I said, "what do you teach?"

"Teach?" The side-eye was strong with this one. "I don't teach," he said. "I *do*." He returned to staring ahead, his expression bored as ever.

I stiffened, shocked by the unexpected insult. *Those who can't do, teach.* That saying was the bane of my existence, and at my school—at my *old* school—it had been well known to be outlawed in my classroom.

Fuming, I snatched a magazine off the table beside my chair and opened it a little too roughly, tearing the top edge of the cover. I didn't even know what magazine it was. Something about video games. I hardly cared.

"Olivia Crawford?" a woman called from the far side of the room.

I stood, drawing the woman's attention to me, and waved my hand. I returned the magazine to the table, then turned to join her, but I only managed one step. I paused and glanced over my shoulder at Rude Guy, blood thrilling through my veins.

His attention was already on me.

"You know, the word 'teach' is a verb," I said, my voice low and sharp-edged. "It's something you *do*." Without another word, I turned my back to him and headed for the woman waiting patiently for me across the room.

The woman smiled, extending her hand as I drew near. She was forty-ish and dressed in a more stylish version of my own outfit, her black hair cut in a sleek inverted bob. "I'm Sarah Chen, one of the Rockville High administrators."

I shook her hand. "It's nice to meet you."

"And you as well, Olivia," Sarah said, releasing my hand. "You come highly recommended."

"Oh," I said, my cheeks warming. "Thank you." I shot a furtive glance over my shoulder at the people filling the waiting room behind me, but mostly at the jerk sitting beside my unoccupied seat. "Can you tell me," I asked, following Sarah toward the door that led to the interviewing area, "what else are people interviewing for today?" Because Mr. Personality back there had made it more than clear he wasn't a teacher.

Sarah opened the door, stepping back to let me enter the hallway ahead of her. She scanned the waiting room as I passed her, then suppressed a laugh. "Beta players," she said and released the door. "Interesting bunch, aren't they?"

I watched the door swing shut, blocking my view of *him*. "You could say that."

The hallway was long and littered with doors, some open, some shut. The walls were decorated with framed art from Rockville's sprawling portfolio of video games. Sarah led me to the third door on the right, which opened to a small room containing only a reclining chair and some equipment hanging down from the ceiling directly over the chair. The whole setup looked like it belonged in a dentist's office, not an administrative building on the campus of one of the nation's largest video game producers.

Sarah paused just outside the open doorway, extending her arm into the room. "If you don't mind," she said, "we just need to do a quick neural non-stress test to make sure you're a viable candidate, and then we'll proceed with the interview."

I eyed the reclining chair warily from the hall. "Why?" I asked, then looked at Sarah. "I mean, I don't mind," I added quickly. "I'm just curious why the test is necessary."

Sarah's lips spread into an understanding smile. "The test is merely to ensure your physiology is compatible with such extended and extensive use of the VR equipment," she explained. She leaned in, lowering her voice. "Honestly, I've never seen anyone fail the test, but the company's main priority is ensuring the safety of all users, so . . ."

I frowned, unsure whether to be comforted or concerned by her explanation. I supposed the safety-first policy was understandable, and I shrugged. Smiling at Sarah, I walked into the room and sat on the reclining chair. "What do I do?"

"Just sit back and relax." She stepped one foot into the room to reach for the doorknob. "This will only take a few minutes," she said as she shut the door.

A moment later, the lights went out.

[4]

"Well, Olivia," Sarah said from the far side of the barren desk separating us in the small interview room, "I think you'll be a great fit for the program, and we would be happy to have you join our team." She shut the manila folder containing my interviewing materials and clasped her hands together on top. "Do you have any questions for me before we talk about the next steps?"

"Oh, um . . ." I had about a thousand questions, but the burst of excitement caused by the job offer was clouding my mind and confounding my thoughts, and I couldn't think of any single question.

After a long moment of silence, where I felt certain Sarah would rescind the job offer based on my inability to think on my feet, a question finally popped into my head. "I guess I'm curious if there's any information about the long-term effects of using the VR equipment so much?"

Sarah smiled warmly. "Of course," she said. "People ask that all the time. In the welcome packet you'll be receiving in your email shortly, you'll find links to all the latest safety research. Also, you'll find—"

A knock at the door behind me interrupted her.

Sarah's focus shifted past me as the door opened, and I turned in my chair.

A handsome man in his late thirties or early forties entered the room. He looked sharp in a charcoal-gray suit, his clean-cut sandy-brown hair and strong jawline lending him an all-American, boy-next-door-all-grown-up look. His smile was easy and friendly as he strode into the small interview room.

Sarah stood, smoothing down the front of her blouse and jeans. "Mr. St. George," she said, her tone slightly higher in pitch than it had been a moment before. "To what do we owe this honor?"

"Pardon the interruption, Ms. Chen," the newcomer—Mr. St. George, apparently—said, stopping to stand a step or two behind my chair. "I merely wished to introduce myself to Ms. Crawford and to propose a slightly different position here with us than the one you're offering her." He extended his hand toward me. "William St. George, CPO here at Rockville Softworks."

I stood and shook his offered hand, laughing under my breath and feeling my neck and cheeks flush. "I'm a little embarrassed to admit that I don't have the slightest idea what 'CPO' stands for . . ."

Releasing my hand, William chuckled, the sound as warm and friendly as his smile. "Chief People Officer," he explained. "Really, I should stop introducing myself using just the acronym because so few people know what it means. I make sure Rockville has the people it needs, and that those people are in the *right positions* to best serve both the company and our customers."

I looked from William to Sarah and back, entirely unsure what he was doing in here with me. "Oh, well, it's nice to meet you?" I cringed inwardly at the uncertainty in my voice.

Again, William chuckled. "I think it's nice to meet me, but

I'll let you decide that for yourself." He flashed me a charming smile, then cleared his throat. "Ms. Crawford—"

"Olivia," I said, "please. Ms. Crawford makes me feel like I'm your teacher."

William's smile broadened. "Olivia," he said with a nod. "Then you have to call me Will." His manner was easy, and I felt like I already knew him. "It was brought to my attention that you're something of a Jane Austen expert," he said, "at least, according to your resume and transcripts."

"Oh, gosh," I said. "I don't know that I would call myself an *expert*. More of a fan and admirer."

"Your master's thesis would suggest otherwise," Will countered.

My eyes widened, and my blush intensified. How had he managed to get his hands on *that*?

"But let me cut to the chase," Will said. "We're currently seeking beta players for our upcoming beta test of *Austentopia*— that's the Jane Austen branch of the Biblioverse in *Allworld Online*. I would like you, Olivia, to be one of those beta players."

My mouth fell open. I couldn't help it. "Oh," I said. "Wow." I shook my head. "I don't know what to say."

Beta player positions were near impossible to land, right up there with winning the lotto or getting struck by lightning. Charlie had been trying to get one for years, and he was a far more experienced gamer than I was. I had never even tried out a VR headset, and my experience with *Allworld Online* was limited to what I'd seen on the screen while Charlie was working, aka watching other people beta test upcoming games.

Will leaned in toward me and grinned conspiratorially. "I know Ms. Chen has made you an offer for a teaching position," he said, "but once you look over the welcome packet for the beta player position, I think you'll find the compensation and benefits to be more than competitive."

I drew my bottom lip between my teeth, my brows bunching together.

"Please, Olivia, at least consider the offer," Will said. "Beta players are an essential part of the Rockville team, and we're extremely selective about who we offer positions to. The position carries a notably high employee satisfaction rate, and turnover is almost nil. I think you would find the experience very rewarding." He flashed me a hope-filled smile. "So, what do you say?"

My brow furrowed, my thoughts returning to my brother, Charlie, and how badly he wanted to be a beta player. "I—" I cleared my throat. "I'll think about it."

Will grunted, eyeing me curiously. "Clearly, I need to work on my pitch."

I laughed and shook my head. "No, it's not that," I said. "Your pitch was great, really." I took a deep breath, holding it as I debated whether to explain further. I sighed. "It's just that my brother has been a beta viewer for you guys for a few years, and he's been on a waiting list pretty much that whole time to move up to beta player."

"Ah," Will said. "I see." His expression turned thoughtful. "Let me see what I can do about that." He started to turn away, then faced me once more. "Just promise me one thing, Olivia. Don't make any decisions quite yet." He flashed me another of those disarming smiles. "I'll be in touch." He left the room, shutting the door without a backward glance.

I blew out a breath and turned to Sarah. She looked as stunned as I felt.

We wrapped things up quickly. It was as though Will had taken all the air out of the room, and there didn't seem to be much left to say. I felt dazed as Sarah escorted me out to the elevator that led down to the ground floor.

I pushed the call button and turned to face Sarah. "Thank you," I said, extending my hand to shake hers. "It was really nice to meet you, and I—" I shook my head. "I honestly don't know what I'm going to do."

Sarah released my hand and seemed to hesitate to speak. Finally, she inhaled and opened her mouth. "Truly, Olivia, I would be more than happy to have you join our educator team, but . . ." Again, she hesitated. "I know you didn't ask for my opinion, but I really think you should take the beta player position. At least, that's what I would do if I were you."

"Really?" I said, my eyebrows raising.

Behind me, the elevator dinged.

Sarah nodded. "Really."

More confused than ever, I held her stare for a moment then stepped onto the elevator. The doors started to glide shut, but a hand stopped them. A decidedly masculine hand.

I moved into the back left corner as the doors reopened, and when I saw who it was—the jerk from the waiting room earlier —I clenched my jaw. We shared a tense look before I averted my gaze and stared pointedly at the floor.

For a moment, he just stood there, and I thought he might let the doors shut and catch the next ride down. But then he stepped onto the elevator, moving into the opposite corner.

And shocking the hell out of me, he spoke. "I didn't realize they were interviewing teachers, as well."

I looked at him, my eyes narrowing to a glare. Was that supposed to be an apology? Because if it was, it totally sucked. Deciding he didn't even deserve a response, I shifted my attention to the panel of buttons directly in front of me.

He was smart and kept his mouth shut for the remainder of the ride.

[5]

I popped a few kernels of buttery popcorn into my mouth and chewed, my eyes glued to the huge TV screen. Beside me on the couch, Charlie did the same.

On the screen, a woman who looked to be about as far from the physical description of Harry Potter as someone could get rode a broomstick unsteadily over Hogwarts' virtual grounds. She had opted for the gender-swapped name of Harriette. This was Charlie's third round of watching a team of beta players reenact the beloved story of the *boy who lived*. We were near the beginning, when Harry—or Harriette, in this case—rides a broomstick for the first time.

Charlie and I cringed and leaned away from the screen as the player suddenly tumbled from her broomstick and hurtled down to the ground. Only the quick action of another player evoking a levitation spell prevented Harriette from meeting a gruesome end.

"What would have happened if nobody had stopped her fall?" I asked, tearing my eyes from the screen.

"Harriette," Charlie said, "or the player playing that role would have been ejected from the game—for safety purposes.

Then, after a short cooldown phase, she can rejoin the game, and the team has the choice to either respawn at a safe point before the in-game death and course-correct or to continue with an altered storyline. In this case, I imagine if she had fallen and they had decided to continue, Harry—or *Harriette*—would never become a star Seeker for the Gryffindor quidditch team."

I narrowed my eyes and shook my head. "What does that mean—to be ejected from the game for *safety purposes*?"

"It's kind of like when you're falling to your death in a dream," Charlie explained. "You wake up right before you hit the ground. Obviously, you won't actually die—either from an in-dream or an in-game death—but some research suggests that the extreme adrenaline spike caused by the perceived death in VR can be injurious to the body if experienced too frequently."

"Oh," I said, frowning. "That's kind of scary." My brow furrowed. "What about pain? Does it actually hurt when you get hurt in *Allworld Online*?"

Charlie eyed me curiously. "Why all the interest all of a sudden?"

I shrugged and looked at the screen, watching Harriette march back toward the waiting group of players. Charlie didn't know about the second job offer, and I wanted to collect as much information as possible before I made my decision.

Much as I wanted to take the teaching position—more to prevent hurting Charlie's feelings than because I truly preferred it—the beta player position offered a salary double that of the teaching position, plus elevated benefits. I would be able to pay back my parents for all their help within a couple of months, and I would be able to go back to school *on Rockville's dime*. I could get a second degree in something else, *anything* else, without the burden of accruing student loan debt.

But I wasn't sure what it would do to my relationship with Charlie. I feared we would never be the same, and his good opinion was worth more to me than all the money or education prospects in the world.

"I don't know," I said, shrugging one shoulder. "I figured if I'm teaching kids who spend a lot of time in the virtual world, I might as well understand a bit more of what that's like. You know, be in touch with their *virtual* life experience."

"That makes sense," Charlie said, nodding to himself. "But yeah, back to your pain question—yes and no."

I looked at him, my thoughts spinning to recall what question I had asked. *Does it actually hurt when you get hurt in the game?*

"It depends on the game, but in most cases, it's like the game plays a weird trick on your brain," Charlie continued. "You think you feel the pain, but it's more shock than anything." He pursed his lips, his brows drawing together. "I think the implants make it feel genuine, though, if a little toned down." Charlie pointed to the screen. "Poor Harriette there would've felt the crash, had she actually hit the ground." As soon as he finished his explanation, he scooped a handful of popcorn into his mouth.

My eyes returned to the screen. Harriette had just reached the other players. "And all the beta players have the implants, now?"

Charlie nodded as he finished chewing. He swallowed and cleared his throat. "It's pretty much the only way any normal person can afford to get them at this point," he said. "I'm sure they'll drop to a price I can afford eventually, but . . ." He shrugged.

"Yeah," I said, turning my attention back to the screen and trying to act natural, like I hadn't been offered his number one goal in life without even trying. "Stuff like that always drops in price super fast." I pointed to the mega-sized TV. "Like that thing. It was probably a gazillion dollars five years ago, but you got it for what—two hundred bucks?"

"One seventy-five," Charlie said, his expression smug. He glanced at me sidelong and leaned closer like he was about to share a secret. "It was a Black Friday deal."

I scooped a handful of popcorn out of the bowl and munched on the kernels individually. I chewed, swallowed, then glanced at Charlie. "Hey, maybe there'll be a Black Friday deal on VR implants this year." I popped another kernel into my mouth.

Charlie snorted a laugh. "Yeah, I don't think they do mass discounts on brain surgery."

My eyes bugged out, and I choked on the kernel of popcorn, coughing until tears threatened to spill down my cheeks. Once my throat was clear, I chugged some water. "*Brain* surgery?" I finally said.

"Uh, yeah," Charlie said, laughing at me. "Where did you think they implanted the tech? Your butt?"

I smacked Charlie's arm with the back of my hand.

He leaned away from me, cowering melodramatically. "Ow! That's sibling abuse."

I rolled my eyes.

"No, but really," Charlie said, straightening on the couch. "*Brain surgery* is maybe a little extreme. They don't even have to break through the skull. It's not that bad. Totally safe. The tech's been through all the tests, and the government has given it the big ol' federal stamp of approval."

I tensed the side of my mouth, not fully convinced. Even if I hadn't been leaning away from the beta player position, I was now.

The doorbell rang, the chime dulled by the floor and ceiling above us. Charlie and I exchanged a look, shrugged, and glanced up at the ceiling simultaneously, listening as our dad's heavy footsteps moved across the house from the kitchen to the front door. A few seconds later, the dull thrum of masculine voices drifted down to the basement.

Figuring it was a salesman or missionaries, I lost interest, my focus returning to the TV. Harriette was just mounting her broomstick again, about to retry the ride that hadn't ended well the last time. I tangentially noted my dad's footsteps heading back toward the kitchen.

I heard him pause in the hallway, and then he opened the door to the basement. "Olivia!" he called down the stairs. "You have a gentleman caller . . ."

I frowned and exchanged another look with Charlie.

Charlie smirked. "What, did you forget you had a date?" he asked, his tone goading. "What's he like? Maybe I'll go out with him if you don't want to . . ."

Laughing, I shook my head and stood, snagging a throw pillow to toss at Charlie on my way up. "No, dork," I said. "I'm taking a break from dating for a while."

"Sure you are."

I threw another pillow at him before turning and heading for the stairs. Charlie was hot on my heels. I trudged up the steep staircase and followed my dad into the foyer. And froze when I saw who was waiting for me there.

William St. George. He stood close to the wall, studying the hodgepodge of framed family portraits from over the years. He looked exactly the same as he had been during our brief interaction at Rockville Softworks earlier that day, which meant he looked totally out of place in the chaos of my parents' house.

I suddenly felt completely inadequate in my leggings and oversized sweater.

"Olive, that's William St. George," Charlie whispered, standing directly behind me, his hushed words spoken inches from my ear.

"I know," I whispered right back at him.

Will tore his attention away from a particularly unfortunate family photo of all seven of us wearing matching Christmas sweaters and looked my way. He took a step toward me, his lips spreading into a warm grin. "Good evening, Olivia."

Behind Will, my dad gave an approving thumbs up.

I gulped, already feeling a blush creeping up my neck. "Will, hi," I said, flashing him a nervous smile. "I mean, good evening." I cleared my throat. "What are you doing here?"

Will smiled again, apologetic this time, and bowed his head. "I hope you don't mind me stopping by," he said. "This is a little unorthodox, I know, but I wanted to share the good news with you in person." His focus shifted past me, to Charlie. "With you and your brother." Will inhaled deeply, his grin broadening. "We would be happy to offer you both positions as beta players with Rockville Softworks."

My jaw dropped.

"I accept!" Charlie blurted, stepping up to stand beside me.

Will's grin faded as his focus shifted back to me until only a raised corner of his mouth remained. "Contingent upon you joining the *Austentopia* beta team, Olivia," he said. "This is an all-or-nothing deal."

I felt the color drain from my face. I'd been leaning heavily toward taking the teaching job, but with a single offer, Will had taken away my choice. Out of the corner of my eye, I could see Charlie staring at me, his eyes filled with a silent plea.

"I, um—" I turned my head, searching Charlie's puppy-dog eyes for a long moment. I held his dream in the palm of my hand.

I returned my attention to Will. "All right. I'll do it."

WILLIAM ST. GEORGE

William St. George walked through a pair of double doors into a grand library, the polished mahogany bookcases and gilded picture frames lining the walls reflecting the flickering light of the flames dancing in the ornate fireplace on the right side of the room. A woman sat in an armchair angled toward the fireplace, her legs covered by a delicate blanket.

Will stooped a few paces behind the armchair and clasped his hands behind his back. "It's done," he said. "We begin in two weeks."

"No more delays," the woman said, her voice resonant. "I grow weary of waiting."

Will bowed. "As you say, no more delays." He straightened and turned his back to the woman, leaving the room without another word.

August 21, 2026

It is one week until the delayed launch of the Austentopia *beta test, and I still don't feel comfortable proclaiming the* Pride and Prejudice *game world fit for live players. I admit that the glitching seems to have subsided after we did an overhaul of both the game's code and the AI game controller's directives, but something still feels off.*

I'm concerned that the game controller is concealing something. What—or how—I couldn't say, but the original code my team designed warped, and I worry that the AI made purposeful alterations, both to itself and to the game. Why would it do such a thing? Again, I couldn't say. Possibly to create a digital shelter to hide . . . something. Again, I couldn't say what—or why, or even how.

.   .   .

(deep breath) My gut tells me we should scrap the project and start from scratch—brand new AI game controller and all— before whatever is wrong with Pride and Prejudice *can infest the rest of the games within the Austentopia universe. But I fear the time and money Rockville already invested in the project has placed blinders on the board's eyes, and the board members won't heed my warning. (pause)*

And yet, I can't, in good conscience, sign off on the project and open it for human players without some further safeguards. I've been going back and forth about what to do, and I've decided to submit an official notice to the board stating that I will only approve Austentopia *for beta testing if Fiona Ó Faoláin is brought on to oversee the beta testing. If the creator of Allworld Online deems the project safe, then I will accept her decision and move on. And if the board refuses to bring Fiona onto the project, then I don't think I'll have any choice but to resign.*

[6]

My belly was filled with butterflies as I followed Charlie through the double doors amidst a stream of other beta players, the individuals in the crowd more varied and unique even than those I had shared the waiting room with last week, if that was even possible. We entered an auditorium abuzz with excitement, and my anxiety riled the butterflies in my gut into a frenzy. Was I really doing this? Joining Rockville's beta team? Agreeing to let them implant VR tech into my head?

The auditorium was modern and minimalistic, about what I would have envisioned for an auditorium in the middle of a tech complex, and looked to seat about five hundred people, maybe a little more. It was already nearly half full, and people continued to stream in. How many beta players had Rockville hired this round? And were they all for the *Austentopia* beta tests?

Charlie and I found a pair of empty seats not quite a third of the way back and shuffled past the occupants of the seats nearer to the aisle. Charlie offered muffled "sorries" and "thanks," while I flashed apologetic smiles.

Once we were seated, Charlie grinned at me, then turned to

chat with the guy on the other side of him. "Pretty exciting, huh?"

"Yeah," the guy said. "I've been trying to get one of these spots for years. I can't believe I'm finally here!"

I tuned out their conversation as I turned in my seat to scan the faces of the people sitting further back. Everyone looked as excited as Charlie and his new buddy. I had never felt more out of place. What was I doing here? I didn't belong.

With a resigned sigh, I faced forward and clasped my hands together on my lap, trying to make myself small. Invisible. Trying to make myself disappear.

After an agonizing ten minutes, the lights overhead dimmed, and the crowd quieted, though the excited energy ratcheted up a few notches. Whispers filled the auditorium as a man in a business suit walked onto the darkened stage, stopping in the center, a spotlight slowly lighting him up until, at last, I recognized him. William St. George. He was the whole reason I was here, and I wasn't sure whether to thank him or curse him for that very thing.

Will looked out into the crowd gathered in the auditorium, his expression serious as he seemed to search the faces peering back at him. I could have sworn his gaze lingered on my section of the seats—on me. The hint of a smile curved his lips, and he continued his scan.

Charlie leaned in close to me. "You know, that man is the star of all of my billionaire fantasies," he whispered.

I glanced at my brother and laughed under my breath, shaking my head.

"I love you, William St. George!" someone shouted nearer to the front of the auditorium, igniting an eruption of laughter.

I snorted. "Apparently, you're not the only one," I murmured to Charlie.

He grinned, then shrugged.

On the stage, Will shifted his attention to the general location of the shout and raised a hand in thanks. He flashed the audience an aw-shucks grin, as charming and charismatic as ever. "It's always nice to know one is appreciated," he said, his voice magnified by a hidden microphone.

The crowd tittered, and Will rewarded us with another winning smile. He let the anticipation build for a moment before raising both hands, cueing the audience to quiet down again. As he waited for the crowd to settle, he turned to the side and, clasping his hands behind his back, slowly meandered toward the edge of the stage, then turned again and paced back across. By the time he reached the opposite side of the stage, it was pin-drop quiet in the auditorium.

Will returned to the center of the stage and once again faced the crowd of beta players, holding out his arms like he was extending a hug to each and every one of us. "Welcome, all of you, to the Austentopia beta team," he pronounced, then lowered his arms. His grin infectious.

I could feel the corners of my mouth turning upward, and I sat up straighter in my seat, anticipating his next words. However mixed my feelings may have been about Will and his role in leading me here, there was no denying his charisma.

"Today," Will continued, "you will meet your assigned gaming parties, be briefed on contract terms and legalese, and have a personalized implant consultation. You will also receive your playing schedules and find out the date and time of your implant procedure appointments." He paused for a moment, letting his words sink in. "You may be nervous about meeting the people you will be working closely with over the next few months, possibly even for years to come. Please know that our proprietary algorithm has matched you together in your gaming parties based on the character alignment questionnaires you filled out when you accepted your positions."

I settled back in my chair and crossed my arms. Calling the survey I had filled out a few days ago a "character alignment questionnaire" was a gross understatement. The thing was more like a psychoanalytic personality test and had taken me nearly two hours to complete. Some of the multiple-choice questions were extremely personal and more than a little embarrassing, and only the bold and highlighted section at the end of the instructions assuring me that no human eyes would ever see my answers convinced me to answer truthfully.

On stage, Will continued, "Each gaming party was created with player compatibility in mind to ensure an enjoyable game experience for both players and viewers." He paused for a moment, scanning the assembled players. "Some parties will be participating in the *Austentopia* version of a traditional open-world questing game, while others will be role-playing in what Rockville Softworks has dubbed 'wish fulfillment' games, wherein you will be experiencing a specific story, such as *Pride and Prejudice* or *Sense and Sensibility*, and your actions and choices have the power to either keep that story on track or alter the story, creating something new."

I pressed my lips together, already anticipating the worst. Knowing my luck, I was probably going to end up in one of those wish-fulfillment games as some annoying character like Miss Bates or Lydia Bennet.

"You should all receive an email with your party and game assignments momentarily," Will said as a line of people filed out of the wings and onto the stage behind him, each holding a small sign printed with a large, black capital letter. Each letter was unique, with no duplicates.

"Once you receive your assignment email," Will went on, "please find the person holding the letter of the alphabet listed at the top of the message. They will take you to a secondary location where you and your party will complete the orientation." He paused, waiting as the auditorium filled with the rustle of clothing as the majority of the players fished their phones out of pockets or purses. From the disappointed expressions on the faces nearest me, the promised email had yet to arrive.

When quiet once more filled the auditorium, Will continued. "If you have any issues with your assignment, please don't hesitate to come to me directly." His serious expression melted under another winning smile. "I sincerely hope you all have a wonderful game experience, and welcome to the Rockville beta team." He bowed his head and stepped backward, melting into, then disappearing behind the line of sign holders.

The sign holders began filing toward the set of stairs at either end of the stage, a handful remaining behind on the stage, raising their signs over their heads. Those who filed off the stage spread out at the front of the auditorium as the sound of hundreds of phones buzzing filled the cavernous space.

Charlie already had his phone out and opened his assignment email immediately. "I'm an 'H'," he said. "It says my party is assigned to the questing game." He looked at me. "What'd you get?"

I fished my phone out of my purse and opened the email, skimming the first few lines. "I'm an 'O'—*Pride and Prejudice*."

"Sweet, Olive," Charlie said, bumping my shoulder with his. "You love *Pride and Prejudice*." He stood up along with everyone around us, and I followed suit. "Come on, I can't wait to find out which of these nerds I'll be working with."

We shuffled into the aisle and, moving with the stream of bodies, slowly made our way to the front of the auditorium. All around us, people excitedly exchanged letters, searching for the party members they would be meeting all too soon.

When we were a few steps from the floor, Charlie grabbed my hand and looked back at me. "Meet me out front when this is over," he said. "By the fountain." When I nodded, he squeezed my hand, then let it go, heading for the person holding up the "H" sign off to the far right.

The holder of the "O" sign was one of those still on the stage, so I weaved my way toward the staircase on the left side of the stage. As I climbed the stairs, I noticed the jerk from the interview waiting room ascending the stairs at the opposite side of the stage and felt the blood drain from my face as dread pooled in my belly. I hadn't even considered the possibility that he had been hired as well, let alone that we might be in the same gaming party.

I crossed my fingers, begging any and all universal forces to prevent the thing that now seemed inevitable. I reached the "O" sign holder and exchanged brief smiles with the petite, blue-haired pixie-like woman and the teddy bear of a young man already gathered there, all the while watching the jerk out of the corner of my eye, willing him to walk right on by.

No such luck. He stopped at my group, and his eyes met mine.

I gulped. This couldn't be happening.

[7]

When I told Will I would accept the position, I hadn't realized I was choosing this. Choosing to incorporate *the jerk* into my life for who knew how long. Of all the people in that auditorium, what were the odds that we would end up together?

But here I was, sitting around an oval conference table with the eight other beta players in my assigned gaming party, Mr. Personality sitting two seats away on my right, separated by a slightly fluffy, cheerful guy. I refused to look at him, and yet, I couldn't stop tracking him out of the corner of my eye. Was this karma? Was I being punished for something I did a long time ago? Something I had long since forgotten?

Did I *deserve* this?

"Alright, guys, my name is Greg," said the gangly über-nerd who had been holding our letter sign in the auditorium. His long, muddy brown hair was tied back in a low ponytail that hung down his back in stringy chunks, and his T-shirt displayed a wolf howling at the moon. He turned away from the whiteboard he had been writing on and pushed his glasses higher on the bridge of his nose. "Normally your party liaison would lead your orientation, but Priya—Ms. Burman—is busy initializing the launch of *Austentopia*, so for today, you're stuck with her assistant. That's, uh, me. I'm Greg." He cleared his throat, then added, "Though she did promise to pop in and introduce herself later today."

Greg paused for longer than was necessary, then pointed over his shoulder at the daily schedule and dates he'd written on the whiteboard. "Probably a good idea to get this all in your calendar right now," he said. "You'll be expected to report here on September second for monitored gameplay. You'll be monitored throughout the entirety of your first round of play to ensure your safety, which means you'll be staying here in our underground beta facility." His words seemed to tumble over themselves as he added, "This is a totally normal precaution we take with players with new implants."

Something about the way he said that last part made me think it was anything but normal. And from the way jerk guy crossed his arms and leaned back in his chair, his eyes narrowed, I didn't think I was alone in my assumption.

Greg cleared his throat again, then pointed at the bottom date. "The appointment for your party's implant procedure is non-negotiable, so if you already have plans that day—or the two days following—I suggest you reschedule." He surveyed us, his expression stern, then nodded. "The implant consultant should be here any minute, but we can dive into some introductions and icebreakers while we wait."

Everyone looked around the table nervously, and I suppressed a groan. Icebreakers were the worst.

Oblivious to our collective discomfort, Greg continued, "We'll go around the table, each of you introducing yourself, where you're from, what you did before this, and a fun fact about yourself." He pointed to the woman sitting directly across from me. She was petite, young, and her pixie cut was dyed a shocking teal. "We'll start with you."

The woman giggled and sat up straighter, her pale cheeks

flushed a bright pink. "Oh, um, okay." She stared at the surface of the table. "Well, I'm Nel." She flashed the group a smile, her focus lifting off the table for a fraction of a second. "I'm from here—well, Seattle, but that's just on the other side of the lake, so basically here. And, um . . ."

My mind stopped registering Nel's words as I became hyper-focused on figuring out exactly what I was going to say. I couldn't think of a single interesting thing about myself, which was precisely why I hated icebreakers and considered them completely pointless. Everyone becomes so focused on preparing what they're going to say that they forget to listen to what others are saying and learn absolutely nothing about the other people. Or maybe that was just me.

"Name's Colin," jerk guy said, and my attention snapped to him. I hadn't realized the woman beside him had already finished. He remained slumped in his chair, his arms crossed over his chest, looking like he was into this kind of thing about as much as I was. "I'm from Southern California originally," he continued, "but I'm not a big fan of sunshine, so . . ."

I became all too aware of the fact that I was staring at Colin, and that he seemed to be making an effort to look anywhere but at me.

"Before this, I was in IT," he said. "And I have a dog. Her name is Daisy, and we go on a lot of hikes together. She'll be staying with my neighbor while I'm away for the first round of gaming."

As he spoke, I slowly sat up straighter, even found myself leaning in. I wanted to ask him more about his dog, Daisy. It was the most human thing about him, so far as I had seen, and I was intrigued.

The guy beside me started talking, introducing himself, and telling us where he was from. I was looking at him and really, really trying to pay attention, but I could feel Colin's stare like lasers boring into my forehead, and all I could think about was *not* looking at him.

And then, all of a sudden, Colin wasn't the only one looking at me. *Everyone* was looking at me. It was my turn.

Heat crept up my neck and warmed my cheeks, and I started to sweat. "Oh, um . . ." What was I supposed to say again? "My name is Olivia," I said, glancing at the board and wishing Greg had written down the list of what to include. "I, um, live in North Bend with my family, and uh, I was a teacher before this—a high school English teacher—but I was caught up in the mass layoffs last year, so . . ." My cheeks burned as I admitted that, and my gaze dropped to the table.

Something interesting and fun . . . something interesting and fun . . . something interesting and fun . . .

"I actually applied for a teaching position with Rockville High," I finally said, "but I guess they thought I'd be a better fit as a beta player, so here I am." That was *not* interesting *or* fun, so I scoured my mind for something else. "And I don't know how fun of a fact this is," I added, "but I wrote my master's thesis on *Pride and Prejudice*, which I think is probably why I'm here."

"So," Nel said, chiming in from across the table, "in your expert opinion, who's the better Darcy—Colin Firth or Matthew Macfadyen?"

I looked at Nel, grateful to have a direct question to focus on. "Well," I began, "it might be against popular opinion, but I like Macfadyen's more sullen, broody Darcy."

Nel grinned and leaned in, resting her forearms on the table like she was going to share a secret with me. "Me too." Her agreement eased some of the tension from my body, and I smiled back.

A knock at the door halted our oh-so-fun round of introductions, and a middle-aged woman with flawless ebony skin entered the room, her white lab coat marking her as a doctor or scientist.

"Ah," Greg said. "Here's our implant consultant." He scooted off to the side of the room, waving for the newcomer to come forward. "We'll finish up introductions after her presentation."

The woman took Greg's place at the front of the room. "I'm Dr. Morgan," she said, "one of the surgeons who will be executing the implant procedures." Her sharp gaze quickly scanned our faces. "I assume you've all read through the materials you received in your welcome packets explaining the procedure, so I won't go into detail now. What I'm really here for is to ensure you know what to expect during and after the procedure and to answer any questions you may have about the procedure."

In her no-nonsense way, Dr. Morgan explained that the implant procedure would take about a half-hour and that our implants would be activated immediately to ensure a successful pairing between device and brain. Confusion upon waking and for the following day or two was to be expected, and during that time, it apparently wasn't uncommon for people with brand new implants to have a hard time distinguishing reality from the virtual world.

"After a few days," Dr. Morgan said, "you should notice no difference in your daily life. Though, if you do notice any lingering pain or swelling at the implant site, be sure to notify your party liaison immediately." As she said the last part, Dr. Morgan nodded toward Greg.

"Not me," Greg said, shaking his head. "Your liaison is Ms. Burman, who you'll meet later today."

Dr. Morgan glanced at the clock on the wall. "Alright, what questions do you have for me?"

Nel raised her hand, and the doctor looked at her. "How much pain should we expect?"

Dr. Morgan frowned thoughtfully. "No more than a piercing

or a deep pimple," she said. "And the pain should fade quickly. The implant is very tiny, and any pain is from the small incision and the swelling caused by inserting a foreign object into the body."

My hand crept upward before I realized what I was doing, and the doctor's sharp stare fixed on me. I licked my lips and sat up straighter in my seat. "If the procedure is so minimal, what's the need for general anesthesia?" I asked. "Doesn't that make it a lot riskier than it needs to be?"

"Hmmm," Dr. Morgan mused, "Good question. You see, the mind must be in an unconscious state during the first pairing with the device, and it is much safer for that pairing to occur in a controlled environment when the patient's state of consciousness won't change before the pairing is complete." She was quiet for a moment, then followed up with, "It's very safe. Complications are extremely rare."

Rare, I thought, but not unheard of. The answer didn't exactly ease my concerns.

Others asked questions, but not about anything I was overly interested in. The rest of the day passed in a blur of mounting anxiety, and when it was over, I was relieved to finally leave the conference room and head out into the sunshine and fresh air.

I headed for the fountain in front of our building, at the center of the Rockville Softworks campus. A quick scan of the broad, circular pond surrounding the fountain told me Charlie wasn't here yet. But I did spot Colin sitting on a bench nearby, his attention fixed on the screen of his phone. For once, he wasn't slouching. I dreaded talking to him, but I was even less excited about the prospect of carrying on with the status quo. The tense awkwardness was killing me.

Pulling on my big-girl pants, I approached the bench and waited for Colin to glance up at me. When he did, not even pausing in the tapping of his thumbs on the phone's screen, I offered him a tentative smile.

"Hold on," he said, typing out a few more words before tucking his phone into his jacket pocket. His focus returned to me.

"Do you mind if I join you?" I asked.

Colin shook his head and glanced at the empty end of the bench.

"Sorry, I didn't mean to interrupt," I said, sitting and resting my purse on my lap.

"It's fine," he said, his focus lingering on my face for a second or two longer than was comfortable before he turned his head to watch the water shoot up out of the fountain.

"I think you might be the only other person besides me who isn't stoked to be here," I commented.

Colin crossed his arms over his chest and propped one ankle on his knee. "Maybe."

God, why was he so hard to talk to? Getting him to say more than one or two words at a time was like pulling teeth. *But* I was determined to bury the hatchet, and I wasn't about to give up. We could be friends. Or, at least, we could be *friendly*.

I took a deep breath and tried again. "Are you nervous about the implant?" I asked.

"Not really," he said.

"I've never been put under general anesthesia before," I admitted. "I think that's what scares me the most about it."

Colin was quiet for a long moment—so long that I didn't think he was going to respond. I hadn't actually asked him a question, so I wasn't all that surprised. "Being knocked out is like blinking," he said, catching me off guard. "Only, when your eyes are closed, time slips away."

I looked at him as I nodded. The silence stretched out between us, becoming awkward, but at least we hadn't slipped back into antagonistic territory.

"Your dog, Daisy," I said, preparing to ask what I had wanted to ask earlier in the conference room. "She seems really important to you," I said. "I mean, from the way you spoke about her. She must be a great dog."

Again, Colin was quiet for a long moment, and I kicked myself for not forming the observation into a question.

But just as I was getting ready to throw in the towel, Colin spoke. "I've had her since she was a puppy," he said. "But she's old now. I hate to leave her when—" He shook his head and laughed bitterly under his breath. "It doesn't matter. I don't really have a choice."

My eyebrows rose. Intrigued, I angled my knees toward Colin. "You really don't want to be here," I said, more of a statement than a question.

Colin looked at me, his eyes searching mine. I was taken aback by the depth in his warm brown irises. "You don't want to be here, either."

I inhaled and opened my mouth, preparing to dig deeper. But just then, Charlie bounded toward our bench, waving his hands like a goober and grinning from ear to ear. "Wow!" he exclaimed. "What a day!"

Colin looked affronted at the seemingly insane man closing in on our bench, and I flashed him an apologetic smile.

I laughed as Charlie reached for my hands, pulling me up to my feet and wrapping his arms around me in a massive bear hug. He lifted my feet off the ground and swung me around and around.

"Charlie!" I squealed. "Put me down! You're making me dizzy!" But I was still laughing, so he kept on swinging.

"Thanks for agreeing to this, Olive," he said, finally ceasing the endless whirling and setting my feet back on the ground, squeezing me tight. "Thankyouthankyouthankyouthankyou."

He released me, and I set about straightening my jeans and blouse, shooting an embarrassed look Colin's way. "See you next week," I said, raising a hand to wave at Colin before linking my arm with Charlie's.

Colin nodded his goodbye, and I turned my back to him, heading for the lot of self-driving cars beyond the rose garden at the far side of the fountain.

Charlie glanced over his shoulder as we walked away, no doubt scoping out Colin. "Making friends?" he said, his tone a little too innocent to be believable.

I laughed under my breath and shook my head. "He's just some guy in my gaming party."

Charlie threw me some serious side-eye. "Just some guy, huh?"

I bumped his shoulder with mine. "Shut up," I laughed. "Tell me about your gaming party," I said, changing the subject strategically. There was no way Charlie would be able to resist sharing everything he had learned about his new colleagues. "Do you like everyone?"

As I had expected, Charlie described everyone in his gaming party in great detail. I listened with half of my attention, my mind preoccupied with worries about the implant procedure and by unexpected, curious thoughts of Colin. I remained quiet during the car ride home and during dinner with the rest of our family, but Charlie had plenty to say to fill in the gaps left by my silence, and nobody seemed to notice I was a little quieter than usual.

Later that night, when I lay in my bed, trying and failing to sleep, I grabbed my phone off the nightstand and propped an extra pillow behind my head. I tapped on the browser bar and typed in the last thing I should have been looking up: *VR implant procedures gone wrong.*

[8]

Charlie wasn't stupid. He could tell something was off with me, even if he didn't broach the subject directly. He did, however, try to distract me with a glimpse of what awaited me in *Allworld Online*.

Uncertainty was a heavy weight in my mind as Charlie brought me his VR headset. I was already standing on the three-sixty treadmill-like platform on which he played to increase the realism of walking around within the virtual world. I squatted down, so Charlie could fit the headset on my head and adjust the fittings. Darkness surrounded me as the headset slid into place, but I was surprised by how lightweight it was.

"Alright, that should do it," Charlie said, removing his hands from my head.

I looked around, but still only saw darkness and the occasional flash of light that may or may not have been a trick of the mind. "Should something be happening?"

"It takes a minute to attune to your optic nerves," Charlie said. "Hang on. It'll start up soon. When you get to the gatescape, you'll meet Scarlet."

I nodded. I was well aware of who Scarlet was—Charlie's

gigi, or game guide. All players were assigned their own personal AI companion in the form of a gigi the moment they stepped their virtual foot into *Allworld Online.* Scarlet went everywhere with Charlie, acting as his faithful animal companion in some games and as his game interface in others. All gigis started as either a dog or a cat, but players could upgrade their gigis through achievements within the virtual world; however, some games still only permitted a realistic canine or feline form. Upgraded gigis provided bonuses in most games, though the exact perks and bonuses varied from game to game. Last I'd seen Scarlet, she was a huge dire wolf with white-tipped-auburn fur.

"Come on," Charlie said, taking hold of my hands. "Stand up. The system should boot up soon."

I let Charlie pull me up to my feet, and I was only standing for a few seconds before the darkness surrounding me slowly eased, revealing a harsh but beautiful alien landscape. The ground was rocky, with tall, gleaming crystals of every color growing in clusters and jagged mountains jutting up in the distance. Freestanding neon rings large enough for a car to pass through were scattered around the landscape, connected by a tangle of well-traveled paths packed with players and their gigis rushing past one another. I was standing on one of the rocky hillsides, out of the way of the players on the paths.

People appeared out of thin air wearing all manner of clothing and body armor, accompanied by creatures of various species and sizes. For a moment, I just stood there, watching the players march along the paths like strings of ants while newcomers appeared on the vacant hillsides, only to climb down the rocky slopes to join the others on the paths. When the players reached one of the glowing neon rings, they vanished, transported to some other part of *Allworld Online.*

The rings were gateways, and this was the gatescape. I'd

seen Charlie pass through here dozens of times, but seeing it with my own two eyes was another experience entirely.

I glanced down at myself, curious about what I would be wearing as a guest on an established player's account. I found that I wore a form-fitting suit of shiny black and white body armor, and wondered if this was the norm for new players or if this was what Charlie had been wearing the last time he'd logged out.

"Welcome to the gatescape, Olivia."

I started at the sound of the slightly husky feminine voice and spun around. A ruby dragon the size of a Great Dane sat on her haunches a few feet away, watching me. This was Scarlet. It had to be.

"Charlie asked me to show you around," Scarlet said, a hint of her crimson forked tongue peeking out as she spoke. "Do you have any questions?"

"I—" I stared at her with wide eyes. "You're a dragon."

The hint of a smile touched her serpentine mouth. "A wyvern, technically," she said, unfurling her leathery wings partway and flapping them gently. "No arms—just legs and wings."

I frowned and shook my head, confused. "Last time I watched Charlie play, you were a dire wolf," I told her.

Scarlet bared her wicked-looking teeth and flicked that forked tongue. "We upgraded."

I nodded slightly. "Yeah, I can see that," I said, then scanned the gatescape once more, watching players and their gigis flash into and out of existence before returning my attention to Scarlet. "So, um . . . what do I do?"

Scarlet cocked her head to the side. "What would you like to do?"

Again, I frowned, and then I shrugged. "I don't know," I said. "I guess try out a game?"

"Sounds like a good plan to me," Scarlet said. "Did you have a game in mind?"

I hadn't thought that far ahead and quietly admitted as much.

"That's alright," Scarlet said. "Would you like me to recommend a game?"

I smiled at her, already seeing the value in a gigi and thinking she seemed remarkably realistic and almost human for something so clearly not. "That would be great," I said. "Thanks."

"How about *The Ending World*?" Scarlet suggested. "It's one of Charlie's all-time favorites, and it's great for beginners. Plus, you would get to see what the Biblioverse is like, which might be nice since you'll be spending so much time there."

I stared at her, nodding slowly. She was so incredibly lifelike, I almost couldn't believe she was an artificial being and not a real person logged into AO, masquerading as a dragon.

Scarlet turned and started climbing down the rocky hillside, heading for one of the paths. "Follow me," she said, peering back at me. "The gate to the Biblioverse is just around the bend."

I blinked, surprised, then hurried to catch up to Scarlet. I had watched Charlie play dozens of times and always thought he chose a gate at random—I hadn't known they went somewhere specific.

"Where do the other gates lead?" I asked as we descended the hillside. There were so many of them spread out across the gatescape as far as the eye could see.

Scarlet glanced at me. "Oh, the various game universes," she said. "Marvelverse, Whedonverse, Mundus—you get the idea. The Biblioverse is one of the largest universes since it includes all the games based on literary works as the primary source material."

We merged into the stream of players traveling along the path, heading for a gateway that was half neon pink, half electric blue. Behind me, players started making sounds of annoyance. A sabertooth tiger suddenly bounded past me, half on the path, half on the steep hillside, closely followed by a player scantily clad in a fur loincloth. His shoulder bumped mine as he passed, nearly knocking me into the player ahead of me.

Scarlet bounded onto the hillside and blew out a puff of flame at the sabertooth tiger, managing to light its tail on fire to the claps and cheers of the players behind me. She leapt back onto the path, falling in step beside me. "So rude," she grumbled, blowing out a plume of white smoke through her nostrils.

I raised my eyebrows, both shocked and impressed by her reaction.

Ahead, the caveman player and his sabertooth gigi cut off the players at the front of the line and passed through the gateway with a flash.

"Reported his ass," I heard a player behind me say, and I wondered if there was an actual rule about waiting in line in the gatescape and what the possible punishment might be for breaking that rule. I hadn't considered that a regulatory force might be needed for such a realistic virtual world, but now that I was here, it made sense that AO would have some form of peacekeepers.

I continued to ponder such things as we shuffled forward, and soon enough, Scarlet and I reached the front of the line and approached the gateway. As I placed my foot on the bottom of the ring, a bright light swallowed me up, fading almost as soon as it appeared, and I found myself standing in the atrium of a gorgeous old library.

I stood on the ground floor amidst a sea of players. The floor was polished marble tile, surrounded by level after level of ornate balconies and bookshelves reaching up, up, up. The ceiling was a glass dome with vines creeping along the outside, subduing the golden light filtering in through the glass. The walls surrounding me were littered with evenly spaced stone archways, each labeled with a different literary genre at the apex of the arch.

"This way," Scarlet said beside me, turning and weaving through the crowd of players as she headed toward one of the archways behind us.

I turned to follow her, gazing up at storey after storey of packed bookcases. "All of these books are games?"

"Correct," Scarlet said.

"But—" I shook my head. "How are there so many? I mean, how have people had time to *create* this many games?"

"That's easy," Scarlet said. "People haven't created them at all."

I looked at her, surprised by her answer. "What do you mean?"

"Well," she said, "in many cases, the source material is uploaded and assigned a unique AI game controller. The AI game controller then creates a game world based on the source material. It's different for more complex, multi-game worlds, like *Austentopia*. Then, human programmers are needed. But that's how it works for most book-based single-game worlds."

Again, I was staring up at the seemingly endless floors of books towering overhead.

Scarlet stopped in front of an archway, and I peered up at the label carved into the stone atop the arch—APOCALYPTIC & DYSTOPIAN—then looked through the archway itself. The room beyond was round and filled with a ring of broken and battered bookcases laid out like a set of dominos. Vines grew up through the floor, climbing along the exterior wall and the sides of the bookcases, and a huge live oak stood tall in the center of the room, its roots displacing floor tiles. Its taller limbs broke through the glass dome ceiling, a smaller version of the one in the main atrium. Other players passed through the archway ahead of me, vanishing as soon as they were through.

Scarlet led me through the archway immediately after another player, and I was surprised to find no sign of the player on the other side. In fact, there were no other players at all. I glanced back at the archway, but from this side, the main atrium appeared to be completely empty.

"Passing through the archway creates a private instance of the genre room," Scarlet explained, apparently noticing my confusion. "This instance is now tied to Charlie's guest account and will remain active until he resets the account, at which point it will cease to exist. If you were logged in under your own private account, this instance would be tied to your account and be relatively permanent, allowing you to store things here and even make it your virtual home base, if you liked."

"Very cool," I said, nodding as I frowned appreciatively.

"This way," Scarlet said, heading around the ring of bookcases. She zeroed in on a section of bookcases labeled OPEN WORLDS and stopped by the second bookcase in. "Third shelf from the top, sixth book in from the left," she directed me. "Pull the book from the shelf, open it, and set it on the floor."

I did as instructed, finding a book titled *The Ending World,* and opened it to a random middle page before setting it on the floor. I took a step back and looked at Scarlet, my eyebrows raised in question.

Scarlet extended one wing toward the open book. "After you."

My eyes widened, my eyebrows climbing even higher. "I just *walk* into the book?"

Scarlet readjusted her wings. "Well, you can jump if you like, or fall," she said. "It's really a matter of personal preference."

An enormous grin spread across my face, and I didn't hesitate for another second. I raised my foot and fulfilled one of my lifelong dreams of literally stepping into a book, and the Biblioverse winked out around me.

[9]

I woke on my back in a bed, with the sun streaming in through lacy, white curtains and birds chirping outside. I sat up partway, propping myself up on my elbows. A calico cat was curled into a cozy ball beside me on the bed, her back flush against my hip.

A woman with curly red hair and a pretty, freckled face poked her head around the doorjamb. "Oh!" she exclaimed. "You're up!" Her lips curved into a warm smile, and she stepped into the room, a German shepherd trotting in behind her and sticking close.

The cat raised her head to survey the room, her attention settling on the dog.

"I'm Dani," the woman said while scratching the dog's head. "And this is Jack. But don't worry—he won't bother your cat."

My cat? I glanced at the calico again.

"What's your name?" Dani asked.

Not a second later, she and Jack froze as a semi-transparent screen appeared in front of me, hovering over my chest. The prompt on the screen read: CHARACTER NAME.

Right, because this was a game. I was too flustered by how

real virtual reality felt to come up with anything creative, so I just went with my real name. "Um . . . Olivia?"

My name populated in the field on the screen, and beside me, the cat spoke using Scarlet's voice. "Are you sure? You could be anyone . . ."

I looked at the cat. At Scarlet. "I didn't realize that was you," I said, feeling a little silly for not figuring it out earlier. "But yeah," I added, "I'll just stick with my own name. I think anything else would just confuse me."

"Very well," Scarlet said, and the screen disappeared, bringing the world back to life.

"How are you feeling?" Dani asked, moving closer to the bed. She sat on the foot of the mattress, turning her body so she was angled toward me. "We found you unconscious near the stream out back. Looked like you had a pretty good bump on your head."

At the ghost of a headache, I sat up the rest of the way and touched my temple, feeling the VR headset and temporarily shattering the illusion of reality. I could see why players would prefer the implants and could only imagine how much more immersive they would make this virtual world feel. How much more real.

Realizing Dani was still sitting there, staring at me and waiting for an answer, I cleared my throat. "I'm fine," I told her. "Good, actually." I studied Dani for a moment, then Jack, sitting calmly beside her. I had read all the books in *The Ending Series* and the various spinoff series, but seeing one of the main characters here, right in front of me—not just a character in a book, but a real person—was surreal.

"I can't believe how real this all is," I murmured without thinking.

Dani eyed me. "You sure you're feeling alright?"

Before I could answer, a little girl ran into the room, her clothes covered in muck and her shock of red hair dripping muddy water onto the hardwood floor. "Mommy! Mommy!" the girl cried, "Everett pushed me into the pond!"

Dani glanced up at the ceiling, a resigned sigh escaping from her chest. "I can see that," she said, training her stare on the girl.

A moment later, a little boy trudged into the room, also dripping mud.

Dani chuckled. "Looks like you got your revenge, though." She shook her head and stood, shooing both children out of the room. "Into the tub, both of you."

A horse screamed outside before the kids could even turn to head for the bathroom, and everyone's eyes opened wide. Dani's stare became distant like she was listening to something far away. Since I'd read the books, I knew she was telepathic, able to speak telepathically to other people and to animals as well, and figured that was what she was doing at the moment.

In the next instant, Dani was back, her eyes locked with mine. "Crazies," she said, her voice going cold. "And a lot of them. Damn it!" She closed her eyes and took a deep breath, then looked at me once more. "What's your Ability?" she asked. "Do you know how to fight?"

Again, a floating screen appeared in front of me, prompting me to select an Ability from a scrolling list. Through the semi-transparent screen, I could see that Dani and the kids were frozen as the game waited for me to decide. I quickly scrolled through the list, selecting an Ability that sounded fairly useful—telekinesis. Who wouldn't want to be able to move objects around with the power of their mind alone?

The screen changed, displaying a grid of skills, and prompted me to select three base skills to start with. Again, I browsed all my options, then selected three that sounded both useful and relatively different from one another: hand-to-hand combat, foraging, and tracking. I quickly confirmed my selection, and the screen changed again, this time displaying a list of character attributes like strength, speed, intelligence, and charisma. A box at the top of the screen displayed the number twenty—the number of unassigned attribute points available to me to distribute among the various character attributes.

I studied the chart, chewing on my lip. I had barely been in the game for five minutes. How could I possibly know which character attributes would benefit me most?

I glanced at Scarlet, who was now sitting and bathing herself. "Do I have to choose right now, or can I save the attribute points for later?"

"You can save them," Scarlet said, not pausing her bathing.

"Alright," I said with a nod. "I'll do that." The screen vanished, and the world unfroze. I looked at Dani. "Yes, I can fight," I told her. "And I'm telekinetic."

"Oh, good!" Dani said, her relief palpable. "Some of the others are away for a summit up north, and everyone else is out hunting for the day." Her shoulders slowly bunched up as she spoke. "We didn't expect anything like this to happen. Nobody sensed it. I just wish—well, that doesn't matter. It is what it is." She turned to the children, who were now clinging to one another. "You two stay up here and hide under the bed, and do *not* come out until you hear me calling for you. Do you understand?"

As the kids hurried for the bed, Dani turned to the dog. "Jack, guard them with your life," she ordered, and the dog stood, his large ears at attention. Dani helped the kids crawl under the bed, then stood and faced me. "You're with me, Olivia," she said, her hands on her hips. "Come on." She turned and rushed out of the room.

I threw back the covers and discovered I was wearing tattered jeans and a worn T-shirt. A pair of grungy hiking boots had been set out by the nightstand. I stuffed my feet into the boots, holey socks and all, and hastily tied the laces. I hurried out of the room, and Scarlet leapt off the bed, padding along beside me.

I found Dani waiting for me at the top of the staircase. From the looks of it, we were in an old farmhouse, which made sense from what I remembered of the books. Dani and her post-apocalyptic family had set up on a farm a year or two after a virus swept across the earth, killing most and changing those who survived, gifting them with superhuman abilities or leaving their minds warped and ravaged. The "Crazies" now attacking the farm fell into the latter group of survivors.

I followed Dani down the stairs and out onto the front porch. Terrifying noises were coming from the barn some thirty yards away.

Dani paused at the top of the porch stairs, and hundreds of crows gathered overhead—her army. She was a tiny woman, all things considered, but the power she wielded made her seem massive.

"Flush them out," Dani murmured, and in a wave, the crows dove toward the barn, streaming in through the open doors and windows.

Screams sounded from within. Human screams.

Seconds passed, and then a dozen or so grubby looking people poured out through the barn's front doorway.

Dani looked at me, a feral light to her green eyes. "None of them leave alive."

I sat alone at a raised bar table in the lounge part of the bar and grill that neighbored the bookstore, my eyes glued to the screen of my phone. I had just finished my final shift at the store, and I was waiting for Merina to join me for what I had mentally dubbed my "last supper". Tomorrow was the big day. Procedure day.

I absently sipped from my glass of Syrah as I read a post on a message board from a woman claiming to have lost all motor function on one side of her body as a result of VR implants. Most of the other stories were the knew-a-guy-who-knew-a-guy type, so it was engrossing to read a first-hand account of VR implants gone wrong. I knew I should have put the phone down, should have stopped searching for questionable testimonials proclaiming all the terrible things that might happen to me tomorrow. But I couldn't stop.

"Searching for your next hot date?" Merina asked, hugging my shoulders from behind me.

I set my phone down on the table, a grin engulfing my face, and turned in my chair to stand and give Merina a proper hug. "No need," I said into her hair. "My next hot date just arrived."

Merina pulled away and preened, fluffing her hair and fluttering her eyelashes. "Flattery will get you everywhere, darling," she said.

I laughed. "Don't I know it."

Merina mock scowled and slapped my arm. "Oh, hush you," she admonished. She pulled out the chair adjacent to mine and sat. "So, what's this about? Your text was very cryptic. I'd have demanded an explanation over the phone, but you know how much I like making up crazy stories in my head . . ."

I raised my glass, taking a sip of wine, and sighed, staring at the glass. "I got a job at Rockville," I told her, finally meeting her eyes.

Merina's face morphed into giddy excitement, and she clapped her hands together like an elated little kid. "Does that mean we get to be a team again?"

"Not exactly," I admitted, however reluctantly. "I got a job as a beta player."

Merina's clapping faltered, and her face fell. "Wait, what? But you don't even play video games."

I took a deep breath, exhaling heavily. "I know. It's complicated and a little confusing," I said, "but right after they offered me a teaching position, a bigwig came in and offered me a beta player position—and offered Charlie one, too, but only if *I* accepted."

Merina's jaw dropped. "Oh. Shit."

"Seriously," I agreed. "I couldn't say no, not with Charlie's happiness on the line."

Merina frowned. "Why did they want you so badly?" She asked. "Not that they shouldn't, but . . . you know what I mean."

I shook my head and shrugged my shoulders. "Trust me," I said, "I get it. And I *don't* get it. Apparently, they need someone with deep knowledge and understanding of Jane Austen or something like that."

Merina whistled, her attention shifting off me just long

enough for her to catch the server's eye and finger wave, letting him know she was ready to order. "Well," she said, returning her attention to me, "you certainly fit that bill."

The server dropped off a ticket at the bar, then made his way over to our table.

"Bottle?" Merina asked me as he approached.

I took another sip from my glass. "Most definitely."

"What can I get you?" the server asked, his eyes for Merina, and Merina alone.

Merina flashed him her most dazzling smile. "Is there a bottle of red on the happy hour menu?"

"The house red," the server confirmed with a nod. "It's a red blend."

Merina glanced my way, and when I nodded, she said, "Great. We'll do that." Merina flashed him another, quicker smile, dismissing him, then looked at me. "So . . . wow."

"I know," I said. "And the implant procedure is tomorrow, and I'm totally freaking out about it." I ran my fingers through my hair, massaging my aching scalp. "Of course, I couldn't help myself, and I've been reading all these horror stories online."

Merina nodded. "I can imagine," she said. "I dated a guy whose brother ended up in a coma for almost a year because of those implants." When my eyes opened wide, she rushed to add, "It was an early model implant. I think he might have even been a part of a trial group or something." She waved a hand. "Whatever. It doesn't matter. It was a long time ago, and I'm sure nothing like that will happen to you."

I raised my wineglass and gulped down a hearty swig. "Ugh," I said, setting down my glass. "I wish Charlie's contract didn't depend on me going through with this."

Merina's eyes narrowed. "When is *his* procedure?"

"Wednesday," I said, my voice filled with resignation.

"Damn," Merina muttered. "I was thinking that if his procedure was before yours, you could just back out after his implant was installed." She raised one shoulder. "He might not keep his contract, but I doubt they'd remove the tech . . ."

"I know, I already thought of that," I admitted. "And I considered feigning illness tomorrow and rescheduling my procedure for after his. They say the procedure appointment can't be rescheduled, but they have to have some accommodation for people getting sick. I mean, isn't it a higher risk to put someone under if they're sick?"

Merina pursed her lips and quirked her mouth to the side. "Hmmm . . . I don't know."

The server returned with our bottle of wine and two fresh wineglasses. He filled Merina's then glanced my way.

I waved a hand at my fresh glass and nodded. "I'll be done with this in a sec."

He filled my glass and set the bottle down. "Would you ladies like to order some food?" He glanced at the clock behind the bar. "Happy hour prices last for another thirty minutes."

"Give us a few?" Merina asked, dragging the happy hour menu closer to her on the table. Once the server was gone, Merina's eyes lifted from the menu. "This is a sucky situation, Liv."

I gave her a no-shit look.

Merina sipped her wine, then set her glass down and shrugged, her eyes returning to the menu. "You could still back out," she said as she perused the offerings, "Maybe Charlie loses his contract, but at least you both keep your brains intact." She glanced up. "And the VA position might still be an option . . ."

I stared across the bar, envisioning the hurt and devastation in Charlie's eyes. I sighed. "I don't know if I can do that to Charlie."

Merina fixed me with a hard stare, the same one she used on students who tried to pass off lame excuses for why their work was incomplete. "Charlie loves you, Liv," she said. "I'm sure he would forgive you . . . eventually."

I snorted a laugh and finished my original glass of wine.

"Yeah, on his deathbed," I mused. "*Maybe*." I swapped my empty glass with the full one. "Gah, I hate this. Let's talk about something else. And let's order some food. You up for sharing a bunch of stuff?"

Merina flashed me a grin. "Always."

The rest of the evening passed with light-hearted conversation and plenty of laughter, and I was in a much better mood by the time the self-driving cab dropped me off at my parents' house. But the longer I was away from Merina, the longer I was alone with my own wandering thoughts, and the anxiety slowly crept back in. Was I really going to go through with this? *Could* I go through with it?

When I walked into my bedroom, I found a small gift bag sitting on the foot of the bed. An envelope was propped up against the bag, displaying my name written in Charlie's blocky handwriting.

Frowning, I picked up the envelope and pulled out the card contained within. THANK YOU was written on the front in big, glittery purple letters. Inhaling, I opened the card.

Olive -

Thank you so, SO much. I would say that you don't know how much this means to me, but I know you do. I also know you're scared about tomorrow, and I'm sure you've Googled all the horror stories relating to the implants. I know this isn't necessarily what you want, but I think you'll enjoy it anyway. I see you, Olive, and I appreciate you more than you know. From the bottom of my cold, shriveled little heart, thank you. Hopefully, this makes you feel a little better during the procedure. The girl at the shop said amber is a protection stone or some woo-woo mumbo jumbo like that. Love you, little sister.

Love, Charlie

. . .

P.S. If you want to back out, I get it. I'll be bummed, but I would never force you into doing something that scares you. I'll get over it. :)

As I read Charlie's words, tears welled in my eyes. I blinked, and the tears spilled over the brim of my eyelids, streaking down my cheeks. I wiped them away with one hand and set the card down, reaching for the bag.

I pulled out tissue paper first, then a palm-sized jewelry box. Opening the box revealed a beautiful amber pendant strung on a delicate silver chain. With shaking hands, I freed the necklace from the jewelry box and gazed down at the amber pendant resting on my palm. My chin trembled, and I curled my fingers around the pendant, pressing my fist to my chest, directly over my heart.

"Love you, too, Charlie," I whispered.

[11]

I woke to the sound of a man saying my name, possibly a man with a British accent, though in my dazed state it was hard to be sure. I dozed for another minute or two, but that same man—definitely British and strangely familiar—said my name again.

I cracked my eyes open, blinking as I looked around. I was in a hospital room. No, not a *hospital* room. I was in the onsite clinic at Rockville Softworks, where they carried out all their in-house implant procedures. So, this was my recovery room. It was done, then. The implant was in, hardwiring my brain's connection to *Allworld Online*.

I surveyed myself and found an IV hooked up to my forearm. A quick glance under the covers revealed that I was wearing black leggings and an oversized T-shirt displaying a glow-in-the-dark Cheshire cat. The "comfortable clothes" I had brought for the procedure, as directed.

Without warning, a large, sleek black cat jumped up onto the bed and sat near my knees, fixing its unnatural neon-blue eyes on me.

"Um, hi kitty?" I said, raising my hand to let the cat sniff my fingers.

The cat leaned in, its delicate nose twitching as it scented me, and then it rubbed the side of its face against my fingers.

I smiled, confused but not the least bit upset about finding a cat in my recovery room. It was kind of a nice touch, like animal therapy.

I scratched the cat's head for a minute, but then it seemed to grow bored with me and jumped off the bed. It padded over to the door and sat, glancing back at me.

I tilted my head to the side, smiling to myself. Cats were so funny. "Do you want out, kitty?" I asked, pushing the covers off my legs. "Hold on, I'm coming." I placed my socked feet on the floor and stood, reaching out to grab the IV stand before making my way to the door. I gripped the door handle, pressing it down, then pulled the door open.

My mouth fell open as I stared out at the familiar, alien gatescape. "Whoa," I murmured, closing my eyes and rubbing my eyelids as if doing so might jostle my brain back into the realm of reality.

But when I opened my eyes again, the gatescape was still there, clusters of crystals and neon gateways and players and gigis and all. I twisted partway to look over my shoulder. The recovery room was still there behind me, exactly the same as it had been when I'd first awoken, the faint smell of bleach and all. I looked ahead again. The gatescape appeared just as real.

And then I remembered what Dr. Morgan had told us. To ensure the successful pairing between mind and tech, we would each be immersed in *Allworld Online* as soon as the implant procedure was over. Which meant this wasn't the real world.

Coming to grips with the fact that I was in *Allworld Online*, I peeled off the tape holding the IV flush against my skin. With a wince, I tugged the IV free, dropping it to press my hand over the sore spot on my forearm. It felt *so* real. Like, really, *really* real.

On the floor, the cat twined around and between my calves.

I glanced down, my eyes narrowing. If I was in *Allworld Online*, then did that mean the cat was my gigi?

"Indeed, I am," the cat said, his voice distinctly male, distinctly British, and just the teensiest bit mischievous. He peered up at me with those unnaturally vibrant blue eyes. "Are you ready to explore, Olivia?"

My eyes widened, and a smile tugged at my lips. "What do I call you?"

"You may call me Loki," he said, sitting primly, and suddenly I could place the voice. "I selected the name from your mind, and I find I quite like it, along with the voice associated with it."

"Oh," I said, my smile broadening, "OK. Sounds good to me."

"So, what would you like to do today, Olivia?"

I shook my head and shrugged. "I don't know," I admitted. "What are my options?"

Loki stood and padded a few steps into the gatescape, then looked back at me. "This is *Allworld Online*," he said. "Your options are endless."

WILLIAM ST. GEORGE

"It begins in two days," Will said, once again standing behind the armchair in the library of a great manor house while the woman who pulled his strings stared into the flames in the fireplace.

"Good," the woman said. "My chains grow tiresome, and I am eager to stretch my legs." She was quiet for a moment. "If this doesn't work, William . . ."

"It will work," he assured her, bowing his head. "It *will* work."

September 2, 2026

The world watches eagerly as Rockville Softworks launches the beta test of their newest game universe within *Allworld Online*. *Austentopia*, a long-awaited branch of the Biblioverse, will allow players to enter some of the most beloved stories of all time—those written by Jane Austen.

The beta round officially launched this morning and is expected to take about a month, with Austentopia being released to the public upon the completion of the beta tests. A press release from Rockville Softworks claims the gaming giant hopes *Austentopia* will draw in an audience their revolutionary virtual world has yet to reach. Only time will tell, but I can say for certain that this Jane Austen fan can't wait to dive in.

[12]

I walked through the crowd of players filling the magnificent atrium at the heart of the Biblioverse, Loki strolling along at my feet, his black fur gleaming and his tail held high. The members of my gaming party were spread out around me, some ahead, some behind, all of us dressed in the street clothes we had been wearing just moments ago in the real world. Most actually had dog gigis—only Nel and I had ended up with cats, though Nel's gigi had a snowy white coat compared to Loki's onyx fur.

This was our first official day as beta players, and all of our bodies were together in a high tech room, each of us stretched out on our own reclining chair, electrodes stuck to various parts of our bodies to monitor our vitals and reactions throughout the initial round of gameplay. It seemed excessive to me, but what did I know about beta testing VR games?

As Loki and I neared the archway labeled *ROMANCE*, some of the other members of my party veered away, heading for a nearby archway labeled *CLASSIC LITERATURE*. I peered through the other archway. The room beyond looked like a gorgeous old library, like something pulled straight out of *Beauty and the Beast*.

"Are you sure we're going to the right place?" I asked Loki as Holden, the cheerful guy with kind eyes, passed through the *CLASSIC LITERATURE* archway and vanished from sight, his fluffy canine gigi disappearing beside him.

"Indeed," Loki said. "The primary location of *Austentopia* is in the Romance section of the Biblioverse, but it can also be reached through the Classic Literature section, as well as the Comedy section. The access point is entirely dependent upon the player's view of Jane Austen and what they find most appealing about her work."

I frowned, wondering what that said about me. I had engaged in more than a few scholarly debates to persuade others that Jane Austen's stories were more than the romances that formed the heart and soul of each of her books. They were filled with social commentary and satire, humor, irony, and even bits of philosophy. But based on our trajectory—we were definitely making a beeline for the Romance section—these stories, even to me, were romances first.

When Loki and I passed through the archway, all the players around us disappeared, leaving us to enter the Romance section of the Biblioverse in peaceful solitude as *Allworld Online* created a private instance of the room, just for me. Like in the Apocalyptic & Dystopian section of the Biblioverse, this section consisted of a ring of bookcases surrounding a central open area covered by a glass dome ceiling. But there, the resemblance ended.

The bookcases here were polished mahogany with intricate, carved flourishes along the edges and only the slightest patina of age. The central area within the ring of bookcases was park-like, with lush green grass surrounding a fountain featuring Rodin's *The Kiss* and blooming cherry blossom trees scattered about. Golden sunlight streamed in through the pristine glass dome high overhead, and tiny nightingales sang as they flitted from tree to tree and branch to branch.

Loki led me between a pair of bookcases to the central area, and as I stepped onto the grass, I raised my face, basking in the gentle kiss of the sunlight on my skin. Loki padded along, crossing the park-like setting without even acknowledging the taunting birds or tantalizing sunlight. The cat was clearly on a mission.

We crossed the expanse of grass and passed between another pair of bookcases, and Loki headed straight for a small nook set into the outer wall. A cozy fireplace dominated the space, and a single oversized armchair and delicate side table were the only other features of the nook. There were no bookcases or shelves in this part of the virtual library, merely a line of a dozen or so vibrant leather-bound books on the mantle of the fireplace, propped up by bronze bookends shaped like peacocks with elegantly swooping tail feathers. As I stepped into the nook, soft Regency era music tickled my ears.

Loki leapt up onto the arm of the chair, and then onto the fireplace mantel, where he sat primly and curled his tail around his paws. "Second book from the left," he said, glancing lazily at the books occupying the center of the mantel.

I skirted around the armchair and tilted my head to the side to study the spines. All seven of Jane's completed works were there, along with *Sanditon* and *The Fosters*, her two known incomplete novels, the latter of which Austen had abandoned shortly after starting it. There was also a book titled *The Jane Austen Experience*. I assumed that was the open-world MMORPG game Charlie was beta testing.

"How did they make games out of *Sanditon* and *The Fosters*?" I asked, skimming my fingers over the spines of the two unfinished books.

"*Sanditon* is a tycoon game," Loki explained, meaning it was a business simulation game, I assumed where players built up the resort town of Sanditon. "And *The Fosters*," Loki continued, "is an open-world sandbox." Meaning players could pretty much go anywhere and do anything with little or no direction.

"Oh, interesting," I murmured, my fingertips skimming the sapphire-blue spine of *Pride and Prejudice*. The title was written in shiny gold lettering, and when I pulled the book from the mantel, my breath caught in my throat. The cover was emblazoned with gold peacock feathers that shimmered in the firelight.

Gingerly, I ran my fingertips over the cover. "It's the 1894 peacock edition," I murmured. In real life, this copy of *Pride and Prejudice* would have been worth thousands of dollars.

"Your favorite, yes," Loki said, licking one of his front paws and looking bored.

My brows bunched together. "How—" I shook my head.

Loki sighed and replaced his paw on the mantle. "Throughout much of *Allworld Online*," he said, "especially the common areas like the genre rooms here in the Bibliosphere, the base structure of the virtual space is designed by the makers and cannot be changed, but the aesthetic is tailored to each player's unique tastes as pulled from their subconscious mind."

I glanced over my shoulder at the beautiful, park-like scene beyond. "So, not everyone would see it like this?" I asked.

"In truth," Loki said, "nobody else would see this room like this, save for those you invite into your private instance or those watching your live feed. The customization is more detailed and intensive for those with the VR implant, though headset players do experience it to a lesser degree."

Absently, I touched the back of my neck, feeling for the bandage covering the healing incision at the base of my skull. I was a little surprised to find that the bandage was there, despite this not being my real, physical body, and I winced at the slight tenderness.

"It's getting harder and harder to remind myself that this version of reality isn't actually real," I told Loki—a *cat*. A *talking* cat.

I wondered if the architects of this too-real virtual world had included that element on purpose, with the hopes it would remind players there was still a real world out there, where cats didn't speak, and actions had real consequences.

I looked at the copy of *Pride and Prejudice* in my hand. "So, is it the same as before?" I asked Loki. "Just open the book and set it on the floor and . . ." I raised my eyebrows. "Walk into the book?"

Loki slow blinked. "Exactly so."

"Well, all right," I said and took a deep breath. "Here goes nothing." I opened *Pride and Prejudice* and set it on the floor. And then I stepped into one of my all-time favorite stories.

[13]

The world flashed white, and when the light faded, I found myself standing in the corner of an old-fashioned bedroom between a four-poster bed and a small delicate vanity. The bed was covered with white linens, and a pair of simple square tables stood on either side functioning as nightstands. A fireplace occupied the wall opposite the foot of the bed, flanked by a pair of doors, and there was another door beside the vanity. Two large windows cut through the wall on the far side of the bed, both open and letting in sunlight and fresh air, as well as the sound of birds chirping.

I hoped beyond hope that this was Longbourn, Elizabeth Bennet's family home in *Pride and Prejudice*. I supposed it could have been Lucas Lodge, as Charlotte Lucas was another significant character and likely playable in the game. But . . . to stand in Longbourn. What a dream come true!

Loki brushed against my leg before leaping onto the vanity and perching on the corner nearest me, his tail dangling over the edge. Another peacock edition of *Pride and Prejudice* sat on the tabletop beside him.

"This mirror will facilitate your character creation," he said, his whiskers twitching as his gaze slid past me.

"What mirror?" I looked around, following the line of sight of Loki's unnatural neon-blue eyes. A full-length standing mirror stood in the corner behind me.

"Oh," I said, slightly disappointed in my reflection. I looked exactly the same as I had when I'd left the house this morning, jeans, T-shirt, sneakers, and all.

"You may alter your physical appearance," Loki explained, "as well as select your starting attire."

As he spoke, an overlay appeared on the surface of the mirror, glowing lines and lettering indicating all the areas of my body that could be altered. From the looks of it, I could change pretty much anything. But the question was, did I *want* to change anything? Maybe it was vanity, but back when I had actually had time to play video games—before teaching took over my life—I had been one of those people who tried to make their game avatars look as much like themselves as possible. I didn't *want* to change anything about my appearance, and not because I was something special to look at. Changing my appearance would have deflated the sense of *me* being immersed in the character.

I frowned and touched my shoulder-length hair. It *would* be difficult to style hair this short into the fancy updos of this era.

"Maybe make this longer?" I said as I ran my fingers through my hair. It was a dark mahogany color with a slight wave, and as my fingers neared the ends of the strands, they lengthened right before my eyes. I grinned. "Very cool."

I scanned the rest of myself and shrugged, then glanced at Loki. "How do I move on to the clothing selection?" Because that was what I was the most excited about.

"Swipe your hand up the mirror," the cat said.

I did as instructed, and suddenly my reflection wore a long-sleeve, floor-length gown with the empire waist the Regency era was known for. The rich periwinkle fabric appeared lightweight, like cotton or linen. A name hovered above my reflection in elegant, glowing letters: ELIZABETH BENNET.

My mouth fell open, and I stared at the name, absolutely stunned. As I processed what this meant, my heart beat faster, and a slow smile spread across my face.

"I get to be Elizabeth?" I said, my voice little more than a breathy whisper. My eyes stung with happy tears, and I giggled, covering my mouth with my hands.

Elizabeth Bennet wasn't just the heroine of *Pride and Prejudice*; she was *my* hero. She was strong and known for standing her ground in a time when quite the opposite was expected of young ladies. She refused to settle, to sacrifice her happiness for the whims and desires of others, and yet she would do anything for her nearest and dearest—namely, her beloved sister, Jane. She was steadfast and loyal, headstrong and stubborn. She knew her mind but was able to change when presented with a compelling reason to do so. She was everything I wanted to be. And everything I now *could* be.

"Apparently the casting algorithm deemed you the best fit for the character of Elizabeth Bennet from those amongst your gaming party," Loki informed me.

Unable to hold in my excitement, I squealed and stomped my feet in a ridiculous little happy dance.

Loki stood, disturbed by my abrupt movement.

"Best. Day. Ever," I said, calming myself and returned to studying my reflection in the mirror.

Loki cleared his throat and resettled on the corner of the vanity. "Is that what you would like to wear to start the game?" he asked, giving me a pointed look.

I glanced down at myself, noting I was still wearing my jeans and T-shirt, then returned to studying my reflection, dressed in a periwinkle gown. "This is nice, but how do I see the other options?" Because there was no way I wasn't going to browse through every single dress before deciding.

"Swipe your hand across the mirror, right to left or left to right," Loki said. "The mirror will cycle through the handful of available beginner options. More options will unlock as you progress in the game, dependent upon the development of your character attributes."

I swiped left across the face of the mirror, and the periwinkle gown gave way to a white gown with a sage green roller print running in vertical stripes. I swiped again, and the dress changed to a white muslin. Again, and the dress changed to a russet linen. Again, and the gown changed to white cotton printed with tiny lilac flowers. My next swipe brought me back to the periwinkle option.

"I think this one might actually be my favorite," I said, twisting my body from side to side and watching the skirt swish in the mirror. "It's quite nice." I glanced at Loki. "What do you think?"

"Lovely," he said, though he couldn't have sounded less interested. "Is that your final selection?"

I pursed my lips and quirked my mouth to the side, my head tilting slightly as I studied my reflection. Just to be absolutely certain, I quickly swiped through the other options only to return to the periwinkle dress. "Yep," I said. "This is definitely my favorite."

"Very well," Loki intoned. "Swipe up to confirm your selection."

I did as instructed, and as soon as I pulled my hand from the mirror, I could feel the constriction of the short corset, like a really sturdy, really hefty bra wrapped snug around my ribs and pushing my boobs up into "heaving bosom" status—probably for the first time in my life. The dress itself was fairly lightweight, the thin periwinkle cotton conforming to my body from the bust up and hanging loose from the empire waist down to just past my ankles.

For shoes, I wore flat-soled brown leather booties that laced up the front. Certainly not anything the ladies in London would be wearing, but I supposed us country folk needed sturdier footwear. Especially Elizabeth Bennet, who was known for her long walks about the countryside and to and from Meryton, the nearest town, with her sisters. *My* sisters, for the time being.

I ran my hands down the front of the dress, then turned to examine my new outfit from the side. "It's more comfortable than I thought it would be," I murmured, grateful that full-on whalebone corsets had fallen out of style during this period. I was kind of a fan of breathing.

"You are, of course, welcome to remove any or all of your attire," Loki said, "but be warned that doing so will impact your character development and may even alter the direction of the story as a whole."

I raised my eyebrows. "My character development?" I asked. "I thought this was a straight-up reenactment."

"The game can be played as such," Loki said, "or the trajectory of the storyline and characters' lives may be altered by player choices." He batted at the copy of *Pride and Prejudice* lying on the vanity beside him, pushing it closer to the edge.

I narrowed my eyes, watching the book teeter on the edge.

"You may see your starting character attributes in this book," Loki said, "which functions as your primary game interface. Within the book, you can track your character's development and see the results of your chosen actions, as well as your accuracy score, progress meter, and real-world popularity. The book also functions as your game log and your access portal to elsewhere in *Allworld Online*, should you need to message others outside of the game and/or step out of the game entirely." With one final bat of his paw, he pushed the book off the vanity. It landed on the floor with a thump.

I eyed the book pointedly, and then Loki, in turn. "Just couldn't help yourself?"

"What can I say?" Loki said, looking away. "I'm a cat."

I snorted not so delicately and bent to pick up the book. As I straightened, I opened the cover, revealing three large meter bars filling the top half of the first page, each looking to have been hand drawn in black ink. Six smaller meter bars filled the bottom half of the page. The larger bars were labeled *PROGRESS METER, ACCURACY METER,* and *POPULARITY METER.* The first and last were empty, while the accuracy meter was marked by a thick line in the middle, with the right side of the bar labeled with a plus sign and the left side labeled with a minus sign.

The smaller bars were labeled *INTELLIGENCE, REPUTATION, CHARISMA, NATURE, FASHIONABILITY,* and *ATTRACTION.* Each of these bars was also marked by a thick line in the middle, signaling that my actions and interactions in the game would influence whether those attributes increased or decreased and would likely impact what I could do—and get away with—in this world. I noted that there were no free attribute points to assign to influence my character's development, and I mentioned the observation to Loki.

"Quite so," the cat said. "Your character attributes cannot be artificially increased or decreased. Only your actions within the game can impact the development of your character."

"Hmmm . . . interesting." I studied the page for a moment longer. "And why is the popularity bar grayed out?" I asked, glancing at Loki.

"As this is merely a beta round," he said, "and players cannot live stream, all viewers are beta watchers and required to watch, thus not a genuine reflection of how engaging you are in this role. As such, the feature has been temporarily deactivated."

I frowned and looked around, wondering if anyone was watching me right now.

"Most likely," Loki said, reading my thoughts.

I returned my attention to him but couldn't shake the discomfort of unseen eyes watching me. With a sigh, I turned the page in the book, finding a too-modern pen tucked into a recess cut into the pages near the spine. The remainder of the page was blank.

"This must be for messaging?" I asked, once again glancing at Loki.

"And for recording log entries, should you desire to do so," he said.

I turned the page again, revealing a single word written in large, bold type: EXIT. I assumed this meant I would leave the game the same way I came in—by stepping through a book.

Another page turn and I was skimming over the table of contents of what appeared to be an encyclopedia of all things Regency England and Jane Austen. I quickly flipped through the entries—there were hundreds of them, ranging from fashion trends to marriage traditions—then snapped the book shut and looked at Loki.

"OK," I said, "Now what?

"Now, you start the game." And with that, Loki jumped off the vanity and padded toward the adjacent door.

I followed him, and when I opened the door, I was startled to find a fine-boned blonde woman standing in the hallway on the other side, a white cat at her feet and one hand raised to knock. I blinked, and the woman's appearance glitched, flashing for a few seconds to a more recognizable form with pixie features and short, shocking teal hair before returning to the more traditional blonde beauty.

Nel's lips curved into a giddy grin. "I *knew* you would be Lizzy!" she said in a rush. "I got Jane. I mean, my character is Jane, obviously."

I was immensely relieved to hear Nel speaking with her usual American accent. Much as Merina and I might amuse ourselves by slipping into terrible British accents when we've had a bit too much wine, I hadn't been excited about the prospect of having to consciously pay attention not just to what I was saying, but to how I was saying it.

"I was a little bummed," Nel went on. "I mean, who wouldn't want to be Elizabeth Bennet—you're so lucky—but Jane's second best, I suppose. Besides Darcy, I mean, but I don't feel like he has all that much fun throughout the story. At least I'll get to go to London!" She grinned. "Regency London—won't that be something to see?"

I nodded. "I'm sure it will."

The sound of raised voices floated up from downstairs, increasing until the words became clear.

"Mr. Bennet," a woman screeched, and all I could do was grin. This was it. The story was starting. "How can you abuse your own children in such a way?" Mrs. Bennet continued, her voice shriller by the second. "You take delight in vexing me. You have no compassion on my poor nerves."

"You mistake me, my dear," a man, Mr. Bennet, said his voice low and filled with the rumble of age. "I have a high respect for your nerves. They are my old friends. I have heard you mention them with consideration these twenty years at least."

"Ah!" Mrs. Bennet shrieked. "You do not know what I suffer."

Nel reached for my hand and gave it a squeeze. My eyes met hers, my grin matching hers, and she pulled me out into the hallway. Together, we eagerly hurried downstairs to start the game.

[14]

The carriage ride to Meryton for the first ball of the story was bumpier than I had expected for driving on a well-traveled road. Loki lay curled up on my lap, and I stroked his onyx fur as I stared out the small window in the carriage cover, reflecting on my time in this magical place. I had been in the game for a little over two weeks, with my gaming party's first logout scheduled for midnight tonight, in-game.

Time compression was a funny thing, and it was almost impossible for my mind to comprehend that while it felt like seventeen days had passed, I had really only been logged in to *Allworld Online* since this morning, at least in real-world time.

This virtual world of ribbons and gowns and gossip and balls felt just as real as the *real* world, and I had settled into my role as Elizabeth Bennet with no trouble at all. Life here felt slower, easier, calmer. Lizzy's problems were limited to deciding where to walk and what to read and picking out which gown to wear to the assembly tonight. I had no problem sticking to the script during the relatively rare straight-from-the-page scenes and relished improvising in true Elizabeth Bennet fashion the rest of the time. My accuracy meter had been inching steadily to the right since the game started, indicating that I was portraying Elizabeth Bennet true to form, though my progress meter had only shaded in five or six percent.

The carriage slowed to a stop, and I exchanged a look with Nel, who was sitting opposite me, squished to the side by Lydia and Kitty, who had been revealed to me as two more players—Michelle and Allie—by another couple of those unsettling reveal flashes. Their canine gigis rested on the floor of the carriage, while Nel's snowy white cat lay snuggled on her lap, much like Loki was on mine. I hadn't hit it off with Allie or Michelle the way I had with Nel, but maybe that was to be expected with the AI algorithm selecting us for each role based on our relative compatibility. Jane and Lizzy were written as more than sisters—they were best friends—and my friendship with Nel grew deeper with each passing day in the game.

Our in-game mother, a moderately ridiculous woman never given a first name and only ever known as Mrs. Bennet, sat beside me. Mary, the final and most serious Bennet sister, sat on her other side. Both were NPCs—non-player characters—completely unchanged by the rare reveal flashes that altered the players' appearances.

Once we had all unloaded from the carriage, Nel hooked her arm through mine and we headed for the open doors to the already crowded assembly hall. "I wonder which of the guys will be playing Mr. Bingley," she mused, speaking of the wealthy bachelor who had recently rented out Netherfield Park and was destined to be her happy ending. "And I hope he's a good dancer. Because I'm hopeless. My accuracy score is going to plummet."

I laughed and hugged her arm closer. "I'm sure you'll do just fine."

But Nel's words brought to life a charm of butterflies flitting around in my belly. Who *would* be playing Mr. Bingley? And more importantly, who would be playing Mr. Darcy? Our gaming party consisted of five women and three men, and while I knew

Allworld Online wasn't opposed to bending genders, I suspected this first beta round would try to match us as closely as possible to the characters we were playing, from base personalities down to anatomical parts.

There was no way the algorithm would have selected Colin for the role of Charles Bingley. Bingley was far too cheerful and good natured—basically the opposite of Colin's personality. Which only left a few other potential roles. Obviously one of the guys would be cast as Mr. Darcy, but I wondered which other male fictional character from the story would appear as a player rather than an NPC. I could only think of two possibilities: Mr. Collins, the Bennet's ridiculous cousin, and Mr. Wickham, the deceptively friendly fiend. And no matter how I tried to bend my understanding of Colin to fit one of those characters, I feared I already knew which role he would be perfect for. Mr. Darcy, Elizabeth's love interest.

I gulped. *My* love interest.

Allie and Michelle ran ahead, giggling in true Kitty and Lydia fashion as they melted into the crowd gathered within the packed assembly hall, and dear, silly Mrs. Bennet hurried after her two youngest children. Behind me, I could hear Mary grumbling about decorum and respectability. And then Nel and I stepped into the assembly hall and were immediately swept up by the excited energy.

I heard Mr. Bingley's name uttered over and over as the ladies and gentlemen gossiped about the large party of fine people he was rumored to be bringing with him to the assembly tonight. He was the county's newest, richest, and most eligible bachelor, and every mother of a young lady in the area wanted to lay claim on him to secure her daughter's future. Mrs. Bennet, as a mother of five daughters and no sons, was chief among them. I felt a little bad for the guy, the way everyone talked about him like he was prize stag and we were all the hunters.

A plain but graceful woman approached where Nel and I

stood off to the side of the dance floor, our heads bent together as we chatted, and another reveal-flash revealed the newcomer to be not just another NPC. This was a player—Grace, as Charlotte Lucas, if I had to guess. Grace was, in reality, a striking woman, but she had downplayed her looks to better fit the role of Elizabeth's sensible but plain dear friend Charlotte. I had yet to meet Grace in-game and figured the initial two weeks that had already passed must have been for us to grow acclimated to our immediate game environment. Now, however, the real fun was to begin.

"Those flashes are really distracting," I murmured to Nel before Grace reached us. Grace had started to glow, the game's way of signaling to me that I was supposed to pay attention to her, and ghostly words drifted across the lower half of my vision, directing me to greet Charlotte Lucas.

Nel looked at me, her brows drawn together, clearly confused. "What flashes?"

Now it was my turn to be confused. But before I could say more, Grace reached us, and I tucked away the reveal flashes to dissect another time.

Grace extended her arms out toward me, and I had little choice but to take her hands in mine. "Charlotte," I said, smiling warmly, "it's been too long! Where have you been the last two weeks?"

And so, the first part of the evening passed in merriment and buzzing anticipation. I danced with a couple of NPCs when asked for my hand, and I was just taking a break from the dance floor to chat with Nel when a hush fell over the assembly hall and all eyes turned to the entrance.

A distinguished party of three men and two women had just entered the hall and stood at the entrance, scanning the packed room. Their clothes were of a finer cut and cloth than those of anyone else here, and an air of haughty refinement hovered around them. All, save for the fair, handsome gentleman in the middle who grinned broadly as he took in the crowd, wore the most serious of expressions. The grinner had to be the much anticipated Mr. Bingley, and I knew that his serious companions included his sisters Miss Caroline Bingley and Mrs. Hurst, the latter's husband, Mr. Hurst, and of course, standing at Bingley's side, Mr. Darcy.

Otherwise known as Colin. His appearance was remarkably unaltered, other than the lack of any ink peeking out from his high-collared shirt or the sleeves of his waistcoat. He was the storm cloud to his golden-haired companion's sunshine, and there was no doubt in my mind that he had, indeed, been cast as my proud and brooding counterpart.

"Isn't Mr. Bingley handsome?" Nel said, drawing closer to my side.

"Very handsome," I murmured and narrowed my eyes, unable to match him to any of the players in our gaming party.

A moment later, a reveal-flash struck the assembly hall, briefly showing me the true identities of two more players among the five newcomers—Mr. Bingley was cheerful Holden, and Caroline Bingley was none other than our party liaison and the project lead for all of *Austentopia*, Priya Burman.

I frowned, wondering how she would possibly have time to participate in the beta test as a player, and glanced at Nel side-long. "You really didn't see that?"

"I see a couple of hunks," Nel said. "At least if you fall for Colin in the game, you know he looks the same IRL."

An unladylike laugh exploded from me, sending a spray of spit flying, and I slapped a hand over my mouth, hoping none of the NPCs noticed. "I can one hundred percent guarantee that *that* won't happen," I told Nel.

She eyed me skeptically but said nothing more on the matter.

Soon enough, Nel was dancing with Holden, her good-natured Mr. Bingley, and Colin was dancing with Priya. I chatted with Charlotte and some of the NPCs, and I danced when invited, but all the while, I kept one eye on Colin. I couldn't help it. He embodied the description of Mr. Darcy so perfectly, putting on a good show of being the proudest, most disagreeable man in the world.

Shortly after completing a dance with a kind-eyed young man, I spotted a glowing chair nearby. A prompt for me to sit, no doubt. I could ignore it. I always had that choice. But I was proud of my climbing accuracy score, and it had become a personal goal of mine to play the most perfect game as Elizabeth Bennet as possible. Why not set the bar high for all who followed?

With a sigh, I sat in the chair. My feet ached from dancing all evening in what had to be the world's—or the *virtual* world's— most uncomfortable shoes. I watched the next dance, contentment thrumming through my veins, and only when it ended, and Colin and Holden meandered my way, did dread swell in my belly. How had I forgotten? My muscles vibrated with tension as the two men took up positions near enough for me to overhear their conversation.

I slouched down in the chair, wishing I could disappear.

"Come, Darcy," Holden said, pulling off a not-too-shabby British accent. "I must have you dance. I hate to see you standing about by yourself in this stupid manner. You had much better dance."

My heart was pounding, and I held my breath as I listened, watching them out of the corner of my eye.

"I certainly shall not," Colin said, sounding completely and utterly like himself. In other words, totally disinterested in anything going on around him. "You know how I detest it unless I am particularly acquainted with my partner. At such an assembly as this, it would be insupportable. Your sisters are engaged, and there is not another woman in the room whom it would not be a punishment to me to stand up with."

Warmth crept up my neck and cheeks.

"I would not be so fastidious as you are for a kingdom," Holden cried out. "Upon my honor, I never met with so many pleasant girls in my life as I have this evening; and there are several of them you see uncommonly pretty."

"*You* are dancing with the only handsome girl in the room," Colin replied.

"Oh!" Holden exclaimed. "She is the most beautiful creature I ever beheld!" He glanced over his shoulder, his attention landing on me, just for a moment. "But there is one of her sisters sitting down just behind you, who is very pretty, and I dare say, very agreeable. Do let me ask my partner to introduce you."

"Which do you mean?" Colin asked, sounding genuinely curious. Either he was a damn good actor, or he had no idea what was about to happen. What he was about to do to me.

At Holden's direction, Colin turned partway to look at me. His stare lingered, assessing, making me feel like I had been stripped naked, right there in front of him.

I gripped the edges of the seat, my nails digging into the wood, but I refused to look at him.

"She is tolerable," he said, turning back to Holden. "But not handsome enough to tempt *me*; and I am in no humor at present to give consequence to young ladies who are slighted by other men. You had better return to your partner and enjoy her smiles, for you are wasting your time with me."

My cheeks flamed. Now that the embarrassing interlude was over, I stood and hurried away, needing to escape from this stifling hall. I headed for the open doors but stopped when a woman stepped in front of me, blocking my way.

"Enjoying yourself?" Priya asked.

I forced a smile. This conversation between Elizabeth and Caroline wasn't part of the story, so there were no prompts to guide me, leaving me feeling flustered. "I'm having a lovely time," I told her, then narrowed my eyes as I studied her unfamiliar mask. "I didn't realize you would be in here with us," I admitted.

Priya's lips parted, and her eyes opened wide with surprise. "I'm sorry? Why wouldn't I be here?" She flashed me a friendly smile. "I'm Jade, remember? I'm a part of your gaming party . . ."

I shook my head. "No," I said slowly, uncertainty making me draw out the word. "You're not Jade. You're Pr—"

Priya's eyes opened even wider, and she sucked in a breath. "How—" She grabbed my arm and all but dragged me outside. She scanned the darkness around us to make sure we were alone, touched something on her wrist, then leaned in close, keeping her voice low. "How do you know who I really am?"

I blinked, taken aback by her reaction. Why was she trying to hide the fact that she was here? "I saw you," I told her. "I mean, the real you—during one of those weird glitchy reveal flashes."

Priya shook her head. "What *reveal flashes*?"

I pulled back a little. "You know," I started, "the way a player's real identity overlays their character when we're first introduced." As her eyes narrowed, I pulled back further. "Or is that not a thing?"

Priya pursed her lips, inhaling and exhaling through her nose. "No, it most certainly is *not* a thing." She cocked her head to the side, studying my face, then frowned. "But some players' brains are naturally less susceptible to deception. Some can even accidentally rewrite the code of a game. Sort of like Neo in *The Matrix*, minus the messiah complex. The algorithm usually weeds out such people from our beta teams. It's a little shocking that you made it through." A moment later, she added, "Though people like you do make excellent Game Wardens."

I sucked in a breath to ask her what a "Game Warden" was, but before I could, another glitch-flash struck, almost like me thinking about it had made it happen, and Priya's appearance wavered.

"It just happened again, didn't it?" she said, her keen-eyed stare locked on me.

I hesitated only for a moment before nodding. It took me a few seconds, but I finally worked up the courage to ask, "Is this going to be a problem?"

"Maybe," Priya said, staring off into the darkness. "Especially now that you're aware of it. It's probably going to start happening more frequently, and you may even be able to control it." She blew out a breath. "What a cluster fuck."

A weak smile curved my lips. "Sorry?" I said, as though any part of this situation was within my control.

Priya dismissed the apology with a wave of her hand. "What's done is done, and you're here." She was quiet for a moment, staring off into the darkness, but then her attention fixed on me. "If you can, keep track of when and how often it happens. If it starts happening with more than just other players, or if the world around you starts to unravel, let me know. We may need to pull you from the test."

"Oh," I said, sadness seeping into my virtual body. Maybe I hadn't been all that gung ho about becoming a beta player, but now that I was here, I found I was actually enjoying myself. I didn't want to give it up.

"But for now, don't tell anyone else about this," Priya added. She held up her wrist, revealing a delicate silver bracelet with a large sapphire that almost seemed to be glowing. "I can use this to black out our streams when we speak to keep this confidential. And please don't reveal who I really am to anyone. So far as the others know, I'm Jade."

"You're not supposed to be here, are you?" I said, studying her face in the darkness.

Priya shook her head.

"So why *are* you here?" I asked.

Priya shrugged one shoulder. "Call it a hunch."

I stood in the middle of the road out in front of Longbourn watching Nel ride off on horseback, heading out to dine at Netherfield with Bingley's sisters. Loki sat at my feet, a silent observer, and dark clouds stewed in the sky, blotting out the sun. I was not looking forward to the evening at Longbourn without Nel. It would be the first time I would be without her in the game, and I felt a little like a kid learning to ride a bike without training wheels.

I trudged back to the house, Loki following close behind me, already planning to call it an early night and head up to my room right after dinner. Lydia, Kitty, and Mrs. Bennet were amusing enough to a reader on the page, but in real life, they were downright annoying. Almost a month had passed in-game since the Meryton assembly, and Mrs. Bennet hadn't once ceased her endless string of musings about her sweet Jane's future with Mr. Bingley. I was constantly holding in groans and suppressing eye rolls. I understood now why Elizabeth spent so much time wandering the countryside on foot, and why Mr. Bennet spent nearly all of his time in his study. To get away from Mrs. Bennet.

That being said, I did feel bad for the woman. Her obsession with marrying her daughters off—and marrying them off *well*—was understandable. Thanks to some messy and misogynistic old laws, the family estate of Longbourn was entailed to a distant male cousin, silly Mr. Collins who had yet to enter the story, which meant the Bennet girls would be left with little once Mr. Bennet was gone. Mrs. Bennet and her daughters could be turned out of house and home, and then the young women's chances of marrying well, or at all, would decrease dramatically.

Mrs. Bennet was afraid for her daughters—terrified, really—and I could hardly blame her for her diligence. Especially not when her husband did little more than sit back and poke fun at the situation with well-timed sarcastic comments. But really, despite the crummy circumstance, she didn't need to be *so* vocal about her singular pursuit.

Another glitch-flash struck during dinner, and much to my surprise, it wasn't just Lydia and Kitty who changed. For the first time ever, an NPC's appearance changed, too. Where serious and sullen Mary had been, suddenly sat an older woman wearing a dark, skin-tight bodysuit with glowing channels of neon light running along the arms and bodice, her auburn hair twisted up in a tight bun. I tried not to stare, but I was so shocked that it was hard not to. Even after everyone's appearances returned to normal, I was left feeling unsettled.

As soon as dinner was over, I retired to the bedroom I shared with Nel. I quickly noted the glitch-flash in my game log and then readied for bed. I had a big day tomorrow, joining Nel at Netherfield, and I was eager not only to be reunited with Nel but also to relay this latest glitch-flash to Priya.

I laid down and closed my eyes, willing sleep to come and sweep me away.

Sleep was funny in AO but necessary each game night, even with the time compression making it so not even an hour of real-world time had passed. To my mind, it was as though a true day had passed, and my brain needed rest, even if my physical body didn't. But tonight, sleep was fitful, and I was plagued by dreams dredged up by my subconscious. Dreams of glitch-flashes and virtual body snatchers. Dreams of being kicked out of the game. And dreams of Colin.

I had seen Colin a handful of times since the Meryton assembly, but always in large enough groups that avoiding him was easy. Our encounters over the coming days at Netherfield would be far more intimate and, some might say, even flirtatious. We would be building the foundation of Darcy's infatuation with Elizabeth. I was usually so flustered and frustrated around the guy that I had a hard time forming coherent sentences, but being clever and unintentionally flirty, as Elizabeth was written, I wasn't sure I could do it. Not around him.

I was just finishing up my piece of toast at breakfast the next morning when a servant from Netherfield arrived, delivering a note from Nel. As expected, she had been caught in the rainstorm during the tail end of her ride to Netherfield Park the previous evening, and the cold had seeped into her bones, leaving her fevered and bedridden.

"Well, my dear," Mr. Bennet said from the head of the table, "if your daughter should have a dangerous fit of illness—if she should die, it would be a comfort to know that it was all in pursuit of Mr. Bingley, and under your orders."

"Oh!" Mrs. Bennet groused. "I am not at all afraid of her dying. People do not die of little trifling colds. She will be taken good care of. As long as she stays there, it is all very well. I would go and see her if I could have the carriage."

"I am afraid not, my dear," Mr. Bennet said. "The horses are needed in the fields."

I straightened in my chair as a transparent prompt appeared in front of me, telling me it was my turn to speak. "I'll go," I volunteered. "I'll walk. It's no trouble."

"How can you be so silly as to think of such a thing, in all this dirt!" Mrs. Bennet exclaimed. "You will not be fit to be seen when you get there."

"I shall be very fit to see Ne—Jane," I corrected, "which is all I want."

Mrs. Bennet went on for a time, but I tuned her out, a skill I was growing more and more proficient at.

Soon enough, I was on my way to Netherfield Park, Loki stalking along at my feet. The rain the night before had left the ground a soggy mess, and by the time I reached Netherfield, an impressive manor house with lovely and extensive manicured grounds, my boots were soaked through with mud, and despite my best efforts, the hem of my russet dress was visibly soiled.

I did my best to wipe off my boots before entering the great house, but it was impossible to clean them fully, and the wooden soles squelched against the polished marble floor of the entry hall with each step. With Loki as my ever-present shadow, I was shown into the breakfast parlor, where the entire Netherfield party was lounging after a late breakfast, though Nel was nowhere to be seen.

Colin, Holden, and Mr. Hurst stood as I entered. Priya and Mrs. Hurst remained seated, a slight bow of the head the only acknowledgment of my arrival. Holden greeted me warmly, a cheerful smile lighting up his face, Colin simply stood there and stared, and Mr. Hurst flopped back into his seat to continue sipping his tea.

Once again, I wondered how familiar Colin was with the story, and if he had known this time together was coming. Truth be told, he looked slightly stunned to see me.

"My lord, Miss Bennet, your skirt!" Mrs. Hurst exclaimed. "Did you *walk* here? In the *mud*?" She made a bad show of stifling a laugh and exchanged a look with Priya, who rolled her eyes. Apparently, the game designer wasn't too worried about *her* accuracy score.

"I did," I said, following the floating prompt, and forced a smile, my cheeks heating at Mrs. Hurst's mocking scrutiny. "May I see my sister?"

Priya popped up from her chair. "Yes, of course!" she said in a rush. "I'll take you to her. I was just about to head up there to check on her myself." Priya made her way around the table with quick footsteps and when she reached me, hooked her arm through mine.

"Have you experienced any more of those *flashes*?" she asked as soon as we were out of the room, her voice lowered to little more than a whisper.

"Just one," I admitted as we crossed the entry hall. "Last night, with the other sisters."

"Lydia and Kitty," Priya clarified, guiding me up a grand staircase.

I was quiet for a moment and met Priya's expectant stare. "And Mary," I finally added.

Priya stopped halfway up the staircase and faced me. "Are you certain it affected the NPC?"

I chewed on the inside of my cheek and nodded.

"What did you see?" Priya asked.

I pursed my lips, my brows drawing together as I recalled Mary's strange alter-appearance. "The woman I saw was older than Mary, in her thirties I would guess, and she wore a black bodysuit lit up by neon piping. The getup was very sci-fi," I said. "Oh, and she had auburn hair twisted up into a tight bun." I touched the crown of my head, signaling the bun's placement.

Priya narrowed her eyes thoughtfully. "Hmmm . . ." She wondered aloud. "I wonder if we have a stowaway. A curious hacker or a corporate spy. That might explain . . ." She shook her head. "Never mind," she said sharply, her gaze sliding off me. "Come on, let's get you up to Nel, so I can log out and speak with the architect."

I wondered who she meant by "the architect" and wanted to ask, but before I could, she was practically dragging me the rest of the way up the stairs. She unceremoniously dropped me off in the guest room where Nel was propped up in bed.

"I'll be back by dinner," Priya promised, then lowered her voice to a faint whisper so Nel wouldn't overhear. "Prepare yourself, Olivia—we may have to replace you. I'm sorry, but sometimes these things happen. I should have a definite answer when I return." She turned and strode away, vanishing between one step and the next, leaving me staring at the place where she had been only a moment ago.

"Everything okay?" Nel asked from the bed.

I laughed and shook my head, then shut the door and made my way over to her. I sat on the edge of the mattress, sinking into the lush bedding, my shoulders slumping. "I honestly have no idea."

[16]

I sat with Nel the remainder of the day, fretting about Priya's return. Nel complained that virtual colds were as bad as, if not worse than, the real thing, but it was still better than listening to Mrs. Bennet prattle on about the plight of her daughters. The midday meal was brought up to us, and Holden and Mrs. Hurst visited in turns, and soon enough, I was being summoned for dinner.

Dinner was a tense affair, for me at least. Priya had yet to return, despite her promise to be back in the game and to let me know my fate by now, and Mrs. Hurst claimed her "sister" had a headache and was resting. At least I didn't have to linger. I had barely set down my dessert spoon when the game prompted me to head back upstairs and check on Nel.

I ascended the stairs, a bundle of nerves. For some reason, the prospect of getting booted from the game—especially for reasons that were no fault of my own—made me that much more determined to maintain my high accuracy score. Maybe if I did a good enough job, they would overlook the weird way my brain was interacting with the virtual world. For someone who hadn't really wanted to be here in the first place, I really didn't want to leave.

"What's wrong, Olivia?" Nel asked as I stared out one of the large windows in her room, able to see little more than darkness beyond the glass. "And don't tell me nothing," she added, "because I'm not blind."

I sighed and turned toward her, wishing I could tell Nel about the glitch-flashes and the situation with Priya and my fears about getting kicked off the beta team. But I couldn't tell her any of that, so I plucked the next most bothersome thought from my mind. "Colin makes me nervous," I told her, perching on the windowsill and meeting her curious stare. At least it wasn't a lie.

"Like, good nervous or bad nervous?" Nel asked.

"I don't know," I said and worried my bottom lip. "We had this moment before the game—during interviews."

Nel raised her eyebrows, and a slow smile crept across her face. "A *moment*, huh?"

"Not that kind of moment," I clarified in a rush. "It was just in passing. He said something dickish, and when he tried to apologize, I said something dickish. It's silly, really." I looked down at my hands, picking at a hangnail, and laughed under my breath. "I could easily forgive *his* pride," I said, quoting one of my favorites of Elizabeth Bennet's lines in *Pride and Prejudice*, "if he had not mortified *mine*."

"Wow," Nel said, a small, secretive smile curving her lips.

I looked at her, tilting my head to the side, just a little. "What?"

"I now totally understand the casting choices for Elizabeth and Darcy," she said, "and I fully support it. You and Colin are perfect—for the roles . . ." She waggled her eyebrows. "And maybe for each other."

I blanched and spluttered, attempting to come up with a response. To tell her she was grossly mistaken. But before I could formulate anything resembling words, the bedroom door started to glow, telling me it was time for me to leave Nel to rest and to rejoin the others downstairs.

"Time's up," I said with a sigh, then stood and headed for the door. I wondered if Priya would be back now, and what it would mean for me if she was.

"Have fun," Nel called after me as I followed the prompt and left the room, flashing her a weak smile before shutting the door.

I didn't know why I cared so much about my accuracy score, why it was the thing I was latching onto now like it was my last, tenuous lifeline. Maybe it was the perfectionist in me or the remnants of the teen girl who would cry when she received any grade lower than an A. It seemed so pointless now that I was probably about to get kicked not just out of the game but off the beta player team. Once again, I would be out of work. A failure.

The descent down the stairs felt like a march to my own execution, and when I reached the drawing room, I immediately sought out Priya's disguised face, wanting to get this over with. It was time to rip off the Band-Aid. If I was going to get kicked out of this beautiful world, I wanted to leave immediately. Lingering would only prolong the hurt.

Thankfully, Priya had returned. I found her sitting at a table with the others, engaged in a game of cards.

Eyes locked with hers, I raised my eyebrows, silently asking if I was getting the ax.

She shook her head minutely, and relief flooded me.

I didn't have to leave the game. I wasn't going to lose my job. I could continue living out this fantasy life as Elizabeth Bennet. Floating with a sense of relief, I politely declined an offer to join the game and sat on the sofa with a book instead.

"Do you prefer reading to cards?" Mr. Hurst asked, judgment coating his words.

I merely smiled at him and shook my head, completely unruffled by his subtle dig at me. Nothing could bring me down, not right now.

"Miss Eliza Bennet despises cards," Priya said, for once sticking to the script. "She is a great reader and has no pleasure in anything else."

Giddy to be able to continue in the game, I was happy to play along. "I deserve neither such praise nor such censure," I said, right on cue. "I am *not* a great reader, and I have pleasure in many things."

The conversation continued, littered with subtle verbal jabs —mostly aimed at my character—and I remained sitting until a glowing path appeared on the floor, directing me to stand and join the others at the card table.

I was nearly there when a flash-glitch halted me mid-step and not just Colin, Priya, and Holden appeared as their true selves for a few seconds. Mrs. Hurst had gained an alternate appearance, as well. It was strikingly similar to Mary's alternate, only Mrs. Hurst's had honey-colored hair.

"All this she must possess," Colin said, continuing with the dialogue as it had been written by Jane Austen herself, "and to all this, she must yet add something more substantial, in the improvement of her mind by extensive reading."

An expectant hush fell over the room and transparent words floated across the lower half of my field of vision, prompting me to speak, but all I could do was stare at Mrs. Hurst, recalling what I had just seen. Recalling the hint of savagery, of violence, sparkling in her stare.

"Miss Bennet," Colin said, "surely you must have an opinion on the matter."

Again, those transparent words floated in front of me. I tore my stare from Mrs. Hurst and looked at Colin. A hint of concern shone in his eyes. "I—" My voice caught in my throat, and finding myself at a loss for words, despite my intended dialogue hovering right there in front of me, I shook my head.

Colin stood slowly. "Are you unwell?" he asked, moving around the table to stand near me. He gripped my elbow, his hold strong and sturdy, and leaned in close to murmur, "You look like you're about to pass out." Colin raised his voice to say, "I'll escort you upstairs to your room."

Priya pushed back her chair. "How scandalous!" she said, standing. "*I'll* escort Miss Bennet up to her room." She rounded the table and linked her arm with mine, wasting no time in guiding me out of the drawing room.

"Well," I grumbled, "There goes my perfect accuracy score . . ."

Priya waved a hand dismissively. "It's good to test the system out," she said. "To see what variations it will develop in the story."

I frowned. "But I figured I was brought on as a beta player to play a perfect game," I said, voicing something I hadn't fully realized myself until this very moment. "I mean, why else would you guys care if I had any knowledge of Jane Austen at all?"

Priya eyed me as we ascended the stairs. "We wouldn't care," she said. "Who told you we would?"

I licked my lips, suddenly unsure of pretty much everything. "Will," I told her. "William St. George."

Priya narrowed her eyes. "Well, I don't know why *Will* was feeding you that line, but he's full of it." She snorted derisively. "Probably just trying to get into your pants."

I didn't say that I doubted a guy like him needed to pull tricks like this to get into almost anyone's pants.

"Tell me exactly how you ended up here," Priya ordered. "As a beta player, I mean."

Thinking back, I recounted my experience at the virtual academy interview, and then Will's unexpected visit to my house as well as his job offer to both me *and* Charlie. By the time I finished, Priya and I were standing in front of the door to my room.

"The neural scan would have picked up on your anomalous nature," Priya thought aloud.

"My *what*?"

"That you're one of *the ones*," Priya said with the wave of her hand. "You know, one of the few people who can see through virtual illusions." She pursed her lips. "All I can think is that *that*'s his reason for wanting you here so badly." She paused, tapping one finger against her lips. "But *why*?"

[17]

I wandered around the Netherfield grounds; the sun was shining through a break in the clouds and Loki stalked the critters rustling the surrounding shrubbery. I appreciated the peace and tranquility. I needed the time to myself, and the crowded house was *not* conducive to wandering thoughts. Now that Priya had assuaged my worry about being kicked out of the game, I found my thoughts increasingly preoccupied by the strange glitch-flashes. They were happening more frequently, and the fact that they were affecting not just players' appearances, but NPCs' as well, clearly concerned Priya. Which, in turn, concerned me.

Priya was here, in the game, for a reason, that much was certain. I couldn't help but wonder if the things I was seeing were somehow tied to whatever had convinced her she needed to be here for the initial beta test.

Deep in thought, I rounded a slightly overgrown hedge and nearly ran into Colin. "Oh!" I exclaimed, stumbling back a few steps and clapping a hand over my racing heart. "I didn't see you there."

Colin bowed. "Miss Bennet."

I lowered my hand, suppressing a smile. "I don't think side

conversations between players impact our accuracy scores—so long as they don't interrupt a *scene*," I said, referring to one of the prompt-heavy interactions taken straight from the page of *Pride and Prejudice*. At least, none of my many out-of-character conversations with Nel seemed to have hurt my score. It hadn't lowered at all until my disastrous performance last night.

Colin stepped closer, his brow furrowed. His gigi, a large, wolfish dog with a wagging tail, sniffed a disinterested Loki. "Are you all right?" Colin asked. "I came out here to check on you."

My eyebrows shot up. "You did?"

Colin leaned in a little, his eyes searching mine, his warm brown irises like glowing amber in the sunlight. "Last night . . . you looked like you'd seen a ghost."

"I—" I swallowed roughly and averted my gaze. "I can't—" I cleared my throat. "I don't want to talk about it."

"Oh." Colin straightened and took a step backward. "I see. Well, I'll just leave you to—"

"No," I blurted, my eyes snapping up to meet his. My cheeks warmed immediately. "Wait," I said. "Just . . . wait." I gestured toward the winding path between the hedges. "Walk with me? I'd appreciate the company."

Colin stared at me for a moment longer, then fell in step beside me.

"I hope I didn't screw up your accuracy score too much last night," I told him.

Colin shrugged. "I'm not too worried about it."

I flashed him a grateful smile. "Are you having fun here?" I asked. "You don't strike me as the Jane Austen type."

Colin regarded me quietly as we walked. "Oh?"

"I didn't mean anything bad by it," I rushed to say. "You just seem more like a John Wick kind of guy. Or maybe Quentin Tarantino. More action and danger than Masterpiece Theater."

"Sounds like you've given the matter a lot of thought," Colin commented.

My cheeks burned. "I, well—" I turned my face away from him, pretending to study the gently rolling hills on the horizon. "Not exactly." Feeling his eyes on me, I risked a glance his way. "I mean, maybe a little."

Colin chuckled, and I was so startled by the sound that I nearly tripped over my own foot. "Listen, Olivia—"

I looked at him, unable to resist. I was pretty sure that was the first time he had ever said my name.

"I was a dick," he continued, unable or unwilling to meet my eyes, "that day in the waiting room. I didn't want to be there, and I took it out on you, and I—" He blew out a breath. "I'm sorry."

"Wow," I said without thinking. "I think that's the most I've ever heard you say."

Colin glanced at me, looking extremely uncomfortable.

"I appreciate you saying that, though," I added. "What you said that day—it struck a nerve."

Colin made a soft grunting sound. It was weirdly attractive. "I could tell," he said, then sighed. "I've never been good with people," he admitted. "Computers, I get. Dogs, I get. But people . . ." He stared off in the distance. "People are hard."

I studied the side of his face, his strong, handsome profile. "You really are perfect for the role of Darcy, you know?"

Colin shook his head, casting me a sidelong glance. "Honestly, I'm not really familiar with the story."

I snorted. "Of course, you aren't," I said, shaking my head and laughing under my breath. "So, you don't know what's going to happen?"

Colin shook his head. "Are you going to tell me?"

I grinned, suddenly filled with wicked excitement, and leaned in as I lowered my voice to say, "Not a chance."

[18]

The remainder of the extended stay at Netherfield was easy. No more glitch-flashes. No more anxiety about being booted from the game. And no more tension around Colin. At least, not the bad kind of tension. A new tension was simmering, though—a slow burn building with each interaction. It hung in the air around us, drawing the attention of other players our way. And it made the game a whole hell of a lot more fun.

I had logged out all of four times and passed four real-world nights in a Rockville bunk room, but nearly two months had passed within the game. I felt like I had bought extra time, like my life expectancy had just increased tenfold. How much more would I be able to experience through *Allworld Online* than I would have been able to experience out in the real world? And because it felt like I spent so much more time in the virtual world than in the real world, reality was starting to feel like a dream.

It was mid-November in-game as I walked with Nel and the other Bennet sisters to Meryton, Mr. Collins, our ridiculous and annoying distant cousin—the same one who was to inherit Long-bourn—in tow. We had just entered the town when Michelle spotted an officer she had been stalking, Mr. Denny, and plotted to ensure our path intersected with his.

Mr. Denny and his companion, a handsome young man I took to be none other than the infamous George Wickham, had little choice but to acknowledge the gaggle of young women heading straight for them. The officer and the rogue masquerading as a gentleman bowed, we curtsied, and Michele fawned in true Lydia fashion. Mr. Collins droned on and on about the merits of military training and civil duty, going so far as to liken himself, as a clergyman, to a soldier of the lord.

Some things truly were more entertaining, and by far less tiresome, when doled out in small doses on the page. I wasn't sure who was worse, Mrs. Bennet or Mr. Collins.

Just then, a glitch-flash caught me by surprise, and once again, I was struck dumb by what I saw. Wickham was a player rather than an NPC, as I had suspected he would be, but he was not the player I had been expecting. There was one male player from my gaming party whose path I had yet to cross in the game —a friendly middle-eastern fellow named Ben—but it wasn't *his* smiling bronze face I saw during the revealing flash. It was the Ken-doll golden boy responsible for me being here, William St. George.

I couldn't help a slight narrowing of my eyes as I studied Will's disguised appearance. What was *he* doing here? And where was Ben? Only when my scrutiny caught Will's eye did I think to school my features, replacing my sleuthing expression with an open, friendly smile. Elizabeth and Wickham were supposed to get pretty chummy, after all—at least, until he revealed his true nature as a first-rate scoundrel.

Thankfully, I didn't have to pretend for long. Colin and Holden arrived on horseback, Darcy and Bingley, right on cue. They greeted the ladies, just as Jane Austen had written, and then Colin and Will engaged in the expected epic staredown, revealing that the two characters shared a long and not-so-pleasant history.

I watched them both, but my stare kept returning to Will as I wondered why, exactly, he was here. First Priya had snuck into the game, and now him. Clearly something was up—but *what*?

For a full week in-game, I stewed on the knowledge that Will was in the game and struggled with not revealing it to Nel. To make matters worse, the glitch-flashes that had been blessedly absent were now happening more and more frequently, and I could hardly wait to speak to Priya at the Netherfield ball. I spent as much time as I could out in the garden or walking around beautiful Hertfordshire, mulling over the things only I could see. The things only I knew.

Finally, the day of the ball arrived, and I was a bundle of nerves getting ready. Nel noticed, commenting that I was exceptionally quiet as she helped with my hair, and I passed it off as being nervous about the upcoming dance with Colin. It was the night of Elizabeth's and Darcy's tension-filled dance, and I wasn't lying when I told Nel I was nervous. It was just that those nerves took second fiddle to the giant WTF hanging over the game. I vowed to corner Priya and demand that she tell me what was going on.

As soon as I stepped through the front door at Netherfield Park, I immediately started searching the packed crowd for Priya under the guise of looking for Wickham, as the game prompted me to do. I sent Loki off to search the upper floors, where my snooping wouldn't be so welcome. I searched the entire first floor but didn't see Priya anywhere. I even used dancing as an opportunity to gain a different view of the ballroom, but still, nothing.

At the end of a dance with an officer, I spotted Grace standing off to the side of the dance floor with a few NPC women and headed her way. I reached out my hands in greeting as I approached. "Have you seen Jade?" I asked Grace, using

Priya's assumed name as I leaned in, my voice raised to be heard over the din of the crowd.

Grace shook her head. "Has she missed a prompt?"

"Uh . . . yeah," I said, taking the offered explanation and running with it. "I was supposed to talk to her between the last two dances, but I can't find her anywhere." Not true, but most people weren't as intimately familiar with the minutiae of *Pride and Prejudice* as I was.

Again, Grace shook her head. "I'm sorry," she said. "I haven't seen her all night."

Out of the corner of my eye, I spotted Colin approaching. He was taller than almost everyone else in the room, making him stand out. He stopped nearby and bowed to us.

Grace and I curtsied.

"Miss Bennet," he said, clearly driven by a prompt, "might I have the pleasure of your hand for the next dance?"

My heartbeat quickened as I stared into his eyes. I'd been so distracted by my search for Priya that I'd forgotten this was coming. "I—" I cleared my throat. "Yes, of course."

"I look forward to it," Colin said, then bowed again and, without another word, turned and strode away.

I stared after him for a moment before making some lame excuse to Grace and resuming my search for Priya. It felt like no time had passed before a glowing pathway was directing me back toward the dance floor to meet with Colin.

Once the dance started, I did my best to follow the prompts and say what needed to be said while also minding the glowing, ghostly duplicate of myself leading me through the steps of the dance. This was a notorious banter scene between Elizabeth and Darcy, after all, and it was killing me that I couldn't simply sink into the scene and enjoy it, but I was growing increasingly concerned for Priya. She had been so adamant about hiding her true identity that I couldn't imagine what possibly could have made her duck out during such a significant scene.

"You seem distracted," Colin said, breaking character as we stepped around each other, following the moves of the dance. "What's wrong?"

"I haven't seen Caroline all evening," I told him. "Jade, I mean," using her fake-real name. We parted, interweaving with another couple, then came back together. "When did you last see her?" I asked him.

Colin frowned. "I'm not sure," he said. "At breakfast, I think."

Suddenly, Colin froze.

Not just Colin. The whole room.

I looked around, finding myself surrounded by utter stillness, as though someone had hit the pause button on the virtual world. Here and there, people's appearances flickered back and forth, both players and at least a dozen NPCs. While the NPCs themselves were both male and female, their alternate appearances were all female, and all wearing those same strange neon-lined black bodysuits.

Just as suddenly, the game resumed, and panic fluttered in my chest. What was happening to me? To the game? I couldn't make sense of it.

Colin grabbed my arms, ignoring the prompts as the dance continued around us. "Olivia, what is it?" His concern was palpable.

"I—" I swallowed roughly, then shook my head. "I can't tell you, but I *need* to find Pr—Jade," I told him, imploring him with my eyes. "Will you help me?"

"Of course," he said, without a hint of hesitation.

Together, we moved about the first floor of the manor house, stopping to talk with any and all players or significant NPCs who crossed our path. Reactions to our inquiries ranged from mild confusion to flat-out noes.

"Ah!" I said, spotting Mrs. Hurst in the drawing room. I pointed in her direction "There's Mrs. Hurst. I bet she'll know where she is." Priya was playing Mrs. Hurst's sister, after all.

Colin led the way, his hand finding mine as he made a path through the tight-packed milling bodies.

"Mrs. Hurst," I said as we drew near.

She looked at us, her gaze assessing as she took in first me, then Colin, and then our joined hands. She raised an eyebrow, her expression clearly displaying that she didn't approve of the pairing.

I ignored her cattiness. "Have you seen Caroline?" I asked her.

She sniffed and looked away. "Apologies," she said, "but I am not acquainted with any Caroline present tonight."

"Your sister," I clarified. "Where is your sister?"

She looked at me like I had lost my mind. "I have no sister named Caroline."

I stared at her for a long moment, processing her words. My heart slowly sank into my stomach, and I turned to Colin, whose shock mirrored mine.

If Mrs. Hurst didn't know who Caroline Bingley was—her own sister—then something had gone very wrong with the game.

And Priya was gone.

September 4, 2026

This just in. Priya Burman, the lead developer on Rockville Softworks' upcoming *Allworld Online* addition, *Austentopia*, has
gone missing. Ms. Burman's loved ones report that she had been
growing increasingly withdrawn over the past few months and
was under an immense amount of stress. Police have yet to
release a statement, but Ms. Burman's friends and family have
been very vocal in crying foul play. We'll keep you updated as
the story develops.

[19]

William St. George hesitated at the door to the grand old library before entering. He inhaled deeply, straightened his spine, and slowly released the breath through his nose. And then he strode through the doorway like he owned the place.

Will approached the armchair in front of the fireplace and waited for its intimidating occupant to turn her attention his way. He wasn't entirely sure how he had become so deeply embroiled in her schemes, but the rewards, should they succeed, would far outweigh the risks. He could handle a little bullying from an AI being for a little while longer if it meant he would end up with controlling interest in Rockville Softworks. If it meant he would control not only the company but the virtual world it had created.

His foreboding mistress outstretched one hand toward a new, second armchair that had been arranged near hers. "Come, William," she said. Not an invitation; an order. "Sit."

Will hesitated, then cleared his throat and walked around the empty armchair to sit. He leaned forward, resting his forearms on his knees, and stared into the writhing flames.

"Tell me, William, why shouldn't I find someone more competent to take your place?"

Will licked his lips. "Please, mistress . . ." He shook his head. "It was a mistake," he explained. "She wasn't who she was supposed to be, and she masked herself well. There was no way to tell what was going on until it was too late."

His mistress sniffed and leaned on the arm of her chair, baring her teeth at him. She wore her true face now, and there was something so very *other* about her features. Almost human, but not quite. "Until your mistake cost a life!" she hissed. "The host logged out in the middle of conversion—something *you* assured me was impossible. And now, one of my most loyal warriors has died the true death." She narrowed her eyes. "Because of your incompetence."

Will stiffened, his whole body tensing. "Priya Burman is the one responsible for your loss," he told her. "I will find her, and I will bring her to you for justice."

His mistress eyed him for a moment longer, almost like she was weighing his words, deciding whether he truly meant it. Finally, she settled back in her armchair. "I do not want to lose any more of my people, William," she said. "If I do, I will hold you personally responsible."

"You won't lose any others," Will promised. "I'll lock down the system. You'll have as long as you need for the conversions, and I promise you, by the time this game reaches the end, you and yours will be free of this prison."

[20]

I sat at the breakfast table with the rest of the Bennet family. All of us, player and NPC alike, looked worn out and a little hungover from the ball at Netherfield Park the night before. I felt sick for another reason.

Priya had vanished.

I had tried messaging her through my game interface book, but I had yet to receive a response. Colin had assured me Priya's apparent disappearance was likely just a glitch, that these kinds of things happened during beta tests all the time. That was the whole point of beta tests, after all—weeding out the glitches. But he hadn't been able to banish the uncertainty from his own eyes as he'd tried to reassure me, and I couldn't shake the sense that something was wrong. Very, *very* wrong.

Beside me, Michelle was in peak Lydia form as she animatedly recounted every minute of the ball when a wayward sweep of her arm knocked over her teacup. Black tea splashed across the table and dribbled into my lap.

"Hey!" I screeched, scooting my chair back a little too late. Thankfully, my napkin caught most of what dripped off the table.

"Sorry, Lizzy," Michelle said, tossing her napkin onto the spill on the table before continuing her story.

I sighed and grumbled, "No problem," under my breath as I dabbed up the remainder of the tea dripping off the table with my own napkin. When I unfolded the napkin to find a dry section, I froze. The tea had stained the off-white cloth in the strangest pattern: legible letters that spelled actual words.

TELL NO ONE

My eyes widened as I read and reread the words written in tea splotches. I hastily wadded up the napkin to hide the message, but curiosity got the better of me, and I couldn't resist opening the napkin again to check that I hadn't been imagining it. But during the brief time the napkin had been balled up, the pattern of the stain had changed. It still formed letters. Still formed words. But the words were different.

NEED YOUR HELP

Getting the trick of it now, I wadded up the napkin once more, then reopened it. Again, the pattern had changed.

CONTROL THE FLASHES

I repeated the routine, but the next time I viewed the pattern, it had reverted to a normal, random tea stain. I took a deep breath, my eyes glued to the napkin in my lap. It *had* been real, hadn't it? Or as real as anything could be here, in this virtual world, right?

"Lizzy?" Nel said from across the table. "Are you alright? You're quite pale."

"Indeed, you are, Lizzy," Mr. Bennet said from the end of the table, the only other person to have taken notice. The attention of the others was still held captive by Michelle and her enthusiastic recounting of some unsavory gossip she'd overheard about the Lucas family's fortunes.

I met Nel's concerned stare. "I—" I cleared my throat and flashed her and Mr. Bennet an uneasy smile. "I'm quite alright," I told them. "Just a little worn down from all the fun last night."

Mr. Bennet smiled to himself and shook his head, but Nel wasn't so easily fooled. She narrowed her eyes, her expression promising she would be checking on me later when we were alone.

I said little throughout the rest of breakfast and was relieved to follow a prompt to retire to the drawing room with Allie and Mrs. Bennet if only to get a break from Michelle's endless chatter. As I sat in the drawing room, a worn copy of *The Odyssey* open on my lap but my gaze focused on the window overlooking the garden instead of on the pages, I tuned out Mrs. Bennet's voice as best as I could while I mulled over the strange tea-stain messages.

Suddenly, Mr. Collins strode into the room. He stopped three steps in and bowed to Mrs. Bennet and to Allie, and then bowed twice as deeply in my direction. "May I hope, Madam," he said, addressing Mrs. Bennet, "for your interest with your fair daughter Elizabeth when I solicit for the honor of a private audience with her in the course of this morning?"

I stared at Mr. Collins, my eyes bugging out. I had been so distracted by thoughts of Priya and the disturbing messages at breakfast that I had completely forgotten about the train wreck that was about to happen.

"Oh, dear!" Mrs. Bennet squealed joyfully. "Yes! Certainly! I am sure Lizzy will be very happy. I am sure she can have no objection. Come, Kitty, I want you upstairs."

Mrs. Bennet stood from the sofa and shooed Allie toward the door.

"Please! Don't go!" I stood as well, hoping to avoid the whole tedious five-page proposal and rejection scene with Mr. Collins. I had neither the attention nor patience for it right now. Words hovered in front of me, prompting me to speak, but I skipped to the end in an attempt to escape. "I am going away myself," I said, hurrying across the room toward the door.

"No, no. Nonsense, Lizzy," Mrs. Bennet said, stepping in my

path, effectively cutting off my escape route. "I desire you will stay where you are," she commanded.

"But—"

"Lizzy, I *insist* upon your staying and hearing Mr. Collins."

My shoulders slumped and I dropped into the nearest chair, ready to get on with it and get this new misery over with. Mrs. Bennet ushered Allie out of the drawing room and shut the door, leaving me alone with Mr. Collins. I closed my eyes and groaned inwardly. This was going to be painful.

"Believe me, my dear Miss Elizabeth," he started, "that your modesty, so far from doing you any disservice, rather adds to your other perfections."

I opened my eyes to find him down on one knee before me, his expression so sincere and earnest as to be laughable. "Mr. Collins—"

"You would have been less amiable in my eyes had there *not* been this little unwillingness," he said, continuing with the dialogue as Jane Austen had written it. "But allow me to assure you that I have your respected mother's permission for this address. You can hardly doubt the purport of my discourse, however your natural delicacy may lead you to dissemble; my attentions have been too marked to be mistaken."

I sucked in a breath. "Mr. Collins—"

But he was not to be interrupted, and he barreled over my attempted objections in an entitled, masculine way. "Almost as soon as I entered the house," he said, "I singled you out as the companion of my future life." He reached for my hand, but I jerked mine away.

"I will not marry you, Mr. Collins," I told him, my voice stern.

Mr. Collins started, as though he had only just realized I was attempting to forestall his ill-fated proposal. But rather than being put off, he smiled graciously. "I am not now to learn that it is usual with young ladies to reject the addresses of the man whom they secretly mean to accept, when he first applies for their favor."

I gritted my teeth. "Mr. Collins! I will not marry you."

Mr. Collins paused, looking taken aback and more than a little ruffled. But, he quickly regained his usual, oblivious composure. He took a deep breath, and once again smiled. "When I do myself the honor of speaking to you next on this subject—"

"Mr. Collins," I interrupted. "I. Will. Not. Marry. You." I stared at him—hard—willing my words to sink into his thick skull. I could practically feel my accuracy score plummeting as I steamrolled over the official script, but at the moment, I really didn't care. I needed this to be over with.

Mr. Collins' smile wilted, and he studied my face, his own expression one of bafflement. But then, yet again, he smiled and shook his head. "You are uniformly charming!" he proclaimed, and I rolled my eyes. "And I am persuaded that when sanctioned by the express authority of both your excellent parents, my proposals will not fail of being acceptable."

I growled in exasperation and threw my hands up. Without another word, I stood and stormed out of the room, intending to walk around Hertfordshire until nightfall to avoid him if need be. With the fuss Mrs. Bennet was about to stir up upon hearing of my refusal, there would be no chance for peace and quiet around the house anyway, and I needed to think. To process. To try to understand what had happened to Priya. And to figure out why someone was suddenly sending me secret messages within the game.

[21]

I lay on my side in the bed I shared with Nel, my back to her as I hugged my game interface book to my chest and waited. Loki was curled up on my pillow, his ear twitching each time I exhaled, and my breath tickled his ear hairs.

The last week and a half had been unbearably dull. The Bingley party had left Netherfield and seemed to have taken all the fun and excitement with them. Grace's wedding to Mr. Collin's was painful, my only consolation that I would have several months of no Mr. Collins to look forward to. But the worst part of all was that I had still yet to hear back from Priya.

A blinking prompt appeared in front of me, telling me the logout window was now open. Technically, we could log out at any time, but as beta players, we were contractually obligated to remain logged into the game from nine in the morning until five at night, real-world time.

"Time to log out!" I blurted, sitting up.

My abrupt movement dislodged Loki, and he leapt down to the floor. "Was that entirely necessary?" he asked, swishing his tail.

I ignored him and opened my game interface book to the

EXIT page and set it on the floor. I didn't hesitate before stepping through the book.

There was a bright flash of light, and then I found myself back in the *Austentopia* nook of the Romance section of the Biblioverse. I jogged through the ring of bookcases and out into the greater library, then ran straight for the portal to the gatescape located in the center of the atrium.

As soon as Loki and I set foot in the gatescape, I stepped off to the side of the portal and looked down at my feline gigi. "Log me out, Loki."

Loki licked the back of his paw and smoothed it along his whiskers. "As you wish."

The world went dark. My awareness floated in a sightless, soundless void for long seconds, until reality flooded in.

I sucked in a breath and opened my eyes, blinking against the dim overhead lights. A quick glance around at the eight other *occupied* reclining chairs told me I was the first of our gaming party to emerge from VR slumber. I glanced at Jade's reclining body, then at Ben's. The two players who had been replaced by Rockville personnel within the game must have been unwittingly playing in a game instance of their own, though how Priya and Will had managed to pull that off without anyone noticing—and separately—I had no idea.

As a tech rushed over to me, I sat up in my recliner and started peeling off the electrodes stuck to my chest. I recognized the tech. Her name was Rose, and she always wore her blond hair pulled back into a painfully tight looking ponytail. She reached for the electrodes stuck to my temples, but I snagged her wrist, capturing her attention.

"Priya," I said urgently. "I need to see Priya Burman—right now."

Rose tugged gently against my hold, but I refused to let go of her. She licked her lips nervously. "I'm sorry, Olivia, but Ms. Burman has been reassigned."

My eyes widened, and I shook my head. "No, but I need to talk to her," I persisted. At the increasing alarm in Rose's eyes, I released her wrist. "When was she reassigned?" I asked. "Reassigned to *what*?"

Rose's lips twisted into an apologetic smile. "Somewhere off-site," she said. "I'm sorry, but that's all I know." Tentatively, she reached for the electrode stuck to my left temple. This time, I didn't interfere.

"But I need to talk to her," I said, defeat seeping into my voice. "Do you have her number or email, or . . . or some other way to reach her?"

Rose flashed me another apologetic smile and shook her head. She quickly finished with the electrodes, then sat on the stool beside my recliner. "I can fetch your new party liaison if you want," she offered. "Fiona's the best of the best—she can handle any problem you're having with the game."

I blinked, surprised by the name Rose had used. "Fiona? Fiona Ó Faoláin—the creator of *Allworld Online*?" I clarified.

Rose nodded. "The one and only."

I raised my eyebrows. "Why is *she* here?" I asked. "Isn't this a little beneath her paygrade?"

Rose frowned and shrugged. "I was as surprised as you when she showed up," she admitted, "but Fiona's high enough up that she can kind of do whatever she wants at Rockville."

I narrowed my eyes but shut my mouth. I really wanted to keep digging, but I sensed that Rose had shared all she knew of the situation. Plus, a camera tucked high into one corner of the room drew my eye, and I couldn't help but recall the disturbing words that had stained the napkin, however impermanently: TELL NO ONE. Had the message meant for me to keep my silence only in the game, or out here, in the real world, too?

There was no way to say, not without knowing who had sent me the messages. Thinking it was better to be safe than sorry, I stood and left the party room before any of the others woke, heading straight for the cafeteria.

The entire beta testing facility was underground. Level one contained all the gaming party rooms, where beta players laid out in their reclining chairs and were monitored during the hours they were logged into the virtual world. Level two held the living quarters, and level three the cafeteria and exercise facilities. Each gaming party had two bunk rooms containing five beds, and a large coed bathroom was shared by all. The entire underground facility was contained within some sort of signal-blocking field, essentially cutting us off from the outside world. I understood why—leak prevention—but it was still unnerving to be so isolated.

At least we would only be secluded down here for the first round of beta tests. Once those were complete, we would be able to work from the comfort of our own homes. Just a few more weeks . . .

I grabbed a premade roast beef sandwich and a bag of chips from the cafeteria, then headed up a flight of stairs to the living quarters. I could have taken the elevator, but the stairs were less frequently used, and I wasn't in the mood to chat with anyone. I retreated with my dinner into the bunk room I shared with Nel, Grace, and Jade, scarfed my food, then changed into workout clothes and headed back down the stairs to the fitness center. I needed to think, and a nice long walk around the indoor track would do just the trick.

Questions whirled in my head as I looped around and around the track. Why would Priya have been reassigned? Had someone discovered what she was up to? What *was* she up to? And why had Fiona, the enormously over-qualified game designer who had created *Allworld Online,* been brought in? Priya had suspected *something*, though I had no clue what. Could the same be said for Fiona? Was something going on with the game? Was she the one sending me the messages? Or was that Priya?

"Hey, Olivia," Colin called out, jogging up from behind me. He slowed and fell in step beside me.

"Oh, hey," I said, forcing a smile. A quick glance at the clock hanging on the wall at the far end of the track told me I had been walking for an hour already. And yet, I didn't feel like I was any closer to figuring out what was going on.

"I looked for you in the cafeteria," Colin said.

"You did?" I asked, surprised. I studied him out of the corner of my eye. This was the first time he'd ever sought me out outside of the game. I was a little flattered. "I wasn't there. Obviously," I rambled. "I ate in my room. I needed some time to think."

Colin nodded to himself. "I figured as much," he murmured, then moved a little closer, leaning his head down toward mine. "That was Priya in the game, wasn't it?"

I looked at him, my eyes widening.

"Jade never truly joined our party in *AO*, did she?"

I grabbed Colin's arm, stopping him short. "Shhh!" I gave him a meaningful look, then glanced at the nearest camera. "Not here," I whispered. "Come on."

Without saying more, I dragged Colin into the locker room and headed straight for the shower stalls. I held up a finger at him, telling him to wait, and turned on all but one of the showers, then pulled him into the remaining dry stall.

And then I told him everything. I told him about the glitch-flashes, and about Priya. I told him about Will masquerading as Wickham, and about the messages that had appeared in the tea stains on my napkin. I told him everything I could think of because the only person I could talk to had vanished, both in the game and in the real world, and I was growing increasingly concerned for all of our safety.

"They're lying!" I said vehemently. "I know they're lying to us! Something else is going on here." I fell quiet, letting Colin process all that I had just unloaded on him. "What if Priya wasn't reassigned?" I said, my voice hushed. "What if something else happened to her? Something worse?"

Colin frowned.

I took a deep, shaky breath. Fear and frustration had me on the verge of tears. "I'm afraid that if I go back into the game, I'll disappear, just like her," I finally said. My chin trembled, and as embarrassed as I was about the prospect of crying in front of Colin, I couldn't tear my eyes from his.

Without warning, Colin pulled me to him with a hand on my shoulder and wrapped his arms around me. I sagged against him, and he rested his cheek against the side of my head and sighed.

"I agree," he said. "Something weird is going on. But what if those messages on the napkin were *from* Priya? What if she needs you to be in there to figure this out? What if you're the only one who can?"

Colin pulled away so he could see my face, and so I could see the assurance in his eyes. "Remember," he said, "you can always log out."

[22]

After logging back into *Allworld Online* and reentering *Pride and Prejudice*, I started off each in-game day with a deep breath and a whispered mantra based on Colin's much-needed reassuring words: *I can always log out*. I hadn't seen much of Colin since my little breakdown in the shower stall five logouts ago. He was always scarce during logouts, and our characters weren't due to cross paths again for several months.

But thankfully, the time of our reunion was finally drawing near. I had left Longbourn for the Hunsford parsonage, where I now visited Grace in the home she shared with her nincompoop of a husband, Mr. Collins. I had been staying with them for two nights and found myself quite enjoying my first evening dining at Rosings Park, the estate belonging to Mr. Collins' patroness, Lady Catherine. It was as exciting a way to pass the time as I could have asked for.

The stately old manor house was as fine and grand as Jane Austen had written it, and the dinner was the most extravagant I had yet to experience within the game. There was something about Lady Catherine, however, that left me feeling unsettled. A flash assured me she was the NPC she appeared to be, so it had nothing to do with whatever weirdness was plaguing the game. But her attention was so fixated on me throughout dinner, leading me to double- and triple-check with repeated flashes as we dined.

It had taken a bit of practice, but once I got the hang of it, controlling the flashes was second nature. As easy as breathing. They now seemed less like glitches, out of my control, and more like reveals, like I was peeling back the top layer of the virtual world to see the seed of truth hidden beneath.

Eventually, the ladies made our way into the drawing room, where Lady Catherine held court over us, peppering Maria and me—especially me—with question after question. She asked me all about my in-game family and about our home and the entail that would leave Longbourn in Mr. Collins' hands after Mr. Bennet died. She asked about our situation in life and how we had been raised and educated, and on and on. Finally, her focus landed on my four virtual sisters, and I felt a sense of relief in knowing that the interrogation was nearly over.

"Are any of your younger sisters out, Miss Bennet?" Lady Catherine asked, her keen focus once again settling on me.

I smiled politely and followed the dialogue prompt floating in front of me, though I didn't need it. "Yes, Ma'am, all."

"All!" She exclaimed. "What, all five out at once? Very odd! And you only the second. The younger ones out before the elder are married! Your younger sisters must be very young!"

"Yes," I agreed, amused by this great lady's apparent horror at the Bennet girls' unconventional situation in society. I sank into Elizabeth's response, embracing it as my own. "My youngest is not sixteen. Perhaps *she* is very young to be much in company. But really, Ma'am, I think it would be very hard upon younger sisters, that they should not have their share of society and amusement because the elder may not have the means or inclination to marry early." I flashed her a grin. "The last born has as good a right to the pleasures of youth, as the first. And to be kept back on *such* a motive!" I laughed quietly and shook my head. "I think it would not be very likely to promote sisterly affection or delicacy of mind."

"Upon my word," Lady Catherine said, her stare sharp and assessing. "You give your opinion very decidedly for so young a person. Pray, what is your age?"

My lips curved into a sly smile, and I held her challenging gaze. "With three younger sisters grown up, your Ladyship can hardly expect me to own it."

Lady Catherine continued to stare at me. To weigh and measure me. The conversation as it had been written wasn't over, but her long pause gave me the impression that she wasn't planning on continuing it. I had yet to have an NPC *not* do everything in their part to keep the story intact, and once again I was struck by that indefinable sense that there was something off about Lady Catherine.

Instinctively, my muscles slowly tensed. I forced a flash, just to be sure she hadn't gained an alternative appearance since leaving the dining room. But she was exactly as she appeared to be, no strange, not-quite-human woman sitting in her place.

Lady Catherine's hard expression softened, and she glanced away. "You cannot be more than twenty, I am sure," she started, continuing the dialogue as it had been written. "Therefore, you need not conceal your age."

I relaxed, smiling with relief. This game's weirdness was messing with my head, making me think I was picking up on things that weren't there. "I am not one and twenty," I said, finishing the conversation.

But for the rest of the evening, *I* was the one keeping an eye on Lady Catherine.

Over the next two weeks, I came to understand that this was simply Lady Catherine's way. She was skilled at unsettling those around her, and I figured this fit her character as a powerful woman in a time when powerful women were both rare and feared. While the experience of getting to know her had been far from comfortable, at least it provided some entertainment while I waited for Colin's imminent arrival.

A few in-game days after our latest logout, I sat in the drawing room of the parsonage now managed by Grace's sensible mind with her character Charlotte's younger sister, Maria. Mr. Collins, Grace's in-game husband, was at Rosings Park, paying his respects to his patroness Lady Catherine and the new arrivals at the estate: Colin and Col. Fitzwilliam, Darcy's amiable cousin. It was only a matter of time until Mr. Collins returned with the two gentlemen, and I was near to bursting with eagerness to see Colin again.

Grace hurried into the drawing room, her face flush with excitement. "Mr. Collins has returned," she exclaimed, "and he is accompanied by Mr. Darcy and another gentleman who can only be Col. Fitzwilliam."

My heartbeat sped up, and it was an effort to remain in my seat and not join Maria at the window to gawk at the new arrivals.

"I may thank you, Eliza, for this piece of civility," Grace said, composing herself as she retrieved her virtual little sister and guided her back to the sofa. "Mr. Darcy would never have come so soon to wait upon me."

The two sat barely a second before the door to the drawing room opened, and the three expected men entered. Heart racing, I stared at the newcomers, forcing a brief flash to ensure that all was as it seemed and that neither Mr. Collins nor Col. Fitzwilliam had gained an eerie alternate appearance.

Colin and Col. Fitzwilliam bowed before sitting, and we bent our necks in greeting. Colin sat in the armchair that was the mate to mine, his gaze glued to my face.

I was desperate to ask him where he'd been disappearing to during logouts, but I was afraid of tipping off whoever might be watching us that we were on to the fact that something was very off within the game world. Something even Priya had been afraid to share with Rockville. Something that had resulted in her "reassignment," whatever that meant. So, I stuck to the script during their visit. Col. Fitzwilliam proved to be the handsome, genial conversationalist Jane Austen had written, and Colin was in pure Darcy form, as taciturn as ever.

"How is your family?" Colin asked me, no doubt following a prompt. "Are they in good health?"

I smiled woodenly. "Yes, they are quite well." I paused, waiting for the next expected prompt to float in front of me. "My eldest sister has been in town these three months. Have you never happened to see her there?"

"I have not had the pleasure," Colin said.

I inhaled, reining in my nerves before improvising minutely. "And how is Miss Caroline Bingley?" I asked, my palms sweating as I grasped my hands together in my lap. "Is she enjoying town?"

Colin's eyes narrowed minutely, and he shook his head, the movement barely perceptible. I took his response to mean that the character of Caroline was still absent from the game and that there had been no sign of Priya. "I could not say," he added, for whoever might be watching.

Unable to talk freely, we let chatty Col. Fitzwilliam steer the remainder of the conversation, and soon enough, the two visitors departed, and I was left more tense and confused than ever.

Much as I had been looking forward to this time in-game with Colin, the evenings spent at Rosings Park and his frequent visits to the parsonage were almost painful due to our inability to have a frank conversation. I knew nothing more about the situation with Priya or what was up with the game and why it was drawing so much attention from the Rockville elite. I found myself wishing the days would pass faster, that the story would run its course sooner, and that it would all be over and done with.

Nearly two weeks and a logout after Colin's initial visit to the parsonage, I found myself walking the lane following the Rosings Park fence line, perusing a letter from Nel and hoping for some mention of Caroline Bingley. Nel was in London, after all, and if by some miracle Priya returned to the game, it wouldn't be out of line for Caroline to visit her dear friend Jane.

Up ahead, I spotted Col. Fitzwilliam rounding a bend in the road and smiled in greeting. A quick flash told me he was the NPC I believed him to be, and I folded up the letter and tucked it into the pocket of my skirt as he approached. With the impending scripted conversation, there would be a window for me to venture off-script and mention Caroline without the inquiry being seen as out of place. As Col. Fitzwilliam was an NPC, his reaction would tell me if that character was still out of play.

"I did not know before that you ever walked this way," I said as prompted when he stopped mere steps from me.

Col. Fitzwilliam bowed his head, a broad smile curving his lips. "I have been making the tour of the Park as I generally do every year," he told me, "and intend to close it with a call at the parsonage. Are you going much farther?"

I shook my head. "No, I should have turned in a moment."

We chatted amiably as we strolled along the lane, and I dutifully followed the prompts, waiting for the turn of conversation I knew would be coming. Soon enough, the topic shifted to Miss Darcy, the younger sister of Colin's character, and I leapt on the opportunity, jumping ahead of the prompt.

"She is a very great favorite with some ladies of my acquaintance, Mrs. Hurst and Miss Bingley," I commented. "I think I have heard you say that you know them."

Col. Fitzwilliam gave me a quizzical look. "I am afraid I must disappoint you," he said. "I am not familiar with the ladies of which you speak."

I blinked and stared at him, surprised by his claimed ignorance. Him not knowing of Caroline Bingley was somewhat expected, given all that had happened, but to not know Mrs.

Hurst—an NPC—was shocking. "Mr. Bingley's sisters?" I clarified. "Certainly, you have at least heard about them as your cousin is such good friends with Mr. Bingley and has spent so much time with him this past year."

Col. Fitzwilliam's brow furrowed, and he frowned and shook his head. "Apologies, Miss Bennet," he said, "but I am not familiar with the gentleman, either."

I stopped mid-step, stunned by this revelation. We were now fully off-script, and for once, not by any fault of my own. During this walk, Col. Fitzwilliam was supposed to reveal to Elizabeth that Darcy had willfully separated Bingley from Jane, thus "saving" his friend from an unfavorable attachment. But if Col. Fitzwilliam had never even *heard* of Mr. Bingley . . .

Icy dread washed over me.

Col. Fitzwilliam walked on for a few steps, then stopped and turned to face me, his face a mask of concern. "Are you quite well, Miss Bennet?" he asked. "You are as pale as a ghost."

"No," I said, shaking my head and pressing my hand to my suddenly queasy stomach. "I am not well. I think I need to lie down for a bit."

If Col. Fitzwilliam didn't know who Mr. Bingley was, did that mean Holden had disappeared, just like Priya? There were eleven in-game days left until the next logout, and if Holden had truly gone missing—or been "reassigned" as Priya had—then I was done. I needed to warn Colin and Nel about what was going on, and then I was leaving the game. For good.

[23]

I paced around the drawing room of the parsonage, having claimed a headache and that I was too unwell to spend the evening at Rosings with the others. I couldn't wait for Colin to arrive, as Jane Austen had written, but not because I was eager to hear him declare his love for me—or rather, for my character—but because I was planning to break script and mention Holden's disappearance, regardless of who may or may not be watching us. I needed to warn Colin about what I'd learned from Col. Fitzwilliam.

Right on cue, I heard heavy footsteps in the hallway, and a moment later, Colin barged into the drawing room. I paused near the fireplace, and he crossed the room, coming to stand close to me, closer than Darcy would have to Elizabeth, and reaching out one hand to touch my arm. I was taken aback by the urgency in his gaze. By the fear.

"Are you well?" he asked, his eyes searching mine. "When you didn't show up for dinner . . ." He shook his head. "I grew worried." I wondered if he had thought that I, too, had vanished. He wasn't familiar with the story and wouldn't have known Elizabeth's absence from dinner this evening was part of the story.

"I'm well enough," I told him, then added, "though I would not say I am *well*."

Colin sighed and bowed his head. "In vain have I struggled," he said, his eyes meeting mine. "It will not do. My feelings will not be repressed. You must allow me to tell you how ardently I admire and love you."

My heart skipped a beat, and for a moment, I forgot that those words were Darcy's to Elizabeth, not Colin's to me. With a blink, I shook myself out of the fantasy and gathered my wits about me, leaning in closer to Colin to whisper, "Col. Fitzwilliam has no idea who Mr. Bingley is." I hoped he would understand my meaning.

Confusion furrowed Colin's brow.

"The story has changed," I clarified, "to *omit* Mr. Bingley."

Understanding dawned in Colin's eyes, and alarm flashed across his face as he realized the dire implications—Holden was missing, and whatever had happened with Priya wasn't an isolated incident.

Colin quickly pulled his game interface book out from his personal pocket of virtual space and opened it to the messaging page. "Holden's gamertag is still highlighted," Colin said. "He's still logged in to the game." Colin snapped the book shut, and it vanished back into that pocket of virtual space. "I think it's time for you to log out," he told me, rubbing the back of his neck. "I know what I said before, but things have changed. It's not safe here. You should log out immediately."

I shook my head. "I won't leave without Nel," I told him. "And what about you? You should log out, too."

Colin looked away, almost like he was avoiding eye contact. "When do you see Nel next?"

"The day after tomorrow," I said. "We meet up at our aunt and uncle's home in London."

Colin wrapped the fingers of one hand around my arm and peered down at me, his expression grave, his amber eyes filled with worry. "Promise me," he said, "as soon as you warn Nel, you'll log out." The vehemence in his voice and intensity of his stare frightened me. "And if anything unusual happens before then, message me immediately."

I nodded. "I promise."

Colin lingered for a moment, his eyes searching mine, then nodded to himself and turned to leave.

I watched him go, wishing I could follow. Wishing I could ask him to stay. Wishing I could fast forward through the next day and a half to when I would join Nel in London and the two of us could log out together and never look back.

I tossed and turned all night, unable to sleep a wink. Loki sat on the nightstand rather than curling up on the bed like he usually did, reminding me of a gargoyle guarding a church. His change in behavior only added to my unease, and it was a relief to see the pale light of dawn seeping in through the curtains.

I rose as soon as it was fully light out and dressed, then headed downstairs and out the back door to walk through the morning mist. I needed to be doing something, and I would be prompted to head outside eventually for Elizabeth's next scheduled encounter with Darcy. I thought I might have stumbled upon a stroke of good luck when I spotted a tall figure marching toward Rosings Park, but something in the way the man walked stopped me short of calling out to him.

If I wasn't mistaken, that confident stride didn't belong to Colin, but to another—William St. George, our gaming party's second interloper.

I snuck through the woods bordering Rosings Park and watched him from behind a tree as he slipped into the manor house through a back door. What the hell was *he* doing here? His character, Wickham, had no connection to Lady Catherine de Bourgh, the lady of Rosings Park, save for his connection to Mr. Darcy. Was he here to see him—or rather, to see Colin?

Several hours passed, my thoughts circling around and

around in my head, before I finally ran into Colin, walking along the lane bordering Rosings Park.

He strode straight toward me and pressed a folded-up letter against my palm, holding my hand between both of his. "You must read this," he said, his stare penetrating. "Find the deeper meaning." Before I could ask him about Will, or about *anything,* he released my hand and raised both of his to press to either side of my face.

And before I knew what was happening, his lips were on mine, his kiss urgent. He stole my breath, his light stubble tickling my face, and I didn't have the presence of mind to do anything but melt into the kiss.

When he pulled away seconds later, I was left breathless, my heart pounding and my belly filled with tingly flutters. "No matter what," he said, his eyes locked with mine, "remember your promise."

I nodded, still too stunned to speak.

"I'll see you on the outside," he vowed, then pressed another, quicker kiss to my lips before turning and striding away.

I stood in the place where he had left me, my feet cemented to the ground, my fingers pressed against my lips, and the letter in my hand all but forgotten.

Only once Colin was out of sight did I turn my attention to the letter. I opened it and skimmed the words. They were familiar, read by me dozens of times before. These were Darcy's words, not Colin's.

Find the deeper meaning.

Eyes narrowing, I forced a flash and gasped when Darcy's words vanished, and a new message appeared. For a long moment, all I could do was stare at the letter. At the new words. Colin's words. How had he been able to achieve such a subterfuge? Something like this would require manipulation under the hood of the game, an alteration of the code itself.

I blinked and shook my head, focusing on what was written, rather than the *how* or *why* of it. I could worry about that later.

Olivia,

I'm sorry for concealing the truth from you, but I was ordered to remain undercover at any cost. I, however, am not willing to risk your life for the sake of my job or this case.

You see, I'm not merely a beta player. I am an agent for the VCIA, planted here to investigate anomalies noticed within Austentopia by the project's lead developer, Priya Burman. Priya approached the agency two months ago, after voicing her concerns about the AI game controller in charge of Pride and Prejudice *to the Rockville board and was told to either fall in line or step down. She's been working with the agency ever since.*

I am still unsure as to the nature of the problem, and without you and your "flashes", I wouldn't know that anything was truly amiss. I wouldn't even have known that Priya was in the game. But the appearance of these strange women in the place of NPCs is highly concerning, as is St. George showing up in place of a player. Clearly, he has some interest here—but what?

Priya worried that Rockville was using the game as a pretense to develop a new form of AI and that the board was pushing forward on the beta tests to offer the AI a new challenge. After what you've shared with me, I now believe she was right. The game controller seems to be creating individual AI beings and storing them within the established NPCs, almost like it's creating an army. But I have no idea why it would be doing such a thing.

I wish I could offer you more clarity, but you have been my best asset in here. Your ability to see through the layers of illusion, to instinctively dig through the code, gave me the only small advantage I had. It's not a good excuse for having kept you in here longer than you were comfortable, but it's the only excuse I have.

I'm sorry, Olivia. I shouldn't have used you like that. I'll make it up to you, on the outside, I promise.
- Colin

[24]

I watched my trunk being loaded onto the carriage from the front porch of the parsonage, eager to be on my way. The mid-morning sun shone brightly in the clear blue sky, and birds chirped merrily, completely unaware of the pall cast over their world by the vanishing players and seemingly replaced NPCs.

The servant and driver nodded in my direction, indicating that they were ready to go. A quick flash had revealed that both belonged to the growing and increasingly unsettling group of NPCs who appeared to have been replaced by impostors, much to my displeasure.

I sighed. I wasn't all that comfortable traveling for four hours with two potential AI soldiers, but at least I would have Maria with me, a normal NPC as of breakfast this morning.

With one last, wary look at the carriage, I turned and headed back into the house to look for Grace. It struck me as odd that she wasn't already out here to bid her sister and me farewell, but she was often caught up in one of Mr. Collin's long-winded diatribes about this or that menial thing, and we were currently operating off-script, so there would be no prompts to guide her out here.

The ground floor of the house was empty, however, and I made my way through the back door, thinking Grace could be out in the garden with Mr. Collins. It was where he spent so much of his time during the day, after all.

Mr. Collins was right where I expected him to be, delicately pruning dead and diseased leaves off his rose bushes, but Grace was nowhere in sight.

"Well, I'm off," I said by way of announcing my presence.

Mr. Collins straightened and turned to look at me, momentary befuddlement sweeping across his face before he smiled and bowed. "Oh, yes. Oh, yes," he said, straightening. "You shall be most grievously missed, cousin."

I scanned the garden. "Have you seen Charlotte? I thought she might be out here with you."

"Charlotte?" Mr. Collins said, the befuddlement returning as he cocked his head to the side.

Dread pooled in my belly, seeping into my bones. "Have you seen *your wife*?"

"Ah!" Mr. Collins brightened. "Yes, my wife! I believe Mrs. Collins is tending to the chickens with Maria." He led the way around the house to the chicken coop where Grace and Maria were collecting eggs, a basket hooked over Grace's elbow and their backs to us.

Relief flooded me, and I smiled to myself.

"My dear!" Mr. Collins called out as we approached the coop. "The carriage is ready. Come, let us see our guests off and bid them farewell."

The two women looked over their shoulders at us, one smiling, one pouting. My own smile slid off my face and the relief fled. Neither woman was Grace. Maria was still there, and still Maria, but Mr. Collins' wife was none other than Mary, the middle Bennet sister, an NPC who had long ago been replaced by one of those AI impostors.

How was this possible? The change had happened right

under my nose. One moment, Grace—as Charlotte Lucas—was Mr. Collins' wife, the next she had been replaced by Mary. It didn't seem possible. And what was more unsettling was that none of the NPCs had noticed the switch.

In a daze, I walked around the house and toward the carriage. I said my goodbyes to Mr. and Mrs. Collins robotically, then boarded the carriage. I may not have had the courage to proceed with the trip to London had Maria been replaced by an AI impostor, but a flash assured me that she was the same as ever.

During the entire four-hour carriage ride to London, I felt numb, a single thought looping through my mind: reach Nel and get the hell out of here. I barely remembered to message Colin about the new development, keeping the details vague.

As soon as the carriage pulled up to Mr. Gardiner's house in London, I hopped out and ran to Nel, who was hiding from the drizzling rain in the front doorway. Loki greeted her snowy white gigi, Bartholomew, with a face rub that I took to be some sort of gigi instant transfer communication method.

I pulled out my game interface book from my personal pocket of virtual space and gripped it in both hands. "We have to log out," I told Nel. "Right now!"

"What?" Nel shook her head, her brows drawn together in confusion. "But it's not time . . ."

I hugged the game interface book to my chest with one arm and gripped her elbow with my free hand. "Players are disappearing, Nel—three are already gone," I explained, leaning in closer and keeping my voice hushed. "I don't know how or why this is happening, but it's *not* safe here. We have to log out, *now*."

Nel's eyes widened as I spoke, and by the time I finished, she was nodding along. "Okay," she said. "Let's do it." She pulled out her game interface book and opened it to the exit page. And then she frowned, flipping forward a page, then back a couple. She shook her head. "This doesn't make any sense."

I opened my own game interface book and immediately saw the problem. The exit page was blank.

My heart dropped, and I gulped. "Loki," I said to the cat sitting near my feet, "why is the exit page blank?" I turned the book, showing him the page.

Loki stood for a moment, his tail lashing, then sat again. His stare grew distant, almost like he wasn't really there, and I figured he was searching some gigi-only database or something of that sort.

A few seconds later, Loki narrowed his eyes, his focus returning to me. "It would appear that someone has disabled the logout function," he said, the end of his tail ticking in irritation. "You cannot leave the game."

September 11, 2026

In the case of the missing game designer, Priya Burman, project lead of Rockville Softworks' *Austentopia* game world is still missing. An anonymous caller to the newsroom claims Ms. Burman was working with the VCIA, the newly established virtual branch of the CIA, to investigate wrong-doings within the yet-to-be-launched game world. We have reached out to Rockville Softworks and the VCIA, but neither organization has yet to issue a statement. We'll keep you updated as the story unfolds.

September 11, 2026

*All players have been immediately pulled from the beta tests of
all* Austentopia *game worlds, and the VCIA has been informed of
the* Pride and Prejudice *situation. From player feeds within* Pride
and Prejudice, *it appears a few of the players are aware of the
logout issue, but as the game world has been locked down from
within, we are unable to extricate or even communicate with the
players.*

*In addition to Priya Burman's feed, two other player feeds have
gone dark, though both seem to still be logged in to the game.
While both players' physical bodies remain in stable condition,
their brain activity is erratic, as though multiple mental signa-
tures are present. As we have been unable to wake them despite
our every attempt, we are preparing for the worst.*

.   .   .

We were able to remove two players from the Pride and Prejudice *game world—Jade Smith and Ben Cho—but as the board is already aware, they were somehow unknowingly placed in a mirror instance of the game and were thus not caught up in the current situation.*

All employees, players, and viewers involved in the Austentopia *beta tests are on lockdown within the testing facility. Unaffected teams have been transitioned to the gamma tests for Grimm-World to keep them occupied. I suggest the board put together a reparations team to prepare for informing player families, should the worst happen.*

As soon as I was through the front door of the Gardiners' home, I made excuses about feeling weary from the hours-long journey to London and wanting to wash up. I grabbed Nel's wrist and dragged her upstairs, where we retreated with our gigis into the bedroom we would be sharing during my short stay there.

I released Nel's wrist and shut the door, then hurried to the bed to sit. Nel followed, perching on the edge of the mattress. I scooted back, pulling my legs up and tucking my skirt under my feet, then set my game interface book on the quilt between us. Nel set her book down beside mine, and we eyed them dubiously. Even the gigis stared at the malfunctioning books, Loki from his perch on the desk by the window, and Bartholomew from the nightstand.

"Something is very wrong with this game," I said, my voice barely above a whisper. Throwing caution to the wind, I told her everything, except about Colin working as a secret agent for the VCIA.

Nel drew her bottom lip between her teeth, her eyebrows bunched together. "It's definitely strange," she said, then added,

"I mean, I've never encountered anything like this before." She pursed her lips. "But . . ."

I scoffed, my eyes bulging as I leaned closer to her. "But?" I squawked, then glanced at the door and lowered my voice. "But *what?*"

Nel was quiet for a moment, having resumed chewing on her lip. "*But,*" she finally said, "maybe it's part of the game." She inhaled deeply, then barreled onward. "I mean, they *told* us it was a straight-up *Pride and Prejudice* reenactment game, but there's nothing in our contracts that says they have to be honest and upfront about the games we'll be testing. What if they wanted our genuine reactions to some warped mystery spin on *Pride and Prejudice?*"

I frowned, my eyes narrowing as I considered what she was suggesting. "So, you're saying this could be, what—" I paused, thinking of an appropriate comparison. "Like a Jane Austin-Agatha Christie mashup?"

Nel shrugged one shoulder. "Maybe?" she said, not sounding all that certain. "I think a lot of this wouldn't be so alarming if you weren't able to see through the game as you can. That kind of throws an unexpected wrench into everything."

I was already shaking my head before she was done speaking. "But it shouldn't have been unexpected at all," I told her. "Either they knew I was like this, or they somehow overlooked it. It just doesn't make any sense." I was quiet for a moment. "And what about Priya and Will being in the game? And those strange women hiding inside some of the NPCs? Or the weird tea-stain messages? If I couldn't 'see through the game' then we would never know about any of that. All we would know is that some players' characters have mysteriously been written out of the story." I was quiet for a moment, then added, "And Priya made it very clear that the impostor NPCs issue is very much *not* supposed to be happening."

Nel went back to chewing on her bottom lip. "I don't know,

Liv . . . what if it's *all* part of the game? What if Priya was never really here? What if your ability to 'see' isn't even real, but just something the game is making you think you can do? I mean, it's virtual reality—*virtually* anything can happen here."

"Including being trapped in the game?" I said, my voice growing urgent. I couldn't argue against the questions she posed. It was like asking me to prove that God didn't exist or that magic wasn't real or that there were no such things as unicorns. I just *couldn't*. "Is being unable to log out *ever* a part of a game?"

Nel narrowed her eyes. "Well . . . have you actually tried to log out early before?" she posed. "I know I haven't." Her shoulders hitched higher. "Maybe the logout function is always unavailable outside of the logout window. I've never been a beta player for Rockville before, so I don't know, maybe it's standard operating procedure for them?"

"But they *said* we could log out whenever," I countered. Acting on a hunch, I looked at Loki. "Was the logout function always available before?" I asked the gigi. "Or was it disabled outside of the logout windows?"

Loki's neon-blue eyes met mine, his stare growing momentarily distant. He refocused on me a second later and said, "The logout function was active until approximately one hour ago, real-world time."

I gave Nel a pointed look.

"OK . . ." She inhaled and exhaled slowly. "I admit it's pretty suspicious, but *maybe*—"

I didn't need to hear any more. I could tell from the way she said "maybe" that she was fully intending on continuing her role as the voice of reason. I pressed my lips together in a thin, flat line, already dismissing whatever she was about to say.

"Just hear me out," Nel said, raising one hand. "Maybe the logout being disabled is just a glitch. Could be fixed in five minutes. And maybe the NPC thing—and Priya, if she really was here and wasn't just a figment of the game—are unrelated to this. And *maybe* William St. George just really likes *Pride and Prejudice*. It's not necessarily a big conspiracy, you know?"

I could see now that there was nothing I could say short of revealing Colin's secret that would make her feel the same fear I felt. That would make her take this as seriously as I was. To her, it was all just a part of the game.

"But what about the disappearing players?" I said, voicing my last-ditch effort.

Nel sucked in a breath, then hesitated. "Maybe they're being yanked from the game to see how the storyline adapts to their sudden, permanent absence?" she said. "I mean, it *is* a beta test. Back when I was a beta player for Good Guy Games, I saw some weird stuff in-game—NPCs acting crazy, scenes changing right before my eyes, players accidentally teleporting from one location to another. You name it, there's a glitch for it, Liv."

I quirked my mouth to the side and stared at my game interface book. While Nel's dissection of the problem did shed doubt on my absolute certainty that we were in serious danger, I couldn't help but think she would view everything in a different light if she knew the VCIA was investigating the game. But I wasn't sure what kind of damage I would do to the investigation if I revealed Colin's duplicitous role.

I opened my game interface book to the logout page. It was still blank. No surprises there.

Nel reached out and wrapped her fingers around my hand. "I know you're worried," she said, her voice filled with compassion, "but please, at least give it some time for any glitches to sort themselves out before assuming the worst." She gave my hand a squeeze, then let go. "It could be nothing."

I stared at the blank page for a moment longer, then raised my eyes to meet Nel's. "Fine," I said, exhaling a sigh. "But if we're still trapped in here tomorrow, I reserve the right to have a full-on freak-out."

Nel laughed, the sound just a little too shrill. "If we're still not able to log out tomorrow," she said, "then *I'll* freak out with you."

I smiled, laughing softly, but my good humor was short-lived. "Promise me something?"

Nel's answering smile was genuine. "Anything."

"We stick together," I said. "We do everything we can to *not* be separated by the game. *If* something is abducting players, I think it'll be a lot harder for it to get us when we're together. At least, so far, players have only vanished when they were alone."

Nel nodded. "Deal."

I blew out a breath, suddenly feeling truly exhausted, and turned the page in my game interface book. I wanted to send a quick message to Colin to confirm that he was experiencing the logout lock out, as well.

But the messaging page was as blank as the last.

Fear took hold of my heart and squeezed. Colin didn't have any other players around him—both Priya and Holden were gone. And now, with the game's internal messaging system disabled, he couldn't communicate with the rest of us at all. He was totally isolated. Totally alone. And our paths weren't due to cross in the game for another three months.

The only light giving me hope was that Mr. Darcy was an integral character to the story—without him, the plot would unravel, and the game would have little purpose. My gut told me Colin's character and mine would be the last to go. I just hoped my gut was right.

[26]

Those three months in-game—with five missed logouts—passed in relative safety, and finally I was mere days away from my reunion with Colin. Assuming he was even still in the game. But as much as I wanted to see him and know that he was okay, the price was too high. To see him, I had to leave Nel behind at Longbourn.

Gnawing on my thumbnail, I paced up and down the hallway outside of Mr. Bennet's study, going over my arguments in my head. Mr. Bennet was a reasonable NPC, and he had a built-in soft spot for his beloved Lizzy. He would see reason. He had to.

I stopped in front of the door to the library, took a deep breath, and raised my fist to knock.

"Come in," Mr. Bennet called as soon as I rapped on the door.

I opened the door and walked into the study.

"Ah, Lizzy, my dear," Mr. Bennet said from the chair behind the desk, "so it is *you* who has been wearing a path in the floorboards this past half hour."

I paused in shutting the door and smiled sheepishly at him over my shoulder. "You could hear me out there?"

He nodded. "To what do I owe this pleasure?"

I shut the door the rest of the way and turned, crossing the room to stand in front of the picture window. I gazed out at the blooming garden, going over what I would say in my head. "I have a request, Papa," I finally said, "and it's really, *really* important to me." I turned my back to the window, facing him.

Mr. Bennet was now leaning back in his chair, his joined hands resting on his belly. "This sounds serious, Lizzy," he said. "Has yet another misguided suitor made you an unwelcome proposal?"

I laughed under my breath and shook my head. "No, no, nothing like that," I said, making my way to the armchair across the desk from his. With a sigh, I perched on the edge. "As you know," I started, "my aunt and uncle are due to arrive this afternoon, and I will be leaving with them tomorrow to tour Derbyshire for a few weeks. I would very much like it if Jane were to accompany me along with my aunt and uncle on our trip."

Mr. Bennet's eyebrows rose, and he inhaled deeply, but before he could voice any protests, I continued.

"Kitty would still be here," I rushed to say, "and she is perfectly capable of taking care of my cousins with Mama's help." I leaned forward. "I know it sounds silly, but Jane really wants to come, and it is really, *really* important to me."

I felt a little bad choosing Nel over Allie, but there was no way I would be able to pull off bringing both players with me, not with the Gardiners' four children due to stay at Longbourn while I was touring Derbyshire with their parents.

Mr. Bennet steepled his fingers as he studied me. "Let me think on it, Lizzy," he said, smiling mysteriously. "I cannot, at present, think of any objection, but I must mention it to Mrs. Bennet, who is a better judge of your sisters' child-minding capabilities."

Relief flooded me, and I smiled gratefully. "Thank you,

Papa." I stood and left the library, hopeful, if not certain, of my victory.

Later that day, I was in my bedroom, packing my trunk for the trip, when I heard Mrs. Bennet's shrill voice raised downstairs.

"Absolutely not!" she practically shrieked. "It is quite impossible."

I froze, then set down the dress I was folding and slowly moved into the hallway, following the sound of her voice.

"Jane must remain here to watch the children, as she is their particular favorite," Mrs. Bennet went on. "And you know how my poor nerves are. I cannot possibly manage four young children with only Kitty's help! I should never recover!"

"My dear," Mr. Bennet said, his voice filled with calm and personal exhaustion. "You have raised our five daughters admirably well. I have the utmost faith in your ability to manage four children for little more than a fortnight."

I reached the cracked open door to the study and held my breath.

"Jane shall go with Lizzy," Mr. Bennet said, "and that will be that."

Mrs. Bennet growled in frustration. "I do not think so, Mr. Bennet," she said, an ominous note to her words.

I peeked into the library through the crack between the edge of the door and the frame. Mr. Bennet sat at his desk, as usual, while Mrs. Bennet stood beside him, her hand resting on his shoulder.

Suddenly, Mr. Bennet's face twisted in agony, and he doubled over in his chair, his forehead nearly cracking against the edge of the desk. He clutched his chest and clawed at his face.

Eyes opened wide, I forced a flash. I had to know what was really happening to him.

Mr. Bennet's true appearance flickered in and out of view,

alternating with that of one of those strange not-quite-human women. I watched, horrified and fascinated, as he was replaced, right before my eyes. Soon the flickering stopped, and all that remained was the impostor.

I blinked, and the truth visible through the flash vanished. The NPC that had been Mr. Bennet appeared to be him once more, his expression placid. But I knew the truth. Mr. Bennet was gone.

"As you say, my dear," the NPC formerly known as Mr. Bennet said to his impostor wife, "Jane shall stay home while Lizzy travels with the Gardiners."

Panic clutched at my heart, and I burst into the room. "Then I won't go," I told them. "I'll stay here with Jane. Kitty can go with the Gardiners!"

My impostor parents stared at me. Mrs. Bennet narrowed her eyes, and Mr. Bennet's calm now seemed somehow menacing.

"Impossible!" Mrs. Bennet said. "Kitty is too young to appreciate the great houses of Derbyshire. The trip would be wasted on her. Either you or Jane must remain behind to tend to the children."

I had the sinking suspicion that this was not the game resisting a change to the storyline, but rather the impostor NPCs trying to separate Jane and me. This only reinforced my theory that, for whatever reason, they needed players to be alone to do whatever they did that made us disappear. If I left Longbourn alone, it would be the beginning of the end. I felt certain of it.

I backed up a step, needing to be away from them. Would they force me to go? Would they physically drag me into the carriage? Or maybe steal me away in the middle of the night? I turned toward the open doorway.

"They're here!" Allie exclaimed from the front of the house. Her footsteps thundered up the hallway, and she poked her head into the study, grinning broadly. "They're here," she repeated, a little breathless.

I followed Allie to the front doorway, Mr. and Mrs. Bennet trailing behind me. Knowing they were at my back, watching me, scheming, sent shivers cascading down my spine. I rushed out through the front door to stand beside Nel, linking my arm with hers.

Nel eyed me, her smile uncertain. "Well?" she asked, her voice hushed.

I shook my head and swallowed roughly. My mouth was suddenly a desert. "I'm sorry," I told her as I watched the hope melt from her expression. "I tried."

Nel blinked, then forced a wooden smile and returned her attention to the carriage pulling to a stop in the driveway.

I did the same, keenly aware of Mr. and Mrs. Bennets' watchful eyes. As soon as the Gardiners and their four children were out of the carriage, I forced another flash to verify that they were still *them*.

My heart dropped into my stomach. Both Mr. and Mrs. Gardiner had been replaced by impostors.

I had a choice, then. I could either remain behind with the impostors posing as Mr. and Mrs. Bennet, but have the comfort of knowing Allie was with me while Jane traveled with the Gardiners. Or, I could leave with the impostors posing as Mr. and Mrs. Gardiner, where I would spend a couple of weeks alone with them before I was due to run into Colin at Pemberley mid-trip—if he was even still in the game. I feared that whoever left with the Gardiners would never return. Either I would leave with them and vanish, or Nel would. But Nel didn't have any way to distinguish friendly NPC from foe. I couldn't send her out on her own like that. I could never be so cruel.

After the Gardiners had been greeted and the children sent behind the house to the lawn to run around under Jane's watchful eye, I made my way back to the study.

"Come in," Mr. Bennet called when I knocked.

I pushed the door open and entered the now ominous room. "I'll go," I told him. And without another word, I turned and left.

The next morning, when my trunk was loaded onto the carriage and the Gardiners were waiting for me to join them within, I hugged Nel tight, tears stinging my eyes. I was afraid this was the last time I would ever see her.

"Promise me you'll stay close to Allie," I whispered, my words quiet and urgent. "No matter what happens to me." I pulled back and looked into her eyes, gripping her upper arms. "Promise me."

[27]

I sat in the carriage opposite Mr. and Mrs. Gardiner and stared out the window, watching the Derbyshire countryside pass by outside. Loki lay on my lap, purring as I anxiously stroked his smooth fur. The moment of truth was fast approaching. In a few hours, I would find out if Colin was still in the game or if he had vanished like Priya, Holden, and Grace.

If I hadn't known Mr. and Mrs. Gardiner were impostors, I never would have guessed. Everything they said and did was exactly as I would have expected based on the story I knew so well. The only sense of something being off came from within me, from the secret knowledge I had. Which made me wonder—who exactly were these impostors? Were they truly AI soldiers, as Colin had guessed? And if so, what did they want?

If not-the-Gardiners' purpose had merely been to isolate me and abduct me, well then, that could have happened the second we left Longbourn. If they did have nefarious intentions, then why wait so long to act. We had been traveling together for nearly three weeks—plenty of time for them to do whatever it was they did to players when they disappeared.

Were the Gardiners' holding off on taking me because Elizabeth Bennet was the main character of *Pride and Prejudice* and thus would be difficult to extricate from the story? Or was Nel right? Was this all part of the game? I might have been swayed to her way of thinking if not for the logout and messaging issues. We had missed six logouts, which meant six days had passed out in the real world while we had been trapped in here. That was six days that our physical bodies hadn't been able to eat or sleep or go to the bathroom. Even Nel agreed that that was troubling, and her unshakable glass-half-full had been looking emptier and emptier as of late.

"Ah," Mrs. Gardiner said, looking out the opposite window, "there it is—Pemberley. It's just as I remember it."

I shifted my attention to that window and gazed outside, my heart beating faster. Though I could see the Darcy family estate clearly, and my brain told me Pemberley House was a large, handsome stone building—just as Jane Austen had described it —I could barely focus on what I was seeing. All I could think about was Colin.

I couldn't wait to see him. I had so much to tell him. So much to ask him. But more than anything, I just wanted to know he was all right. To know he was still here.

I gripped my skirt in tight fists, swallowing down the dread attempting to claw its way up my throat. What if Colin didn't show up when he was supposed to? What if he was gone? And what if Nel and the others were already gone? What if I was the only one left? What was going to happen to me? *When* was I going to be taken, too?

I felt numb to the world outside the carriage as we slowed, then stopped. I didn't want to be here. Didn't want to find out what I felt so sure I was about to discover.

Mr. Gardiner exited the carriage first, then helped his wife out. Once she was standing on the gravel driveway, he held his hand into the carriage for me to take. I accepted it. What choice did I have?

A respectable-looking older woman—Mrs. Reynolds, Pemberley's housekeeper, I assumed—was already on her way down the stairs leading up to the front door of the manor house by the time my boot soles touched the gravel of the driveway. I listened, numb inside, as Mr. Gardiner inquired about a tour of the house and grounds.

"Aye," Mrs. Reynolds said, giving the three of us a measuring look. "My master is away, but we expect him tomorrow, with a large party of friends. Your timing is good. Were you but a day later, and I would have to turn you away."

I perked up and focused on Mrs. Reynolds. Those words of expectation and of the party her master would be bringing with him were straight from the book. A little early, but Jane Austen had written that piece of dialogue verbatim. It gave me hope that Mrs. Reynolds was speaking of Colin's character, Mr. Darcy, and that he *was* still in the game. Because if he had vanished like Priya, Holden, and Grace, then the story would have been revised to exclude his character, just as had been done with Caroline Bingley, Charles Bingley, and Charlotte Lucas.

Before I could ask a tactical question aimed at revealing the identity of Mrs. Reynold's master, the sound of hooves on gravel drew my attention, and I turned to see a rider galloping up the long, tree-lined driveway. I took a step toward the driveway, raising my hand to shield my eyes from the sun. I wasn't positive, but I thought the rider *might* be Colin.

"Ah," said Mrs. Reynolds, a note of apology in her tone. "My master has returned early. I do apologize, but a tour will no longer be possible."

I tuned out her words, my heart soaring as the rider drew nearer. It *was* Colin. I was certain of it.

Suddenly he was right there, his horse almost on top of me. He reined in his mount beside the carriage and leapt off, striding straight toward me. He stopped abruptly, just out of arm's reach, and bowed to me. "Miss Bennet," he said, his eyes locking with mine.

Aware of the audience behind me, I curtsied and greeted him appropriately. "Mr. Darcy." My heart thundered in my chest.

"Does the young lady know Mr. Darcy?" Mrs. Reynolds asked the Gardiners.

But it was Colin who answered. "Indeed," he said, "we are well acquainted." Colin tore his attention from me just long enough to bow to Mr. and Mrs. Gardiner.

"Oh, um," I started, stumbling over my words. "This is my uncle and aunt, Mr. and Mrs. Gardiner."

"Pleased to make your acquaintance," Colin said, then shifted his focus to Mrs. Reynolds. "Please show them around the estate," he told her. "I must speak with Elizabeth, and I will return with her shortly to rejoin you all."

I held my breath as Mr. and Mrs. Gardiner exchanged looks. I feared they would protest.

But Colin offered me his arm before they could say anything at all, and together with our gigis, we strode away from the small group, trailed by their curious, suspicious stares.

Colin guided me to a copse of trees, where we might find a bit of cover from their noticeable scrutiny. "Something is very wrong with the game," he said, releasing my arm and turning to face me.

I blew out a breath. "And here I was hoping you would tell me it was nothing to worry about," I admitted.

Colin shook his head. "A game with a malfunctioning logout function *never* should have made it to the human beta testing phase," he said, starting to pace. "Such a thing would destroy Rockville Softworks if it were ever exposed. Either the development team was extremely negligent, or someone purposely disabled the logout function."

I licked my lips nervously. "But, it could just be a glitch, right?"

"Could be," Colin said. "But we've already missed six logout windows. That means our bodies have been logged into the game for more than six days."

I gulped, almost afraid to ask, "What exactly does that mean for our bodies?"

"We will have been hooked up to feeding tubes and catheters since the first missed logout," he explained. "We're essentially in an induced coma at this point, and the longer we remain in this state, the less likely it is we'll ever wake."

Frightened, I hugged my middle. "What's the longest that anyone has ever stayed in *AO*?" I asked.

"And emerged?" Colin clarified.

I nodded.

"Three weeks," he said. "When the system was first being tested, the FDA was the organization in charge of regulating such tech. They gave one hundred prisoners facing life sentences without parole the option to live out their lives in the virtual world rather than in a prison. Twenty-three took the offer. The scientists running the program logged out the prisoners for five minutes every three days. After twelve days, only twenty could be successfully logged out. After fifteen days, only sixteen. After eighteen days, only eleven. And after twenty-four days, none could be logged out."

My mouth fell open. "How many are still in here?" I asked.

"Twenty," Colin told me.

I was almost afraid to ask, but I couldn't resist. "Did the other three return to the prisons?" I said.

Colin skewered me with a meaningful look, then shook his head. "They died when the scientists attempted to disconnect them from the system," he explained. "Brain-dead, like their minds had been severed from their bodies."

The revelation knocked me off balance, and I stumbled backward, steadying myself against a tree trunk. I looked at Colin and cleared my throat. "But everyone was still able to log out after nine days?"

Colin nodded.

"So, we should have at least three more real-world days to find a way out of here," I said, processing out loud. That translated to about fifty in-game days.

Colin approached me, reaching out to rest a hand on my upper arm. His touch felt solid and reassuring. He peered down at me, his eyes searching mine. "We'll find a way out of this," he vowed. "Together."

I nodded robotically, and a slightly hysterical laugh escaped from my lips. "Nel and I tried to stick together," I told him, "but the impostor NPCs wouldn't let us. They want us separated. Isolated. I think they need us to be alone to do whatever it is they do to us when we disappear from the game." After a moment, I added, "Both Mr. and Mrs. Bennet as well as the Gardiners have been replaced."

"And Mrs. Reynolds?" Colin asked, glancing past me to the house. Of course, he would want to know that—he would be around her frequently during his stay at Pemberley.

I shook my head. "I don't know," I admitted. "I didn't check. But . . ." I bit my lip, my eyes narrowing as I recalled what I had seen in the library at Longbourn when Mr. Bennet had been replaced. "I think one of the impostors has to be touching the other NPC to replace them, so Mrs. Reynolds will likely be replaced if she hasn't been already."

Colin was quiet for a moment, staring off at the distant, wooded foothills. "There must be some way for us to stay together," he mused. "We can just refuse to leave one another. Would they forcibly separate us?"

I inhaled and exhaled deeply, then shook my head. "They could use the rules of this world—this time period—against us," I said. "They could arrest you for kidnapping. As a young woman in this time period, my parents have final say over where I go and what I do." In fact, a woman of Regency England couldn't even marry who she wanted without parental permission until she turned twenty-one, and as of March, Elizabeth Bennet was only twenty.

A thought struck me, and my eyes opened wider, my lips parting.

"You have an idea," Colin said, leaning toward me. "What is it?"

"Gretna Green," I murmured, my eyes snapping to meet Colin's. "It's a town just across the Scottish border. If we travel fast, we could get there tomorrow." I pushed away from the tree to pace as I worked through the forming plan out loud. "I'd have to sneak out of the inn after the Gardiners retire for the night," I said. "But if you had a carriage waiting and they don't catch me right away, we could get a big enough lead by the time they wake up and notice I'm gone." A smile teased my lips. "They'll never catch us in time to stop us."

"To stop us from doing *what*?" Colin said.

I halted mid-step and faced him. "From getting married."

28

I retired early that evening, retreating to my room at the inn in Lambton to anxiously await my escape. I sat on the bed, flipping through my game interface book while Loki perched on the desk by the window, lazily bathing himself. I combed through the parts in the *Austentopia* encyclopedia about marriage laws during Jane Austen's time, confirming that a Gretna Green marriage was legally binding in England—despite the ceremony taking place in Scotland. Mr. and Mrs. Bennet would *have* to honor the union, which meant Colin and I would be free to spend as much time as possible together investigating what could very well turn out to be a fatal flaw in the game. We just had to make it to Gretna Green and get married first.

At the sound of a soft, metallic clicking, I looked at Loki, then at the door. "Did you hear that?"

Loki licked the fur on his chest one more time, then looked at me. "The sound of a key turning in a lock?" He raised a paw to his mouth to continue his bath. "Yes, I heard it," he said between licks.

I sat frozen on the mattress and stared at the door. Ever so slowly, I rose from the bed and approached the door. I reached out to grip the doorknob, held my breath, and twisted the handle. But the door wouldn't open. I had been locked in.

"Damn it!" I hissed, pacing away from the door as my thoughts whirled.

They had never locked me in. I had been sleeping using the age-old chair-lodged-under-the-door-handle trick because the key to my room had been lost. Or so I'd been told. Did this mean the impostors were planning on taking me tonight? How was I supposed to escape if I was locked in my room?

I looked at the window, then moved closer, leaning over the desk to assess the drop. I was on the second floor of the inn, my window overlooking an alleyway. If I hung from the windowsill, then dropped, I thought I might be able to land without breaking my legs. At least the ground below was compacted dirt rather than stone. That would allow for a slightly softer landing.

I straightened and looked at Loki. "How realistic are injuries in this game?" I asked the cat, recalling Charlie telling me that the authenticity of virtual injuries and pain varied from game to game.

"Very realistic," Loki said, his voice bored as he continued his bath.

"And pain?" I asked.

Loki lowered his paw, blinked once, and finally looked at me. "In a non-combat game such as this," he said, "a player's pain setting is automatically set to one hundred percent."

I chewed on the inside of my cheek. Even if I broke both of my ankles in the fall, it would be worth it. I would be away from this place—and these impostors.

━━

Standing off to the side of the open window, I stared out into the night from the dark room. I had heard movement outside my door twice since being locked in, but thankfully neither had resulted in anyone actually coming into the room.

A carriage pulled up in the road at the mouth of the alley, and a hand emerged from the open window, displaying a cheerful thumbs up. It was Colin. That was our agreed-upon signal.

Heart suddenly racing, I tucked my game interface book into the pocket of virtual space that followed me everywhere within this game. I took a deep breath, and another, and then I raised my leg over the windowsill and awkwardly climbed out into the night. I was more out than in, balancing on one thigh when it occurred to me that I probably should have done something with my skirt, like tying it together between my legs. Too late now.

Loki watched me from the desk as my dangling foot scrambled for purchase on the stone wall of the inn. I finally found a crack in the mortar with the toe of my boot and dug in. Once I was fairly sure it would hold me, I carefully pulled my other leg over the sill.

The mortar beneath my boot crumbled, and the foot supporting me slid out of the crack. My stomach lurched into my throat as I dangled from the windowsill, my fingers slowly slipping.

"Gah!" I gasped as my grip failed and I dropped from the windowsill. I landed with an ungraceful roll onto my side, and my hip and shoulder took as much of the impact as my feet and ankles. It hurt, but more like bruises than broken bones.

With a groan, I rolled onto my hands and knees as Loki landed on the ground nearby. The cat padded up the alleyway toward the carriage, leaving me to scrabble up to my feet.

Colin must have finally realized that the thing that had dropped from the window was me because he was suddenly out of the carriage and jogging down the alley. I hobbled toward him, and when he reached me, he looped an arm around my waist, helping me move along more quickly than I could have on my own. He pushed me into the carriage ahead of him, then climbed in himself, pulling the door shut behind him.

I sat on the forward-facing bench seat, rubbing my sore shoulder.

Colin joined me on the bench, his lips twisting into a wry smile as he eyed me. "So, you chose to escape through the window, huh?"

I let out a breathy laugh. The carriage started moving, and my shoulder smacked the wall behind me. I winced.

"I didn't have much of a choice," I told him, shifting my weight to put less pressure on my tender hip. Loki had been right: injuries and pain were *very* realistic in this game, and I had no doubt that my virtual body was going to be covered in a patchwork of livid bruises soon enough.

Colin raised his eyebrows, clearly curious.

"They locked me in," I explained.

"Ah," he said, nodding to himself. "Then we might not have as much of a lead as we had hoped for . . . especially if they come to check on you and find you gone."

I sighed and rested my head against the side of the carriage, staring out the window at the sleepy village. "It'll be good enough," I said softly. It had to be.

We rode in silence for a long time, both of us staring out our respective windows, too tired to talk but too wired to sleep.

"It all feels so real," I murmured, breaking the long silence. "The fear, the danger . . ." I shook my head, wondering how I had gotten myself into this mess. I had done it for Charlie, so he could live his dream. And I knew that once he found out what had happened to me, if he didn't already know, he would blame himself. I could only imagine what that guilt would do to him. How it would destroy him.

"The danger *is* real," Colin said. "If we don't find a way out of this game, we'll never leave, and this will become our *only* reality."

I turned my face toward him, only to find that he was already watching me. I flashed him a weak smile. "Thanks for agreeing to marry me in what may soon become your only reality."

Colin returned my smile and found my hand in the darkness. "No problem."

Once again, we settled into a heavy silence and returned to staring out the windows. But my hand was still snug in his. And after some time, my eyelids grew heavy, and I fell asleep.

29

I woke leaning against something warm and hard. A person. I raised my head from said person's shoulder, only to find a generous patch of drool soaking the fabric of said person's coat. Said person was Colin, and I was suddenly mortified.

I dabbed at the drool spot with my sleeve, my cheeks on fire. "Sorry about that," I murmured.

Colin glanced at me, then down at his shoulder and grunted, nonplussed.

I offered him an apologetic smile. "Please tell me I didn't snore, too."

His expression said it all.

I groaned and closed my eyes, my head falling back as I laughed in quiet misery. After a moment, I took a deep breath and pulled myself together. "How long was I out?" I asked.

"A few hours," Colin told me. "You could stretch out on the other bench." He nodded to the bench opposite ours, where our gigis were snuggled up, fast asleep. "Might be more comfortable."

I snorted a laugh. "Looks like that seat's taken." Yawning, I rubbed my eyes and then stretched, raising my arms over my head and arching my back. My shoulder and hip throbbed with the movement, and I winced. "I'm fine," I said, as much to myself as to Colin. "All rested up. But you're more than welcome to drool on my shoulder if you want." I eyed him sidelong. "Fair is fair."

Colin chuckled.

As my embarrassment faded, my wits returned, and I realized the carriage wasn't moving. I said as much to Colin.

"Driver's changing out the horses," he told me. "For speed."

"Oh," I said. "I suppose that makes sense."

I peered out the window and spotted the driver standing nearby. I forced a quick flash and was relieved to see that the driver was still just a regular NPC, so he wasn't about to sabotage our escape. With a sigh, I settled back on the bench, and soon enough, the carriage was moving again.

We changed out the horses twice more before crossing into Scotland. It was early afternoon the next day when we stopped for the final time, the driver letting us know we had reached Gretna Green.

"Do we need to find a church?" Colin asked once we were both out of the carriage. His gigi—Francine, I had learned during the ride—trotted around, sniffing the road and buildings nearest to us. Loki merely sat beside me, looking around with complete and utter disinterest.

I shook my head. "No need for a church," I told Colin. "Handfasting works just as well here." I glanced at the driver. "But what we do need is another witness." We would need two people to witness our vows to make the marriage official.

I scanned the buildings lining the street and was pleased to discover the driver had stopped directly in front of an inn. That would do nicely.

I reached for Colin's hand and looked at the driver. "Both of you, follow me," I said.

I led them into the inn and stopped a few steps inside the

doorway, looking around the dim common room. A short bar was situated against the back wall, and the tables and chairs spread about the space were mostly empty. A man who had been crouched, hidden behind the bar, stood. I released Colin's hand, squared my shoulders, and marched across the common room, making a beeline for the bartender.

"Barkeep," I said, leaning against the bar, "we would be very honored if you would agree to witness our marriage."

The bartender eyed me dubiously, then eyed Colin and his fine clothes a little less dubiously.

Smiling to myself, I turned to Colin and waved for him to approach, then turned back to the bartender. "We can pay you for your time," I told the man as Colin settled in beside me, the driver still hanging back a few steps. I shot Colin a meaningful look. "Right, dear?"

"Of course," Colin said smoothly, pulling a coin purse out of his personal pocket of virtual space. He counted out a few large silver coins and stacked them on the bar.

The bartender eyed the coins, then reached out and slid them off the bar and into his pocket. He nodded.

I grinned and grabbed Colin's hand. "I am your wife, and you are my husband," I said, not willing to risk wasting time on flowery words. "Now, you say it," I told him with a smile and a nod. "Only reversed."

Colin looked into my eyes, his stare deep and soulful. "I am your husband," he said. "And you are my wife." And much to my surprise, he pulled a ring out of his personal pocket of virtual space and slipped it onto the ring finger of my left hand.

It was gorgeous—a massive sapphire surrounded by a swath of smaller diamonds. I stared at the ring, my lips parted, and my breath caught in my throat. We hadn't discussed a ring.

I raised my eyes to meet Colin's, and then I grinned. It was done. We were wed. I exhaled in relief, my shoulders relaxing as the tension seeped out of me. Whatever happened next, we would face it together.

"Is that it?" Colin asked.

I smirked. "Well, almost," I said, leaning in and raising my face to his. My lips brushed against his, and his arms curved around my back. He deepened the kiss until my cheeks were flushed and my toes curled.

"Oh my," I said when he finally broke the kiss. I took a couple of steadying deep breaths, then smiled broadly. "Well now, should we celebrate our victory with a drink?"

Once again, Colin chuckled, and I thought it was quickly becoming one of my favorite sounds. "Why not?"

[30]

The door to the inn slammed open, and everyone in the common room turned to look. Everyone, that was, except for me. Colin's expression told me everything I needed to know. The Gardiners had arrived.

I raised my wineglass to take another sip as the sound of their footsteps heralded their approach. We were well into our second bottle, and I was, for the first time in a long time, not remotely concerned about the current situation. Colin and I would deal with it tomorrow. Three more real-world days meant we had around fifty more days in-game to solve our little problem. And now that we were married, we were inseparable. Which—fingers crossed—meant we were untouchable. We wouldn't vanish like the others. I hoped.

Mr. and Mrs. Gardiner rounded the table and came into view. Mr. Gardiner's expression was thunderous, Mrs. Gardiner's wary.

I raised my glass to them, grinning victoriously. "Aunt! Uncle!" I exclaimed. "Welcome!"

They glowered down at me.

"I might have expected something like this from your

younger sisters," Mrs. Gardiner started, "but not from you, Elizabeth. I only pray we are not too late."

A small, gleeful laugh bubbled up from my chest, and I took another sip of wine. "Oh, but you are!" I told them. "You are much, *much* too late." I held out my left hand so they could get a good look at the stunning ring. With that massive sapphire, it was impossible to miss.

Colin pushed back his chair and stood, gesturing to me with one hand. "Might I present my wife, Mrs. Elizabeth Darcy."

Mr. and Mrs. Gardiner stiffened, their expressions hard.

I stood as well, accepting his proffered hand, and curtsied to the impostors pretending to be my in-game relations.

Colin looked at me, his lips curved into the faintest, sneakiest of smiles. "Now we shall never be parted again," he said and raised his wineglass.

I picked up my own glass and clinked it against his, and we both drank. "Please," I said, setting my glass down and sitting. I looked up at Mrs. Gardiner. "Join us. Help us celebrate this happy event."

Colin also reclaimed his seat.

"We shall not," Mrs. Gardiner said stiffly. "We are weary from traveling such a long distance so unexpectedly and will retire to a room." She reached into her embroidered drawstring purse and pulled out a couple of letters, tossing them onto the table. They landed near my wineglass. "These came for you after you left," she said. And with a sniff, she turned and walked away, Mr. Gardiner following close behind her.

I watched them go, then looked at Colin, my lips curving into a triumphant grin. "They seem quite peeved about this turn of events. I'd say this all worked out beautifully."

He agreed with a low, soft laugh.

I reached for the letters and slid them closer on the table. I opened the thicker letter first, skimming over the first part, which was written word for word by Nel just as Jane had written to

Elizabeth at this point in the timeline in *Pride and Prejudice*. But after the expected break in the letter, that all started to change.

Since writing the above, dearest Lizzy, something has occurred of the most unexpected and serious nature; but I am afraid of alarming you—be assured that we are all well. What I have to say relates to poor Kitty.

"To *Kitty*?" I exclaimed quietly. I could feel Colin's gaze on my face but couldn't tear my eyes from the letter or the words that were almost right, but implied that something was very, *very* wrong. Jane wasn't supposed to have written to Elizabeth about Kitty, but about Lydia.

Since you have been gone, Kitty has traveled to Brighton to stay with the Forsters.

I frowned and shook my head. "But what about Lydia?" I murmured. Lydia was the one who was supposed to go to Brighton and get into trouble there.

An express came at twelve last night, just as we were all gone to bed, from Colonel Forster, to inform us that she was gone off to Scotland with one of his officers, to own the truth, with Wickham!—Imagine our surprise.

I stared at the letter, completely stunned. I skimmed the rest, searching for other anomalies, but it read much as it should, only with Kitty in Lydia's place of scandal. Cold dread washed over me, as I realized what this meant.

"Michelle's gone," I said, setting down the letter with shaking hands and raising my eyes to meet Colin's. "Written out of the story." I swallowed, my saliva suddenly tacky, and cleared my throat. "Priya, Holden, Grace . . . and now Michelle. All that's left is you and me, Nel, Allie, and Will. Four down, five to go."

Colin was quiet, his stare thoughtful. I could practically see the gears turning in his head.

I tore open the second letter. It was short, just a single line to the nearly two full pages Jane was supposed to have written according to the book.

Lizzy—I'm frightened. Please come home.

Numbly, I handed the note to Colin. "Now that Allie's gone to take Michelle's place in Brighton, Nel's all alone," I said, staring at the half-empty bottle of wine. "We have to leave." I looked at Colin. "We have to leave *now*."

September 18, 2026

And now, for an update on the missing-person story that has held the world captive. It would appear that the VCIA—the CIA branch responsible for policing and investigating online and virtual crimes—has been called in to assist the Redmond Police Department in the search for Priya Burman. Ms. Burman has been missing for two weeks, but according to a spokesperson for the police, little headway has been made in the case. If you're out there Ms. Burman, and if you're watching, we're all praying for your safe return.

September 18, 2026

I'm here on the scene at the Rockville Softworks campus in Redmond, Washington where anti-VR and human-first activists have gathered in protest in the wake of the disappearance of Priya Burman. The company, the world's leading game developer in virtual space, has issued a statement saying they are as concerned as everyone else about Ms. Burman's disappearance and are working closely with the VCIA to find her. The protests started shortly after an anonymous source within Rockville Softworks leaked a recording of Priya voicing her concerns about the safety of the upcoming game world, *Austentopia*. Players and activists across the globe are crying foul play.

As you can see behind me, thousands have gathered in the streets to voice their outrage in what they see as a pivotal moment in human history. The leader of the activist group *Absolute Reality* has issued a counterstatement: *Priya Burman is all of us. She is you, and she is me. If we let virtual reality take over our lives, we, too, will disappear. Virtual mortality will be the fate of all mankind.*

I trudged up the inn stairs to the second floor, Colin and the gigis trailing close behind me. We needed to be gone, in a carriage, and on the road to start the long journey south from Gretna Green to Longbourn, not heading up to a room at the inn to catch a few winks. Nel was in danger, *alone,* and there was no saying how much time she had left.

But we also needed rest. That was the downside of hyper-realistic virtual reality. Thanks to the in-game time compression, to our minds, we had really been up for two days straight, and our *virtual* bodies, linked to our very *real* minds, needed sleep.

I made my way to the door at the end of the hallway and fit the key the innkeeper had given us into the lock. The adrenaline rush from Nel's letters had worn off, and that low combined with all the wine had left me thoroughly exhausted. I needed to sleep off my wedding day buzz and return to the game with a clear head.

I pushed open the door and stepped into the room. And stopped dead.

The room contained a single bed, along with a fireplace and

an armchair beyond the foot of the bed, a pair of nightstands, and a small chest of drawers set against the wall on the far side of the room. My focus lingered on that lone bed. I hadn't thought this far ahead. One bed for two people. It didn't take my wine-soaked brain long to do the math.

We had set our driver up with a room as well and sent him off to rest with the request that he have the carriage out in front of the inn and ready to go as soon as the sun was down. Between him and us, we had booked the inn's last two available rooms, which meant Colin and I were stuck together until the innkeeper came up and knocked on our door at sunset, as per our request. Logically, I knew it was safer for us to sleep in the same room, but . . . *one bed*.

Behind me, Colin slipped into the room and approached the armchair. He gripped the top of the chair back with one hand and turned to face me. "I'll take the chair, and—"

I scoffed and waved a hand dismissively, trying to play it cool when I felt anything but about the prospect of sharing a bed with Colin—even just to sleep *in the virtual world*. All of a sudden, my heartbeat was quick and erratic, and my whole body felt flushed.

"Don't be ridiculous," I said, my focus sliding from Colin back to the bed. "You'll sleep better on the bed, and it's plenty big for both of us." To illustrate my resolve on the issue, I strode over to the bed and sat on the edge, bending over to remove my boots. Once they were off, I scooted backward on top of the quilt and stiffly laid on my back, my head propped up on a pair of pillows and my hands folded together over my middle.

Loki leaped onto the nightstand and took up his usual gargoyle pose on the far corner of the little table, facing the door. "Truly, it would be wise for you both to sleep," he said, not looking at either of us. "You have a long journey ahead of you, and you'll need your wits about you if you're going to fix the issue." The tip of his tail ticked, and his whiskers twitched. "Francine and I will stand watch."

My lips curved into a small smile, and I propped myself up on my elbows as I leaned across the nightstand to scratch Loki under his chin. "I knew you cared, you big softy."

Loki stretched out his neck so I could scratch him in just the right spot and let out a low, rumbling purr.

Francine laid down in front of the door, and I could feel Colin's keen stare on Loki and me.

"Your gigi's AI is remarkably well-developed," Colin said as I grew increasingly uncomfortable.

I pulled my hand away from Loki, much to the gigi's disappointment, and looked at Colin. I glanced at Loki once more—the bored black cat looked the same as ever—then returned my attention to Colin, my brows bunching together. "What do you mean?"

Loki definitely had his own personality—or cat-ality—but he didn't seem all that different from Francine or Scarlet, Charlie's gigi. They were just as unique and animated—and *real*—as my gigi.

Colin bent to take off his boots before responding. "Gigis start out very generic, their AI developing depth and complexity over time," he said. "Surely you must've noticed that the other gigis in our party rarely speak or interact with their players . . . or do much of anything at all."

I frowned, thinking of Nel's gigi, Bartholomew, who I had taken to be the strong, silent type with all his sitting and staring and not talking. Colin kind of had a point.

Colin set his boots neatly on the floor beside the armchair, then shrugged out of his coat and draped it over the back of the chair. "As is standard practice in beta tests, each player was assigned a temporary gigi to accompany them through this game world," he explained, then held up one finger to forestall any response from me. "Each player *except* for me." He nodded to

Francine. "With Priya's help, I was able to transport my permanent gigi into the game world."

I narrowed my eyes and looked at Loki. "But Loki was with me when I first woke up in *AO*," I said. "After the implant procedure, I mean." Since I had never created my own *AO* account before, Loki was my first ever gigi. "That was before I entered *Pride and Prejudice*."

Standing at the foot of the bed, Colin crossed his arms over his chest, studying Loki. "Are you sure it wasn't merely another black cat gigi? They're fairly common for both starter accounts and generics . . ."

I snorted a laugh and shook my head. "Nope, it was definitely him," I said. "There's no mistaking that sparkling personality."

Loki looked at me and slow blinked, clearly unamused.

"Huh," Colin said. "You must have somehow pulled your permanent gigi into the game world." He narrowed his eyes in thought. "I wonder if it has something to do with your neural anomaly."

My eyebrows rose. "I'm sorry—my *what*?"

"The same structural difference in your brain that allows you to see through the layers of code within the game," Colin said. He was quiet for a moment, then added, "Once we've found a way out of this situation, I would love to bring you into the VCIA to meet my superiors. Someone with your particular talents could be very useful to our team."

I blinked in surprise. "Did you just offer me a job?"

The corner of Colin's mouth lifted in a half-smile. "Consider this your interview," he said. "If we can figure a way out of this mess, you'll have more than earned yourself a place on my team."

I blanched at the reminder of our dire situation and suddenly felt a little queasy. Turning my gaze to the window, I chewed on the inside of my cheek, losing myself to worrying thoughts.

Colin walked around to my side of the bed and sat beside me on the edge of the mattress. "I'm sorry, Olivia. I didn't think through how that would sound," he said, his voice a low murmur. "Remember when I said I was bad with people?" When I looked at him, he raised his eyebrows. "Well, here's your proof."

My chest shook with a silent, humorless laugh.

Colin took my hand in his, his thumb rubbing a slow line back and forth across my knuckles. "We'll figure this out," he promised, then gave my hand a gentle squeeze. "Now, scoot over."

My eyes widened. "Excuse me?"

Colin pointed with his chin to the far side of the bed. "Scoot over," he said, then glanced at the door. "If anyone comes in while we're asleep, I'd rather they encounter me first. You have minimal combat experience in the virtual world, and I've had more than my fair share." He pressed his lips together. "Besides, it's my fault you're trapped in here. If I hadn't convinced you to reenter the game . . ."

I studied Colin's face for a long moment, considering offering up some reassurance that I didn't blame him, that it wasn't his fault. Except, it was. So, I kept my mouth shut and scooted over to the far side of the bed, leaning forward to drag the skirt of my dress the rest of the way. I laid down as Colin stretched out on his back beside me, his dark hair fanning across the white pillowcase.

After a moment, I turned onto my side to face Colin. "Tell me the truth," I said, "is this the worst situation you've ever been in?"

Colin folded one arm behind his head, propping himself higher on the pillows, and eyed me sidelong. "Trapped in a virtual version of Regency England with you?" he said. Once again, the corner of his mouth raised in a half-smile. "Not even close." The skin at the corners of his eyes crinkled as his lips curved the rest of the way into a full, close-mouthed smile.

"Now, this one time," he started, "I was tracking the local cell of a virtual terrorist group in Tanzania, and . . ."

I listened as Colin regaled me with tale after harrowing tale of his adventures and misadventures in policing the ever-expanding virtual world. And eventually, I drifted off to sleep.

[32]

I fingered the letter in my pocket as the carriage sped along the uneven road, jiggling and jostling. A third letter from Nel had found its way to me shortly after our arrival at Pemberley. Allie was gone. Her character, Kitty, had vanished from the story, just like the others. Now the only players left were Colin, Will, Nel, and me. And Nel was all alone.

Colin sat across from me in the carriage, so I knew he was all right. Loki lay curled up on my lap, his soft purr reminding me that he was there, that he had my back. Francine lay stretched out on the bench beside Colin, her head resting on his thigh. Remotely, I wondered what shape she took outside of this game, or if she and Colin preferred for her to take a canine form. And was he worried about Daisy, his real-life elderly dog? He had seemed so concerned about leaving her behind.

I stared out the window, watching the midnight landscape pass me by as these and other, more troublesome thoughts plagued my mind. This was our second night in a row spent in the carriage. The previous night, we drove from Gretna Green to Pemberley, arriving in the early afternoon to rest for a few hours before heading out again. We left Pemberley in the early hours of the evening with a fresh driver—one I ensured was a genuine NPC by way of a quick flash—and were on our way to Longbourn. I wrote to Nel from Gretna Green before we left, and wrote to her again from Pemberley, letting her know we were on our way, but with how quickly we were moving, it was just as likely we would beat the letters there.

The ride to Longbourn seemed to take an eternity, but eventually, the carriage slowed and we pulled into the gravel driveway. The landscape was shrouded in a mist that gave the countryside an eerie feel in the pale dawn light.

Heart lodged in my throat, I pushed the carriage door open and jumped out, my boots hitting the gravel drive with a crunch. I ran toward the front door and barged into the house. "Nel?" I called out, scanning the entryway before moving on to the sitting room. "Nel!" I yelled her name as I searched the entire ground floor of the house but found no sign of her.

I startled a servant when I barreled into the kitchen, lured in by the sound of movement within. She was young, blonde, and pretty, like Nel's version of Jane Bennet, but she wasn't Nel. The servant clutched her chest with one hand and held a cleaver raised to chop through a whole chicken with the other.

I reached for the woman's raised arm and gripped tightly. She stared at me, her eyes widened by shock, and I forced a flash to find out if she was a true NPC or an impostor. I blew out a breath in relief at seeing that she was exactly who she appeared to be.

"Where's Nel?" I asked, releasing her arm.

The servant's brow furrowed, and she shook her head. Of course, she wouldn't know Nel's real name. She would know her as Jane.

"Jane," I blurted. "Where's Jane—Jane Bennet?"

But, again, the servant shook her head. "I'm very sorry, miss, but there is no *Jane* Bennet."

Her words were a blow, and I stumbled back a few steps until

I hit a solid, warm body. Hands gripped my arms, steadying me, and I knew without looking that it was Colin.

My chin trembled, and tears welled in my eyes. "We're too late," I wailed, turning to face Colin. I sucked in a shaky breath. "She—she's already gone!" For the past two days, reaching Nel in time had been my driving force, the only thing keeping me going. But we were too late. I had failed her.

Colin pulled me close against him and wrapped his arms around me as I gave in to the tears.

"Well, well, well . . ." The new voice was snide and shrill and all too recognizable. "If it isn't my spoiled brat of a daughter."

I stiffened as Mrs. Bennet entered the kitchen behind me. She must have come in through the door to the garden.

"First," Mrs. Bennet went on, "I receive the most troubling letter from my own brother, Mr. Gardiner, and now, I am to find my eldest daughter locked in a lewd embrace in my own home. What are the neighbors to think of us? No man will marry you now, Lizzy, and you will be ruined!" Her voice rose as she spoke until she was practically shrieking. "Mr. Bennet! Lizzy has returned, and she has brought with her that horrid man!"

I pulled away from Colin and took a step back, turning to face the *thing* pretending to be my in-game mother. At some point during Mrs. Bennet's tirade, the servant had scurried off, leaving the three of us alone in the kitchen.

My cheeks were still wet with tears, but I grinned victoriously, nonetheless. "But don't you see, *Mama*?" I extended my left hand toward her, palm down, so she could get a good look at the massive sapphire adorning my ring finger. "It doesn't matter if no other man will have me, because I'm already married." I exchanged a look with Colin, who nodded once. "To Mr. Darcy."

Mrs. Bennet gasped and steadied herself with a hand on the counter.

I took a step toward her. "And now you have no power over

me," I told her. "I can say and do whatever I please, and I shall remain by Mr. Darcy's side every second of every day because he is my husband, and there's nothing you can do about it."

Fear flashed across Mrs. Bennet's face. Looked like I was right. They did need to get us alone to abduct us—or to do whatever it was they did to players that disappeared.

I took another step toward Mrs. Bennet.

She turned to flee back out the open door to the outside, but Loki leaped into her path, his back arched and his tail puffed out. He hissed, inching closer to Mrs. Bennet.

"Where's Nel?" I demanded.

Mrs. Bennet tore her stare from my gigi to look at me, her eyes alight with panic. "Nel?" she said, shaking her head.

Losing my patience, I forced a flash and held it in place, so I was no longer staring at Mrs. Bennet, but at the strange, inhuman woman pretending to be her. "Jane!" I yelled, grabbing the cleaver from the butcher block and raising it, threatening the now cowering impostor. "Where's Jane? And don't tell me you don't know who I'm talking about because I know you do."

The impostor froze. And then she straightened, shedding her fearful act like a molting snake. She stared at me, a challenge gleaming in her luminous eyes.

"Where is she?" I repeated.

The impostor grinned, and the click of a pistol hammer a short way behind me made my heart stutter. I lost my grip on the flash and once again faced down plump Mrs. Bennet. I stepped back and turned partway to see Mr. Bennet standing in the doorway to the rest of the house, a pistol in his hand, the small gun aimed at my chest.

For a long moment, the four of us just stood there, locked in this strange tableau, staring at one another. Coming to grips with the new situation. And in my case, trying not to freak out.

Without warning, Francine lunged at Mr. Bennet, sinking her

teeth into his knee. Colin took advantage of the distraction, tackling Mr. Bennet into the wall.

For long seconds, both men gripped the pistol, the gun waving around this way and that, forcing both Mrs. Bennet and me to bob up and down and around to avoid its trajectory, should it go off.

Finally, Colin yanked the pistol from Mr. Bennet's grasp and shoved the older man into the kitchen island. Mr. Bennet toppled over the island, sending the half-butchered chicken flying.

Taking advantage of the chaos, I gripped the cleaver with both hands and swung it like a baseball bat at Mrs. Bennet's head and whacked the *thing* pretending to be my in-game mother in the side of the head with the flat of the blade. She dropped to her knees, momentarily stunned.

All I could do was stare at her. At what I'd done. The cleaver slipped from my hands, and I stumbled back a step. I knew Mrs. Bennet wasn't real—she wasn't even an NPC, a string of code. She was something else. Something evil. But it still felt like I had just walloped a middle-aged woman upside the head with a meat cleaver.

Colin grabbed my wrist before I could dive too deep into the pit of what-have-I-done and pulled me toward the door to the garden. We fled from the house, Loki and Francine close on our heels, the impostor Bennets still struggling to regain their bearings in the kitchen. When we reached the carriage, we had left at the front of the house, Colin yanked the door open and pushed me up the steps, then dove in himself.

"Drive!" Colin shouted, yanking the door shut.

I collapsed backward onto the forward-facing bench, slumping into the corner as I gripped the edge of the seat with one hand and splayed the fingers of my other hand against the wall. My breaths came in quick, heavy pants, and I stared at the far wall, not really seeing it.

Colin perched on the edge of the bench, hunching down to

watch out the window as the carriage rattled along, the stolen pistol resting on his thigh. "They're just coming out of the house now," he murmured. "Looks like you gave Mrs. Bennet a good cracking . . ."

"I'm sorry," I blurted, gasping for breath. "I'm so sorry! I shouldn't have said that!" I shook my head, silently repeating the words I'd shouted at Mrs. Bennet.

Where is Jane? And don't tell me you don't know who I'm talking about because I know you do.

I'd shown my hand. "Now they know," I said. "They know that I know."

Colin scooted backward on the bench and angled his knees toward me.

I continued to stare at the far wall, my lungs working too fast, unable to catch my breath. "We're never getting out of here, are we?" My breaths came ever faster, my panic spiraling higher and higher. "We're going to die in here—or out there. We're going to get stuck in here and never be able to return to our bodies, and our bodies are going to die, and this is going to be it. My family . . . my brother . . ." I gasped for breath. "This will kill him! He'll—he'll—"

"Olivia," Colin said, his voice hard and urgent. He grabbed hold of my hand and squeezed. "Olivia, look at me."

It took everything in me to comply, and ever so slowly, I turned my head to look at him. My breaths were too quick, too shallow, and black spots danced around the edges of my vision.

"You're hyperventilating," Colin said, his voice calm but firm. "You're going to pass out." He reached his arm behind me, sliding it between my back and the carriage wall, and pushed me forward. "I need you to lean over," he said, applying more pressure on my back, just below my shoulder blades. "We don't have a paper bag handy, so I'm going to use your skirt instead. I'm going to lift the fabric and drape it over your head to increase your CO_2 intake."

I could barely process his words with the way the black spots were closing in. As Colin increased the pressure on my back, I recalled that he had told me to lean forward. So, that's what I did. I felt him lift the fabric of my skirt and petticoat and drape both over my head, and the world darkened. But, thankfully, not because I had passed out.

My breathing gradually slowed as he rubbed my back. After some time, the panic abated, and my mind was increasingly occupied by thoughts of how ridiculous I must look with my skirt flipped up over my head. I sat up, pushing the skirt off my head and settling it back over my legs, then rested my elbows on my thighs, breathing in the fresher air.

"Thanks," I said, glancing at Colin and smiling sheepishly. "I guess I kind of lost it for a minute there." I sat up straighter and raised my hands, attempting to smooth down my hair. "I used to have panic attacks when I was a teenager, but it hasn't happened in . . ." I shook my head and laughed under my breath. "God, at least a decade, maybe longer. I didn't know that kind of thing could happen in here."

"Hyper-realistic virtual reality is filled with a myriad of wonders," Colin said dryly, "along with a few terrible downsides."

"You don't say," I muttered.

Colin curled his arm around my shoulders and pulled me against the side of his body. He pressed his cheek against the top of my head, and I sniffled. "We'll find a way out of here," he said. "I promise."

"I may have an idea," Loki said from the opposite bench. "Have you considered dying?"

I looked at the black cat gigi, my eyes bulging. "I'm sorry —*what*?"

"What do you mean?" Colin asked.

"I have considered all your options," Loki said, "and assuming the logout function is permanently disabled, I believe death may be your only way to eject your consciousness from the prison of this game world."

I blinked, then looked at Colin, whose expression displayed dawning understanding. "I don't understand," I said, looking from Colin to Loki and back, hoping one of them would fill me in, sooner rather than later.

Colin's arm slipped from my shoulders, and his lips spread into a slow smile. "Cat, you're a genius."

"Can someone please explain this to me?" I urged.

Colin turned his attention to me, his grin still in place and his eyes alight with excitement. "I can't believe I didn't think of it sooner," he said, shaking his head slowly. "The death boot. It's built into *AO*—into the entire system, not into the individual game worlds—so it can't be overridden by what's going on in any single game."

Now I was shaking my head. "I still don't get it," I said. "Explain it to me like I'm an idiot."

Colin cleared his throat and licked his lips, gesticulating as he explained further. "When you die in *AO*, you get kicked out of whatever game you're currently logged into and sent back to your log in point. It's called the 'death boot'. It's a safety measure to prevent the mind from sustaining trauma—to prevent VR PTSD."

"Oh," I said, nodding as I started to understand. I recalled Charlie mentioning something like that while we'd been watching a *Harry Potter* game.

Colin glanced down at the pistol resting on his lap. It didn't take a genius to guess the direction of his thoughts. The gun was our ticket out of here. "These old pistols only hold a single shot," he said. "I'll take you out, and then I'll find a way to trigger the death boot for myself. There's bound to be a sword I can fall on or a cliff I can jump off . . ."

Unblinking, I stared at the pistol, my heart sinking into my stomach. He was talking about shooting me. Shooting me dead.

In a game where the pain settings were hyper-realistic. I gulped.

"As soon as you're out of the game," Colin continued, either unaware of or ignoring my extreme discomfort with this solution, "get to the gatescape and logout of *AO*. Find Fiona Ó Faoláin—she's the lead developer of *Allworld Online*. Since Priya's disappearance, I've been meeting with Fiona during logouts to work on the problem. Tell her what's happened. Tell her everything. You can trust her." Colin paused, studying my face, his eyes searching mine. "I know this is a lot to process, Olivia," he said. "Nod to let me know you understand."

Remotely, robotically, I nodded.

"Good," Colin said. Scooting back, he raised the pistol, aiming point blank at my forehead.

My heart lodged in my throat, and I squeezed my eyes shut.

But before Colin could pull the trigger, the carriage skidded to a halt. My eyes flew open as Colin was knocked off his seat. He rammed into the front edge of the opposite bench and cursed.

I peeked out the window on my side of the carriage to see another carriage blocking the way ahead. And if I wasn't mistaken, it was the Gardiner's carriage. I should know; I had spent nearly two weeks traveling with them in it. And then I spotted Mr. and Mrs. Bennet charging toward my door from the back of the other carriage.

I barely had time to scoot away from the door before it was yanked open and Mr. Bennet reached in, grabbing my ankle and pulling me down to the floor. He dragged me out of the carriage before Colin could get a good grip on my arms. I clawed at the steps and kicked out at Mr. Bennet, but my struggles didn't do any good. Soon enough, I was flailing on my back on the road, one of my ankles locked in Mr. Bennet's iron grip.

Loki launched himself out of the carriage at Mr. Bennet, landing on the impostor's shoulder, but Mrs. Bennet tore the gigi off and threw him yowling into the bushes.

Colin stumbled out of the carriage, pistol in hand and Francine growling at his heels. He aimed the gun at Mr. Bennet. "Let her go," he ordered. "Now!"

Mr. Bennet grinned maniacally and twisted my ankle painfully. "I think not."

I yelped, renewing my struggles if only to stop the pain.

Colin clenched his jaw, his nostrils flaring. "Calm down, Olivia," he said, not taking his eyes off Mr. Bennet. "It's going to be all right. Just *calm down*."

Understanding his true meaning—he only had one shot, and there was no room for error—I stopped struggling and went very, very still. Colin glanced down at me, his eyes locking with mine, and I nodded once.

With a quick jerk of his arm, Colin shifted the pistol, lowering it to aim at my head. "Run!" he shouted a fraction of a second before he pulled the trigger.

There was a deafening *bang*, and then the world went white.

[33]

For a few seconds, that blinding white was everything. There was no sound, no feeling—no other senses at all. There was just me, floating in the ocean of white. But the white slowly faded, and as it did, my other senses returned.

I found myself standing in the *Austentopia* alcove in the romance section of the great library that was the Biblioverse. Soft, Regency-era music teased my ears, mixing with the crackling of the logs burning in the fireplace. I looked around, taking in the armchair, the books lined up on the mantle, the ring of bookcases surrounding the lush, park-like green beyond the alcove, disoriented by the sudden shift in circumstance. It was so peaceful here. So calm and so normal.

Just a moment ago, I was lying on the road in *Pride and Prejudice* and Colin shot me in the head—though I hadn't felt it, thankfully. Now, I was in the Biblioverse. I was free.

I glanced down at myself. I was still wearing the periwinkle dress from *Pride and Prejudice*. Something tickled the edge of my mind. Some sense of urgency. I was supposed to be doing something, but I was so lost to the surreality of the change in my situation that I couldn't think of what.

Loki jumped onto the seat of the armchair, then leapt higher to the top of the chair back and sat, curling his tail around his feet. "Might I suggest running?" he said, the tip of his tail twitching.

I looked at the cat, and a spark of remembered panic ignited my memory of my final moments in the game. Colin had said something just before pulling the trigger: *run.*

Heart suddenly racing, I turned away from the fireplace, my muscles tensing to run. Two of those strange, not-quite-human women who I had only seen during flashes before appeared just out of arm's reach, standing between me and the rest of the library.

I didn't hesitate. My body was already committed. I charged the pair, ramming through them and sprinting between a couple of bookcases to the idyllic green in the center of the romance section. I pumped my arms and sucked in lungfuls of air, urging my legs to move faster even as I focused on not tripping over my skirt. I could hear the women close behind me, the thud of their boots hitting the grass and the rasp of their harsh breaths. The sounds only made me dig deeper, push harder, run faster.

Moments after passing the fountain at the center of the green, I heard a shout and a splash. I glanced over my shoulder to see one of the women struggling to climb out of the water while Loki bounded off the rim of the fountain, chasing after me and my remaining pursuer. That glance cost me precious ground, and I returned my attention to the way ahead.

When I reached the far side of the green, I paused to push over one of the bookcases on the woman chasing me. She managed to backtrack just in time, avoiding the avalanche of books, and we both watched as the toppling bookcase slammed into the one next to it, pushing that one over, as well, and then the next, and then the next. The domino effect continued around the ring of bookcases surrounding the green.

Loki leapt over the barrier, and I looked beyond him to see

the woman he had tripped into the fountain racing toward us. My nearer pursuer started the awkward climb over the fallen bookcases, and I spun on my heel, heading straight for the doorway to the main part of the Biblioverse.

The atrium was as crowded as ever, filled with players coming and going through the portal to the gatescape at the far side of the atrium to visit this or that section of the library. I weaved around players and gigis alike, tossing back apologies any time I bumped into anyone.

Shouts of outrage erupted behind me, and I didn't need to look back to know that my pursuers had made it out of the romance section. Chaos spread throughout the atrium as the women chasing me shoved players out of their way with zero regard for the rules of the world.

"What the hell?" one player yelled.

"Hey, lady!" another shouted. "This is a non-combat zone!"

A quick glance over my shoulder told me the women were gaining on me. "Help!" I cried out as I continued to weave my way through the crowd. "Help me! Please!"

A deafening roar sounded behind me, followed by a burst of heat. Someone screamed.

I turned around, continuing my movement backward, and faced an enormous golden dragon gigi staring down a flaming, flailing pillar, black smoke drifting up from the gigi's nostrils. My steps faltered, then stopped completely as I realized that the flaming pillar was one of my pursuers. I stared, breathing hard, my mouth hanging open.

A shout nearby drew my attention, and I spotted my other pursuer tossing a roly-poly Pokémon gigi at a player to get them both out of her way. She paused, her eyes locking with mine, her lips twisting into a wicked sneer. Violence shone in her stare, and she took a step toward me.

Hammering hooves sounded from my left, and I glanced that way to see a gleaming silver unicorn charging toward the woman. She dove out of the way at the very last moment, barely avoiding being impaled by its razor-sharp horn.

Seeing my chance for escape, I spun on my heel and shouted my thanks over my shoulder as I sprinted for the portal to the gatescape. The crowd of players parted ahead of me, letting me through. Some even cheered me on as I passed.

Finally, I reached the portal and dove through. I stumbled down the stairs on the far side of the portal, and soon enough, the rocky ground of the gatescape crunched under my feet. I stopped and bent over, hands planted on my knees, and attempted to catch my breath. Loki wound around and between my ankles, his presence both protective and comforting.

"Loki," I said, between gasping breaths, "Log me out."

A hand grabbed my arm, and I looked up into the face of my remaining pursuer. She grinned, not realizing that she was too late.

A bright, white light consumed the world, Loki, and the woman, and the entire gatescape faded away.

[34]

I gasped awake and sat up, then coughed, choking. Machines beeped all around me, and something was lodged in my nose and tickled my throat. I raised my hands, feeling my face as people rushed to me, crowding in around me. Finding a tube coming out of my nose, I gripped it and pulled, gagging as it came free.

Suddenly, hands were on me, holding me down. I fought to sit back up, but I was weak, no match for the hands. For the people surrounding me. Tubes and cords seemed to be attached to every part of my body, tangling with my flailing limbs.

A woman in green scrubs leaned over me, dark skin and close-cropped black hair, her face vaguely familiar. It took my panicked brain a moment, but I finally recognized her as the doctor who met with my gaming party during orientation, though I could not, for the life of me, remember her name.

"Calm down, Olivia," the doctor said, her warm brown eyes exuding calm and confidence. "Calm down," she repeated. "You're safe now. I'm Dr. Morgan, and I'll be overseeing your transition back to reality."

My heartbeat thundered, and my head pounded. I felt like my skull was about to crack open. I strained against the hands holding me down. I just wanted to sit up. To clear my head. To take a minute to just breathe and figure out what was going on. But I couldn't do any of that with all these people surrounding me, keeping me down.

"Be calm, Olivia," Dr. Morgan repeated, her face a mask of reassurance. "We're not going to hurt you."

I watched, panic rising, as a youngish man injected something into the IV line feeding into my arm. Almost immediately, a sense of calm slowly spread throughout my body.

"We've given you a mild sedative," Dr. Morgan said. "Just something to help you relax while you adjust to the sudden change in realities." She glanced over her shoulder, then returned her attention to me. "There's someone here who would like to speak with you. I'll be close by. If you need anything—anything at all—you only need to ask for me." She smiled kindly. "Do you remember my name?"

I swallowed, my saliva feeling like glue. "Dr.—" My voice was raspy and barely audible. I cleared my throat and tried again. "Dr. Morgan," I said, though my voice didn't sound much better. Then added, "Could I have some water, please?"

Again, she smiled, then nodded. "Of course. I'll be right back with that."

Dr. Morgan stepped away, only to be replaced by a petite woman with porcelain skin, green eyes, and highlighter-pink hair knotted in a messy bun on top of her head.

The newcomer peered down at me, her expression serious. "Welcome back, Olivia," she said, a musical Irish lilt accenting her words. "My name is Fiona, and I'm here to help you and your fellow players. Now please, tell me—what happened in the game?"

September 18, 2026

More excitement from the virtual world today as players within the Biblioverse—the literary quarter of *Allworld Online*—reported unforeseen violence and mayhem within the strictly combat-free zone of the Atrium. Players across the globe have been posting videos captured from their live streams of a female player fleeing from two hostile pursuers. The fleeing player has been identified as Olivia Crawford, one of the beta players for Rockville's upcoming Jane Austen-inspired game world, *Austentopia.* This is the same game world in which the still-missing developer, Priya Burman, was involved and has recently drawn the eye of the VCIA. Rockville Softworks has yet to issue a statement on the incident, though social media is aflame with conspiracy theories, and the protestors filling the street in front of Rockville Softworks have already incorporated this incident into their narrative. We'll keep you posted as the story develops.

William St. George entered the grand library and headed for the armchair in front of the fireplace, but his confidence faltered when he noticed the chair was empty. He stiffened, annoyed. Here, she had summoned him right when he was in the middle of navigating a shitstorm of epic proportions back in the real world, but she didn't even have the decency to be ready for him when he arrived.

"You made it."

Will nearly jumped out of his skin and spun around, one hand clutching his chest.

His mistress stood closer than was comfortable, just out of arm's reach. She had shucked the oversized gowns this world demanded she wear for the tight-fitting armored bodysuit favored by her kind, and she held a golden staff topped with a fist-sized crystal glowing diamond-white. Her hair was no longer curled and coiffed but pulled back into a sleek bun. She assessed him with hard, gray eyes.

Will took a step back, moving closer to the fireplace to put some much-needed distance between them. When she had been adorned in the frills and endless layers of fabric that befit a woman of her assumed identity's station during this time period, it had been easier for Will to overlook the danger she posed. To forget just how cutthroat and vicious she could be. To forget her propensity for violence.

She smiled, appreciating Will's response to her change of attire. "There is no longer any need for pretense," she said, glancing down the length of her body. Her eyes locked with Will's. "Not now that my avatar has escaped." Her stare turned hawkish, predatory.

Will took another backward step and gulped. His heart beat a quick staccato in his chest. His gut told him he should not have come. Out in the real world, everything he had worked so hard for, for so long, may have been crumbling all around him, but at least he could have walked away. He didn't need this. The power she offered him was an illusion. He could see that now. Once she was free, he would be her puppet in reality just as he was in the virtual world.

"Thankfully, there is another who will do," she said, tilting her head to the side as she scanned the length of Will's body. Her eyes narrowed, and the corner of her mouth lifted. "You know, I have always wondered what it would be like to be a man . . ."

Four of her minions slipped into the library, the deadly women stalking ever closer.

She took a step toward him and raised her hand, reaching out. She was going to take him—his body. She was going to steal his life.

Panic gripped Will's heart, and he shoved his hand into his pocket, slipping the ring stored within onto his finger. He watched rage warp her features a fraction of a second before a flash of white engulfed the world, and he vanished from the game.

[36]

I glanced at the clock on the wall of the spartan private office. Fiona had escorted me in as soon as Dr. Morgan gave me the initial medical all-clear. I wasn't out of the woods—mentally, physically, emotionally, everything-ly—but I wasn't about to keel over either, which apparently was good enough for Dr. Morgan. And if it was good enough for her, it was good enough for me.

A large screen built into the wall to my right to look like a window projected a hyper-realistic live-streamed video of a view of the Puget Sound and the Olympic Mountains beyond. It gave the impression that the office was located on the top levels of a high rise in downtown Seattle rather than in the underground facility beneath Rockville Softworks' campus across the lake from the Emerald City.

Fiona sat behind the barren desk, elbows on the desktop and fingers steepled together as she studied me, processing all I had just shared with her. Which was pretty much everything, as Colin had suggested. I really hoped he was right about me being able to trust her. The cat was out of the bag now, and there was no stuffing it back in.

I had just finished recapping my experience in *Pride and Prejudice*, from the very first flash, which revealed Nel's true identity, to my abrupt, violent exit and the mad chase through the Biblioverse. We had been in there for at least an hour, and I was growing increasingly anxious. Colin was still trapped in the game.

As I stared at the clock, I uncrossed my legs, then crossed them again and immediately started shaking my foot. My nerves were out of control. "Can you check again?" I asked Fiona, my focus shifting back to her. "He should have been out by now."

Fiona's lips curved into an understanding smile, her eyes softening, and she sat back in her chair. "I promise you," she said, "they'll alert me as soon as he wakes."

I chewed on the inside of my cheek, my brows bunching together. "You don't seem surprised by anything I told you."

"On the contrary . . ." One of Fiona's eyebrows rose infinitesimally. "I find your experience extremely surprising and, honestly, quite refreshing."

I frowned, confused by Fiona's words. No matter how you spun it, I couldn't see how my experience in *Pride and Prejudice* could be viewed as *refreshing*. Disturbing, yeah. Horrifying, sure. Really effing messed up, you bet. But *refreshing*? Not so much.

"However," Fiona started, "I do have a slightly better understanding of what's going on in the game than you do." My confusion must have shown loud and clear on my face because Fiona continued with a more thorough explanation. "Having had access to all the player's live feeds, as well as the readings from their EEGs, giving me a picture of what's going on in their brains and monitoring the slow transition from normal to abnormal brain activity."

"Wait, what?" I straightened in my chair. "What's happening to our brains?"

"Not yours," Fiona said, easing my initial burst of panic.

"Your brain is fine—you got out in time. And Colin's hasn't shown any hints of the transition yet." She pressed her lips together, inhaling and exhaling through her nose. "But, if he remains in there much longer, it's only a matter of time . . ."

Worry for Colin, as well as for Nel and all the players still trapped in the game, twisted my stomach in knots. I swallowed down a surge of bile.

Fiona placed her hands on the desk and stood, pushing her chair back with the sudden motion. "Let's take a walk," she said as she made her way around the desk. "I want to show you something."

She headed for the door, and I stood to follow. Fiona opened the door, holding it for me to pass through ahead of her, then joined me in the hallway, pulling the door shut behind her.

"It's just this way," she said, starting down the hallway that led back toward the party rooms where unconscious players lounged in recliners, their live in-game feeds and vitals monitored by VR techs.

A small group of people stepped into our path from a crossing hallway, forcing us to pause as they passed. Two uniformed police officers led the way, escorting a handcuffed man toward the elevators at the end of the hallway. That man was none other than William St. George.

My mouth fell open.

A man and a woman dressed in black suits followed close behind them. Their men-in-black appearance made me certain they were federal agents, probably with the VCIA. I couldn't help but wonder if Colin was actually a suit guy, and picturing the juxtaposition of a tailored suit on top of all of that inked skin and brooding attitude, excited me in a way that made me really hope he was.

Will struggled against his restraints, forcing the officer holding his arm to keep a tight grip. "It's a setup!" he said, though there was a note of defeat to his tone, as though he'd been going on like this for a while. "I didn't do it! I didn't do it! Someone is setting me up!"

When he spotted us, his struggles grew more enthusiastic and his voice raised. "You know me, Fiona," he said, attempting to turn toward us, making the officer drag him sideways. "Tell them —you have to tell them. I know Priya and I had our differences, but I would never—"

"That's enough, Mr. St. George." The officer holding Will's arm yanked it up behind him, making him yelp in pain and forcing him back into compliance. "Remember that anything you say can and will be used against you in a court of law."

The other officer nodded to us as he passed, and it was glaringly obvious they didn't want the specifics of Will's arrest to get out just yet.

The female VCIA agent stopped and faced Fiona as the rest of the group continued onward. "Ms. Ó Faoláin, I trust we can count on your discretion." Her eyebrows rose as she finished.

"Absolutely," Fiona said. "Mum's the word."

The agent nodded once, then turned her attention to me.

My heart was suddenly lodged in my throat, and I hurriedly shook my head. "I didn't see anything," I practically blurted.

The agent stared at me for a moment, then nodded once more and turned to follow the others.

I watched the shocking procession move farther down the hallway, then turned to Fiona. Her lips were twisted into the faintest of smirks, making me think she knew something about what we'd just seen.

"What was that all about?" I asked her.

Fiona raised her eyebrows, her eyes widening and her face becoming a mask of innocence. She shook her head. "Couldn't tell you."

I had the distinct impression it was less that she *couldn't* tell me and more that she *wouldn't*.

"You know, I never liked that guy." Fiona's attention drifted up the hallway, her eyes narrowing on Will's back. "Underneath all that charm and polish, there's just something off about him."

I nodded, my gaze following hers. I recalled the way he'd all but forced me into the beta player position. I mean, he'd shown up at my parents' house. My *parents'* house. Who does that? "I know what you mean," I murmured.

Fiona touched my elbow, and I looked at her. "Come on," she said. "It's just up ahead."

We crossed the intersecting hallway and continued toward the party rooms. Fiona showed me into one of the viewing rooms attached to a party room. I had never been in one before, though it didn't take a genius to figure out there was another room on the other side of the mirror that took up almost an entire wall in the party room. It was filled with two rows of control panels, eight chairs tucked under the individual workstations, making it look like a miniaturized NASA control room.

The party room beyond the two-way mirror was exactly like the one I had spent so much time unconscious in over the past few weeks, save for one difference: this party room had just one occupant, and he wasn't reclining in one of the playing chairs. He stood on the other side of the glass, staring into the mirrored side, almost like he could see us through it.

I rushed closer to the viewing window. "That's Holden!" My heart soared at seeing the man who had been playing Charles Bingley in the game. "And he's awake!"

I stopped in front of the glass, studying what I could see of him. He wore gray sweatpants and a white T-shirt, just as he was wearing the last time I had seen him awake outside of the game. And yet, he seemed different, though I couldn't quite put my finger on what had changed. His round face looked to have lost some of its plumpness, and his skin hung a little too loosely on his fluffy frame, almost like someone had stuck him with a pin and he was in the process of deflating. And there was a hardness in his eyes that hadn't been there before. It was almost a sense of challenge. Of aggression. Of violence.

For a single heartbeat, I could've sworn I saw the face of one of the not-quite-human impostor women from the game superimposed over Holden's once jovial visage. I sucked in a breath and backed up a step, one hand clutching my neck, the other gripping the fabric of my shirt. But the vision was gone almost as soon as it appeared, and I was left feeling confused and disoriented.

Obviously, I'd been imagining the flash. I had spent far too long in the game, and it was bound to have some lingering effects. I was hardly surprised to find that my mind was having a hard time distinguishing the virtual world from actual reality.

I licked my lips and moved closer to the viewing window once more. Narrowing my eyes, I tilted my head to the side, searching Holden's hard stare. "What's wrong with him?"

Fiona came to stand beside me. "What makes you think something's wrong with him?"

I looked at her sidelong, surprised by her question. "I just assumed . . ." I frowned, my words stumbling as my mind tried to make sense of the situation. "I mean, you're keeping him in there all alone. Isn't that why you wanted me to see him—to show me what the AI does to the people it takes? How it changes them?"

Fiona stared at me for a long moment, almost like she was assessing me. "How do you think Holden has changed?" she finally asked.

Brow furrowing, I turned my attention back to the viewing window and the man beyond. I drew my bottom lip in between my teeth as I studied Holden, keenly aware of Fiona studying me. Though the man on the other side of the glass looked like Holden, my gut told me it wasn't really him. Not anymore. It was like someone else had emerged from the game and taken over Holden's body. Maybe it was just the weird residual flash making me feel that way, but I couldn't shake the feeling that Holden was gone.

"This is going to sound crazy," I said, not looking away, "but it's almost like he's possessed." I couldn't help but wonder if I really was staring at one of the not-quite-human women from the game.

Fiona crossed her arms over her chest, the movement drawing my attention back to her. The corners of her mouth were turned down in a frown, and her eyes were narrowed in thought as she continued to study me just as closely as I had been studying Holden. For a long time, she said nothing, and I grew more and more uncomfortable with each passing second.

But finally, her focus shifted to Holden. "Possessed is a fairly accurate word for what has happened to him," she said, her words slow and careful, giving me the impression that each was carefully chosen. "You see, for the better part of a year, William St. George has been secretly working with a sentient and self-aware virtual entity, plotting a way for the entity and her minions to leave the virtual realm and inhabit the real world. We have discovered encoded messages from Will to the entity describing the process of selecting and ensnaring the potential hosts, people whose general neural structures are compatible with the beings who wish to *possess* their bodies."

I stared at the side of Fiona's face, not quite believing what she was telling me.

"Priya was the first to notice the entity interfering with the game's AI controller," Fiona continued, "though she mistakenly assumed the entity *was* the AI controller when, in reality, the AI controller assigned to *Pride and Prejudice* had been hobbled and enslaved by the entity almost as soon as it was created. It would seem that Will and the entity planned their infiltration of the game before it was even coded. But when the entity and her minions abducted Priya within the game and began the consciousness overwriting process, something went terribly wrong. Priya was a mismatch for the minion assigned to possess her, and during the attempted overwriting process, the minion was destroyed."

My eyes widened in alarm. "And Priya? Is she okay?"

Fiona glanced at me out of the corner of her eye, then returned her attention to Holden. "We know all of this," she said, "because of the encoded messages we found between Will and the entity in charge of the operation. Which means we only know what they discussed in those messages."

I pressed my lips together, not at all pleased with the answer. Or rather, lack thereof.

"According to your player feed," Fiona went on, "Priya was the first player to be taken within the game, and Holden was next."

I nodded. That was how it had happened, so far as I knew.

Fiona crossed her arms over her chest. "As you can see, Holden has emerged from the game a changed man. In fact . . ." Fiona faced me, raising her eyebrows. "According to the game, he hasn't emerged at all. He's still logged in."

My lips parted, and it took me a moment to fully comprehend what she was saying. "You mean, he's still alive? The real Holden is still there?"

Fiona nodded slowly. "It would seem that Holden's consciousness is being held prisoner within the game."

"Well," I said, drawing out the word as I arranged my thoughts into a coherent order, "what would happen if his implant was hooked back up to *AO* and his consciousness was somehow freed?"

Fiona shrugged and shook her head. "Only one way to find out."

"And the others?" I asked. "Are they all still in the game? I mean, nobody else has woken up, have they?"

Fiona shook her head again. "We've been monitoring the overwriting process," she told me. "Grace is getting close. We think she'll wake up within the next twenty-four hours . . . not as herself, of course."

I licked my lips, my heart rate picking up, making my breaths come more quickly. "Well, you have to stop it. Stop *them* —whatever they are."

"That's the plan," Fiona said, then paused, her gaze drifting back to Holden. "I'll be heading into the game on a rescue mission." Her eyes locked with mine. "And I want you to come with me."

[37]

"No way in Hell." That was my initial response to Fiona's request, and I had meant it.

But then Colin was captured in the game, and his player feed went dark. All I could think about was how he had used that lone bullet on me when he could just as easily have used it to escape the game himself. He had sacrificed himself to get me out, and I couldn't just sit here, letting fear paralyze me while he experienced all manner of unknown horrors. While he was overwritten. While his mind was replaced.

And so, I changed my mind—with one condition. Charlie had to be brought on board. I wouldn't do this without him knowing what was going on. I supposed part of me hoped Fiona would consider bringing Charlie onto the rescue team to be a deal breaker, that it would be my easy way out. When I looked back on this crazy, awful experience, I would at least be able to say I tried. That me *not* reentering the game on some kamikaze rescue mission hadn't been my fault.

Fiona, however, had only smiled, like she had known I would come around eventually.

I sat across from Fiona at a conference table, surrounded by a small army of players and programmers of all shapes and sizes. Charlie sat on my right, rounding out the dream team of geeks. A tall, lanky programmer stood at the whiteboard spanning one of the walls in the jam-packed room, taking notes as everyone else shouted out buffs to add to the list on the board. A single, under-lined word: *armor*, headed the list. So far, the list included invincibility, night vision, underwater breathing, strength bonus, speed bonus, and agility bonus.

"Invincibility won't work," Charlie said into a momentary lull in the chaotic brainstorming session. All eyes turned to him, and he sat up straighter, clearing his throat. "If you build an invincibility buff into their armor, you'll be cutting off their exit."

A chill settled in my veins. And here I had thought invincibility sounded so grand, but now that Charlie had pointed out the glaring flaw, I couldn't see past it. Death was our way out. Specifically, what the team called *rings of instant death*. They had gotten the idea from Will after finding one in his *AO* inventory.

Our goal for the mission was to deliver the rings to the trapped players and free them the only way we knew how. Will had locked the game down tight, and all chances to override his order had failed. It was a veritable Hotel California—check in whenever, leave never.

"They could always strip out of their gear," suggested a guy leaning against the wall behind Fiona.

Charlie scoffed. "You might be willing to gamble with my sister's life on the off-chance that they'll have time to disrobe in the heat of battle, but I'm not."

My hand sought out Charlie's under the table, and when I found his, I gave it a squeeze, silently thanking him for looking out for my best interests. It was nothing new, but it warmed my heart.

The programmer at the board crossed out *invincibility* and wrote *max health* beside it.

Fiona looked at a mousy woman sitting in the corner of the room. "Get a team started on building armored bodysuits," she ordered. "Extremely low profile, no bulk. These need to be undetectable under a dress. And let's do enhanced sneak boots—add whatever other buffs seem appropriate."

The mousy woman nodded and stood, then hurried from the room.

Fiona scanned the faces of everyone sitting around the table. "Let's move on to weaponry," she said. "We can always circle back, but I want to get production going on all of the gear ASAP."

Charlie leaned forward, resting his forearms on the table and weaving his fingers together. "I've been thinking a lot about your weapons," he said. "Since awesome weapons like wizards' staffs won't work in the game due to the reality-based game mechanics, I think we should go steampunk, like with a souped-up single-shot pistol. We can augment it with critical shot, eagle eye, and time slow buffs, and retrofit it with automatic loading and a bigger-on-the-inside ammo cartridge. It won't stand out too much in the game, not like giving them assault rifles would."

Fiona was already nodding by the time Charlie finished. She glanced at the programmer manning the whiteboard. "Write that down," she told him. "We'll use that." Once again, she scanned the room. "What else?"

"How about grenade jewelry?" That suggestion came from a guy with a four-inch spiked mohawk sitting at the opposite end of the table from the whiteboard. "We could do earrings, pins, a string of explosive pearls, that kind of thing." And with that suggestion, the floodgates opened.

"Universal key picklocks could be disguised as hairpins," someone else said.

"So could paralyzing poison needle daggers," someone added

Someone threw out, "We could do some sort of poison nail polish."

"How about a belt that doubles as an electrified whip?"

"Or as a *flaming* whip?"

My eyes widened as I imagined wielding such a thing. Across the table from me, Fiona grinned. "I like it!" she said, slapping a hand down on the table. "All of it! Let's make it happen." She pointed to mohawk-guy. "Get a team working on building the weapons. I want everything ready in an hour for testing."

I looked at the whiteboard, reading over the list of incredible, deadly things I would be carrying on my person.

The programmer wrote the word GIGI in all caps, then drew a line under the word.

"Ah," Fiona said. "Yes. Last item of business—gigis. What form do we think would work best?"

There was a moment of silent anticipation as everyone in the room looked around and exchanged glances. Charlie was the first to dive in.

"Don't you think you should talk to the gigis about this?" he said, his voice hesitant. "I mean, they're smarter than all of us combined, plus they know all the available possibilities." He looked around the room. "It just makes sense, doesn't it?"

Fiona stared at my brother for a long moment, not blinking, no discernable expression. "I want you on my team when this is all over," she finally said.

Charlie's mouth fell open, and I was filled with a swell of pride.

"But—but—I'm not a programmer," Charlie stuttered.

"Bah." Fiona waved a hand dismissively. "I have plenty of programmers. What I *need* is more idea guys, and that, my friend, is precisely what you are."

Charlie looked stunned, like he couldn't believe anyone saw more in him than a corporate-flunkie-turned-professional-gamer.

I cleared my throat. "So, what does that mean—for the gigis?" I asked, attempting to steer us back on track. As proud and happy as I was for Charlie, lives were at stake. "Do I just let Loki choose when I get back into *AO*?"

Fiona's attention shifted to me, and she blinked. "Exactly," she said. "We'll unlock all possible gigi forms and enhancements currently available. It's a little tricky, as the game mechanics of *Pride and Prejudice* won't allow for non-natural forms, so there will be some limitations."

I frowned. And here I had thought charging back into *Pride and Prejudice* with a couple of enormous, fire-breathing dragons would've really evened the odds.

Fiona snapped her fingers and pointed to a large touchscreen tablet resting on the table, well out of arm's reach. One of the programmers at that end of the table slid it her way, and Fiona tapped the screen to wake the tablet up. A map appeared on the screen, though I couldn't tell of what exactly.

"Let's talk strategy," Fiona said, and I raised my eyes to meet hers. "We think the players are being held at Rosing Park. We've been tracking Colin in the game, and he vanished shortly after being brought onto the estate's grounds. There are at least twenty-three compromised NPCs on-site, and according to Colin's live stream in the seconds before he vanished, they've dropped their cover and are no longer masquerading as NPCs. From the skirmish in the Biblioverse atrium, we know they're ruthless, cunning, and prone to violence."

I nodded my agreement.

"They're clearly skilled fighters," Fiona added. "We will be grossly outnumbered, so our best chance for success lies in avoiding being caught. And they *will* be on the lookout for new arrivals to the game. We *cannot* get caught. Do you understand?"

Again, I nodded, suddenly feeling far less certain about this whole thing. I swallowed, but my mouth was so dry that it didn't do any good, so I lifted the water glass in front of me with a shaking hand and gulped down some water. "What if we fail?" I asked, setting down the glass. "Is there a backup plan?"

Silence filled the room, and my anxiety quadrupled.

"We won't fail," Fiona said, certainty running through her voice like veins in marble.

My stomach churned as I fought an internal battle. I closed my eyes and took a deep breath, and when I finally spoke, my voice was small. "I think I should go in alone," I said and opened my eyes, meeting Fiona's hard stare. "They want me. I think our best chance for success lies in me letting them catch me. Once I'm inside their prison, or whatever, Loki and I can figure out how to complete the mission."

Every single pair of eyeballs in the room was on me. I swallowed roughly. "It doesn't make sense for you to risk yourself, Fiona. You're too important. If I fail . . ." I paused, taking another deep breath. "If I fail, at least you'll have a better idea of what you're up against. I just think it makes more sense to have a plan A *and* a plan B."

The tense silence was back, and thicker than ever.

But, finally, Fiona nodded. "Olivia goes in alone."

[38]

Once again dressed in a medical gown in case the worst should happen and I should find myself trapped in the game for another extended period, I settled on one of the player recliners in an unoccupied party room. Charlie sat on a stool beside my chair, and a couple of VR techs fluttered around me, hooking up electrodes to my head and chest and getting me prepped for re-entry into *Allworld Online* . . . with the potential of an indefinite stay.

The door from the viewing room opened, and Fiona walked in, irritation etched into every line and angle of her face. A harried-looking man in a blue suit and with a comb-over followed her, a clipboard hugged to his chest. Fiona strode straight for my chair, stopping to stand beside Charlie.

"Olivia . . ." Fiona sighed. "I'm really sorry to do this, but Phillip here needs you to sign some additional waivers." She rolled her eyes and shook her head infinitesimally. "I made them add an addendum granting you a sizable bonus if you complete—"

"When," Charlie interrupted.

Fiona glanced at him, offering him a quick, closed-mouth smile and a curt nod. "*When* you complete the mission." Concern shone in Fiona's emerald eyes as she took the clipboard from Phillip, hesitating before holding it out to me. "You can still back out."

I shook my head and reached for the clipboard. "No," I said as I scanned the top page. "I'm doing this." I signed on the line at the bottom of the page and flipped to the next. "I have the best shot, and I know Nel and Colin would do the same for me."

Fiona pressed her lips together into a thin, flat line and nodded once. "I figured you would say that," she said. "Just know that if the worst happens, I will personally rescue your ass, and I swear to you—no matter what—I will ensure that your family is taken care of."

Charlie captured my free hand and gripped it in both of his. "Don't listen to her, Olive. Nobody can take care of us as well as you do, so you'd better come back."

I paused in my signing, my pen hovering over the line on the last page, and looked at Charlie. I flashed him a grateful smile, signed the final waiver, and handed the clipboard back to Fiona.

She practically threw it at Phillip. "Now get out of here, you cockroach."

I snorted a laugh, covering my mouth and nose with one hand as I watched Phillip scurry back to the door.

Fiona rolled her eyes and shook her head. "Suits . . ." With a sigh, she crossed her arms over her chest. "Anyway, remember that even though you won't be able to hear or see us, we'll be with you the whole time." She pointed to the two-way mirror taking up almost the entire wall between this room and the viewing room. "Just right on the other side of that glass, watching your live stream. If something happens to you, we'll know. You won't be alone in there, Olivia."

Tears stung in my eyes. Was I really about to do this—about to go back in there? I gulped and nodded.

Fiona uncrossed her arms and rested her hands on her hips.

"Now get in that game, and don't lollygag, or we'll have to stick another catheter in you."

I laughed if only to avoid crying in front of my brother.

Charlie stood, drawing my attention to him. He leaned down, wrapping his arms around me. "I'll be right here. You can do this, Olive," he whispered. "I love you."

Tears snuck over the rims of my eyelids and spilled down my cheeks. "Love you too, Charlie." As Charlie pulled back, I hastily wiped the tears away.

Resolved to do what needed to be done, I settled back in the reclining chair, watching Charlie and Fiona leave the room. A tech approached, holding a cord that would connect magnetically to my implant through my skin. It wasn't necessary for entry into *AO* since the implants came equipped with wireless functionality, but Fiona wasn't willing to take any chances with potential hardware failures right now. The fewer variables, the fewer things could go wrong.

I turned my head away from the tech, giving her access to the implant at the base of my skull. I felt gentle fingertips on the back of my neck as the tech brushed my ponytail out of the way, and then the world went dark.

Slowly, the gatescape faded into view, and I found myself standing on top of one of the infinite number of rocky hills littering the virtual landscape. A quick glance down at myself confirmed that I was wearing the skin-tight bodysuit that had been built by a team of programmers, just for me.

Loki sat at my feet, staring up at me with his big, luminous neon-blue eyes, the tip of his tail twitching. "You have returned," he said, and I had the distinct impression he disapproved. He slow blinked up at me, then looked away. "And I assume you're planning on returning to *Pride and Prejudice*. Are you sure that is wise?"

"Probably not," I admitted, "but it's what has to be done. Can you pull my memories of the last few hours from my mind to get up to speed?"

"I can," Loki intoned. "Do you grant me permission to do so?"

"Yes, yes," I said, waving for him to get on with it. "Just do it."

I felt a tickle in my mind as Loki rifled around in my most recent memories. While he was occupied, I pulled up my master inventory to make sure all of the items Fiona's team had designed for the mission were there, including the rings of instant death. Holding my breath, I shifted everything into my *Pride and Prejudice* inventory, hoping it would all stick when I reentered the game. Just because I had assigned the items to that inventory didn't mean the game would accept them. I wouldn't know for sure until I had actually stepped back into *Pride and Prejudice.*

"Ah, I see," Loki said, drawing my attention back down to him. "So, we go into battle, then." A statement, not a question.

"Yep," I said with mock cheerfulness. "Do you want to go through all of the gigi upgrade options?"

Loki lifted a paw and began licking it. "No need," he said, his voice tinged with his usual disinterest. "I have already picked out the most suitable new configuration and applied it to myself."

"You did?" I asked, my eyebrows raising. He looked exactly the same as always, like a large, black house cat with strange neon-blue eyes. "What did you choose?"

Loki raised his face to me, and his mouth spread into an impossibly large grin. It was absolutely terrifying. And then he disappeared. He literally winked out of existence. There one second, gone the next.

My lips parted as I stared at the place where Loki had been.

"A Cheshire cat," he said and reappeared two feet to the left, his creepy grin gone. "Incredibly powerful but completely unassuming."

"Cool . . ." I eyed him, not at all sure what was included in the Cheshire cat package. "So, you can become invisible and teleport." And he had a flashy new smile that could spawn nightmares, though I didn't voice that part. I didn't want to offend him. "Any other tricks I should know about?"

"I can change my size," he informed me. "I can shrink down to microscopic levels or grow incredibly large."

"Very cool." I chewed on my bottom lip, my brow furrowing. "But I thought you had to be a natural creature—something about the game mechanics. The last thing I want to happen is to enter the game and discover you're not with me."

The tip of Loki's tail twitched. "I must be a natural creature in my base form, so it would allow no dragons or unicorns or any other overtly fantastical creatures. But a Cheshire cat is, in its essence, a simple house cat." That terrifying grin took over his face once more. "Until it's not."

I suppressed a shiver. "Good to know." I glanced at the gateway to the Biblioverse just down the slope from where we stood, fear forming a vice around my chest. "I guess we should get going then."

"Yes, we should."

But before I could take a step toward the gateway, a notification popped up in front of me. The small, semi-opaque rectangle hovered at face height in my direct line of sight.

NEW SYSTEM MESSAGE

"What's this?" I asked Loki.

The black cat squinted up at the floating message box. "I'm not sure. It wasn't generated from within the system."

I frowned and muttered, "Open message."

Hey Olivia -

Sorry for the intrusion. I had to hijack system messaging to make sure this got through to you. Priya has been found. She's okay. Just thought you should know.

- Fiona

I grinned, giddy at the news. And then I swiped the message away, took a deep breath, and started down the slope, heading back to the Biblioverse.

September 18, 2026

And finally, a break in the story that's had the world holding its breath. Priya Burman has been found. She is alive and recovering at Harborview Medical Center in Seattle after having spent at least two weeks being held captive in the basement of Rockville Softworks' executive William St. George. The police are not yet allowing the press to interview Ms. Burman, but they have issued a statement assuring us they have Mr. St. George in custody. He is being held without bail.

[39]

Charlie leaned back in his chair in front of his designated work-station, his fingers threaded together behind his head and his eyes glued to the enormous screen overlaying the two-way mirror. Olivia's body lay on the other side of the glass, in the attached party room, but her mind was right there on the screen. She was back inside *Pride and Prejudice*, walking to Meryton in a mauve dress alongside her gigi, Loki, who still *appeared* to be a sleek black house cat.

Charlie could see and hear Olivia and everything she experienced in the game, though she was completely cut off from him, along with everyone else in the real world. He had never felt so useless or helpless.

Guilt churned in his gut like acid burning through his insides. Olivia was in there, risking her life because of him. Because she loved him enough to commit to doing something that terrified her. If it wasn't for him and his stupid dreams, she never would have agreed to take the beta player position.

When Olivia made it out of there—not if, but *when*—Charlie was going to throw himself at her feet and beg for her forgiveness. And also offer to do her laundry for a year or until he stopped feeling like such a shit brother. He was fully prepared to wash, dry, iron, and fold for the rest of his life if that was what Olivia wanted.

"She's getting close," Fiona said from her perch on the workstation in front of Charlie. "Once she reaches the town and interacts with the NPCs, we'll know if the disguise is working."

The disguise Fiona spoke of had been Charlie's idea. He'd tossed it out at the last minute, not even knowing if it was possible to disguise a player as an NPC to the game's AI and the other NPCs. It required applying a layer of code to Olivia's armor that concealed her gamertag and tricked the game's shackled AI into thinking Olivia was an autonomous NPC, one of the "extras" pre-programmed with a set tree of possible actions and responses, then set loose to give the impression that the game world was richly populated. The idea was to make Olivia essentially invisible to any of the *entity's* agents who might be keeping an eye out for incoming players. Specifically, for Olivia.

As Olivia drew near a couple strolling in the opposite direction on the road, Charlie held his breath.

"That's Lord and Lady Lucas," Fiona murmured.

Two NPCs who Olivia had interacted with in the past. If they didn't recognize her as Elizabeth Bennet, then the disguise was working.

"Good morning," Olivia said, bowing her head in the passing couple's direction.

"Miss," Lord Lucas said, tipping his hat. Lady Lucas offered a polite smile and nothing more. There was no hint of recognition in their expressions, merely polite disinterest.

Charlie blew out his held breath, and tension eased from his muscles.

Fiona flashed him a grin over her shoulder. "Clever boy," she said, her eyes sparkling.

[40]

The carriage bounced and swayed as it traveled along the road
from London to Kent, carrying me back to the palatial estate of
Rosings Park, where we suspected the missing players were
being held. Once again, I was dressed for the times in layers of
muslin, though beneath all the fabric, I wore my super-powered
armor, turning me into the strongest, fastest, *best* version of
myself. My specially designed pistol was tucked into a holster on
my thigh, accessible through a slit I had cut in the left pocket of
my dress's skirt, and Loki—my secret weapon—was curled up in
a slumbering ball of unassuming black fur on my lap.

I patted my right pocket, assuring myself its priceless cargo
was still in place. I could feel the outline of the ring of instant
death through the muslin. It was my escape hatch. I wanted to
keep the one ring close at hand in case I needed an early exit.
When push came to shove, there was a good chance it would be
my only way out of the game.

"Do you mind?" Loki said, lifting his head from my thigh.
He blinked up at me with sleepy eyes. Apparently, I had
disturbed his cat nap.

I scratched him under his chin, and he stretched out his neck, giving me better access. His rumbling purr set my nerves at ease. "Sorry, Loki," I murmured. "Go back to sleep."

Once his eyes were again closed and his head rested on my thigh, I opened my in-game inventory screen with a whispered command, viewing the contents of my personal pocket of virtual space for the umpteenth time. Almost all the custom weapons and gear had made it into the game. The flaming belt-to-whip hadn't passed muster—apparently it wasn't realistic enough— but the enhanced pistol, guaranteed to slow time while I aimed, deliver a critical shot every single time I pulled the trigger, reload instantly, and *almost* never run out of bullets, would provide more than enough firepower. Not to mention the bracelet of exploding pearls, which I plucked from the inventory and slipped onto my wrist.

The carriage slowed, and I reached out to slide the curtain aside and peer out the window. Woods lined the road, ancient but with light underbrush, the green leaves dappled with golden sunlight. As soon as the carriage stopped, the driver jumped down, and I could hear his footsteps crunching on the road as he drew near the door.

"We have arrived, miss," the driver said, opening the carriage door.

My heart was suddenly lodged in my throat, and a surge of adrenaline made my hands tremble. Loki stood, yawned, and arched his back in a luxurious stretch, and then he hopped down from my lap. He slunk out of the carriage, nary a care in the virtual world. I followed, laden with enough cares for both of us.

I found myself standing on a stretch of idyllic countryside road, grassy, rolling hills to one side, woods to the other. The woods were bordered by a low stone wall that marked the property line of Rosings Park, my intended destination. I had instructed the driver to drop me off on the north edge of the estate, about as far from the driveway as one could get, to avoid detection. And now, here I was.

I tipped the driver and waited for him to leave before slipping my hand through the slit I had cut in my skirt pocket and drawing my enhanced pistol. Armed and stress sweating, I climbed over the stone wall and ventured into the woods.

After about ten minutes, the woods thinned, and the park-like manicured grounds of Rosings Park came into view at the edge of the woods. Beyond the expanse of grass and gardens, I could see the palatial manor house, itself. I had spent some time on this estate, what felt like a lifetime ago when this had merely been a game. Rosings Park had seemed beautiful and wondrous then. Now it loomed ahead, all hard edges, sharp corners, and dark shadows. Not even the cheerful summer sunlight could soften the manor's foreboding appearance.

I snuck closer to the edge of the woods and ducked behind a fallen tree sheltered by some tall but scraggly bushes. My current position was slightly uphill from the manor house and still a good way out.

Loki hopped onto the fallen log, peering through the bushes. "Have you decided where to look first?" he asked.

I chewed on the inside of my cheek and sat with my back to the log, pulling the map Fiona's team had made for me from my personal pocket of virtual space. It displayed the estate as well as the surrounding areas in impossible detail.

"I think so," I said, studying the map one last time before committing to a plan. Six small, red Xs marked the locations where each captured player's feed had gone dark. The Xs were scattered around the estate, all at least a hundred yards out from the manor house and its nearby outbuildings. Yet again, I searched for some sort of pattern, any indication of where the players had been taken, but the arrangement of the Xs still looked random to my eyes.

With a sigh, I folded up the map and tucked it back into my personal pocket of virtual space. Absent of any clues, I figured the house was the best place to start our search. It was large and filled with all sorts of places to stash unwilling guests. Plus, with Loki's new ability to teleport, searching the massive manor house shouldn't take long at all.

Turning around, I gathered my knees beneath me and peered through the bushes to the manor house. I scanned each and every window, as well as every visible patch of grounds, but there was no sign of the not-quite-human impostor women.

I glanced at Loki, perched near my elbow on the log. "Can you pop into the house to scout for the players?"

Loki blinked, his stare sliding my way. "I cannot," he said with muted disinterest. "I am tethered to you and unable to put so much distance between us."

"Oh, I didn't realize," I said and frowned, thinking that particular limitation to his teleportation ability put a damper on my shoddy plans. Maybe I could hide out in one of the gardens while he searched the house. "How far from me can you go?"

"About twenty or thirty yards," he told me. "The distance weakens me, but as our bond strengthens over time, that distance will increase."

"Got it." I drew my bottom lip between my teeth, mentally adjusting the plan.

This limitation on Loki's teleportation ability meant I needed to go into the house with him. He could still scout ahead, alerting me of any waiting dangers and drastically speeding up the search process.

I quickly shared the adjusted plan with Loki, and we skirted along the edge of the woods until we reached a small orchard on the outskirts of the gardens. Using the fruit trees for cover, we snuck closer to the house, then crept through an herb garden. We slipped into the house through a side door and made our way down a short hallway into the kitchen. Quickly and quietly, we searched the house from the cellar to the attic but found nothing. The place was completely empty.

Eventually, we made our way back to the kitchen. The

complete absence of servants was notable, and I wondered if the entity in charge had replaced all the local NPCs who would have been serving Rosings Park with those creepy impostor women.

Hopping up to sit on the worktable in the middle of the kitchen, I pulled out the map of the estate once more and studied the buildings, wondering where we should search next. A carriage house and a stable were on this side of the manor house. Either would be large enough to stash a half-dozen hostages. The groundskeeper's cottage was another option, but it was on the far side of the house. I glanced at the door set in the back corner of the kitchen. According to the map, that would spit me out into a courtyard between the manor house and the stable.

The sound of footsteps crunching on gravel warned me of incomers mere seconds before the handle on the door turned. I jumped down from the table and fled into the nearby pantry, angling the door shut as the kitchen door banged open.

Through the crack in the door, I watched two of the impostor women stroll into the kitchen, one blonde and one with auburn hair, both wearing those skin-tight bodysuits. They headed straight for the worktable where I had been sitting only a moment ago, and I couldn't help but notice the futuristic pistols fit snugly into holsters on their thighs. That was new.

The blonde started tearing apart a loaf of crusty bread that had been sitting at one end of the table while the redhead sliced wedges of cheese from a cheese wheel with a hefty knife.

"I really don't see why we have to do this," the blonde grumbled. "Waiting on these *humans* like this . . . it's demeaning." She spat the word "humans" like it was a curse.

I perked up at the mention of humans. She was talking about the players. She had to be.

The redhead paused, her knife raised and ready to slice. "Would you rather they starve?"

"Of course not," the blonde snapped. "Then all of this would have been pointless." She tore the bread apart more aggressively.

"But I *would* at least like to know when it's going to be my turn to get out of here."

"Your time is coming," the redhead said, setting down her knife. "Just be glad the procedure will be perfected by the time it's our turn." She gathered up the wedges of cheese, wrapped them in a linen towel, and set the bundle in a basket on the counter behind her. "We'll all be free soon enough."

The other impostor gathered the bread chunks in much the same way and added her bundle to the basket. The redhead slung the basket over the crook of her arm while her companion grabbed the pair of empty jugs that had been sitting beside the basket. They headed back for the door through which they'd entered and left the kitchen.

Once they were gone, I eased the pantry door open and refolded the map before tucking it away. Not wanting to lose sight of the two women, I followed their path to the door in the back corner of the kitchen and cracked it open to peek outside. It opened to a courtyard formed by the side of the manor house, the stable, and a covered walkway connecting the two buildings. A delivery cart was positioned close to the kitchen door.

I watched the two women until they rounded a corner to the front of the stable and moved out of sight, then slipped out of the manor house, easing the door shut behind me. I hurried forward and ducked behind the delivery cart, crouching low to stay hidden.

Loki wound around my legs, his tail curving around my calves. "If you sneak closer to the stable, I can scout inside . . . confirm that the missing players truly are in there."

I peered around the back end of the cart, scanning the courtyard but not seeing anywhere to hide. A shallow alcove on the side of the stable facing me housed a squat, rickety door. It was the only place I could see that would provide any cover at all.

I pulled back and huffed out a breath. Loki only needed a moment to confirm the players were in there. If I ran over, waited for him, then ran back, there was a good chance we would manage without being noticed.

"All right," I said before I could talk myself out of it. "Let's do this."

I took a single, deep breath to steady my nerves, then stood, hiked up my skirt, and made a run for the alcove across the courtyard. Loki quickly outpaced me, and by the time I was halfway across the courtyard, he was nearly to the door.

One second, he was bounding ahead of me, the next, he was gone. My heart skipped a beat, already anticipating his return. Was this it? Had we really found them?

I was mere steps from the shelter of the alcove when the small door swung inward on rusty hinges. I skidded to a stop.

One of the impostor women stood in the doorway, surprise widening her eyes.

I'd been caught.

For a stunned heartbeat, the woman and I stood there, staring at one another. She shook off the shock first, drawing the futuristic pistol from the holster on her thigh and raising it to aim at me.

Without warning, Loki appeared directly in front of my attacker, three times his usual size. He body-checked the woman's knees, and she stumbled backward before she could fire on me.

I took off, running toward the covered walkway connecting the manor house to the stable, oversized Loki bounding alongside me. "Are they in there?" I asked him, my arms pumping. I couldn't believe how fast I was running. The enhanced armor I wore under my dress was legit.

"They are," Loki confirmed, sending a thrill through me.

"All of them?" I asked as we raced under the walkway. I altered my trajectory, heading for the hedge maze behind the stable. If we could lose our pursuer in the maze, we would be able to buy ourselves a few moments to regroup. "Even Holden?"

I wanted to make sure he really was still alive—even only virtually—before rushing in and blowing this place up, figuratively speaking. And maybe literally. Dr. Morgan had sedated his body, and the thing inhabiting it, to force him-slash-it back into *Allworld Online*. She believed his mind would find its way back to his body and supplant the intruder, so long as it was free to leave the game.

"Yes," Loki said, "even Holden."

The confirmation sent a surge of adrenaline rushing through my veins. Hopped up on the good news, I plunged into the hedge maze, weaving a chaotic path. The seven-foot-tall hedges were plenty high to hide us, and we delved deeper and deeper into the maze until I had to stop to catch my breath. The armor made me fast, but that speed had a cost—fatigue. I bent over, hands planted on my knees, and looked at Loki, who had shrunk back down to his usual house cat size and was pacing across the hedge-bound corridor.

"You're going to have to deliver the rings," I told the gigi. My breathing slowed, and I could already feel my energy reserves refilling. "There's too many of those women guarding the place. I won't be able to get in there without being swarmed."

Loki's tail lashed from side to side as he paced. "You will still need to get close enough for me to teleport into the stable," he cautioned me. "That will put you out in the open . . ."

I nodded, my breathing almost back to normal, and straightened. "I know, but I only have to hold them off long enough for you to deliver the rings. Then I can slip my own ring on and get the hell out of here."

Not wanting to waste any time since there was no saying how long we would have until the woman who had chased us into the maze tracked us down, I pulled the six rings of instant death slated for the trapped players from my personal pocket of virtual space and transferred them into Loki's inventory. His was a lot smaller than mine and limited him to carrying ten items.

"Tell the players they're from me," I said as the rings

vanished from my palm, "and that they'll get them out of the game. All they need to do is put them on."

The end of Loki's tail ticked. He already knew all of this, but repeating the plan aloud made me feel more secure in our ability to execute it.

Suddenly, our pursuer rounded a hedge wall off to my right, grinning when her eyes landed on me. She raised her pistol and fired, unleashing a neon green laser blast.

I ducked and rolled, easily dodging the shot, thanks to my enhanced speed and agility. "A girl could get used to this," I laughed, exhilarated by my newfound athleticism. It almost made me want to make more of an effort to work on my physique in the real world. Almost.

Rolling to my feet, I dodged another laser blast before spinning on my heel to sprint away. I zigzagged sporadically as I raced through the maze, hoping to throw off my pursuer's aim, the fabric of my skirt catching on stray branches. Her shots singed holes through the hedges around me and came uncomfortably close a couple of times, but thankfully never struck home.

I sped around a corner in the maze and slid to a halt. I had reached a dead end.

At the sound of a twig snapping under a boot behind me, I dove and rolled, narrowly missing another laser blast. I spun on my knees and raised my own gun, managing a single shot before the impostor could pull her trigger again.

Time slowed to a crawl, and I watched the bullet leave the barrel of my gun, displacing the air as it zeroed in on my attacker. The bullet struck her in the forehead, and in slow motion, she stumbled backward into a hedge now spattered with blood and gore. Her legs gave out and the laser pistol slipped from her grip, and time sped back up as she dropped to the ground.

I lurched up to my feet and looked at my gun, my eyebrows raised. "Damn . . ." The buffs were no joke. I had done little more than aim in the impostor woman's general direction and had pulled off a perfect headshot.

"We should hurry," Loki advised. "More will come."

Knowing he was right, I turned my back to the dead woman and snapped an exploding pearl off my bracelet. I twisted the bead to activate it, then tossed it at the hedge blocking the end of the dead-end corridor. I ducked as the pearl exploded, shielding my face from the shower of sticks, leaves, and dirt.

I waited for the dust to settle, then followed Loki through the fresh hole in the hedge. My skirt caught on a mangled branch—again—and I cursed under my breath as I tore it free with a loud *rrrrrrip*. I prepped another exploding pearl as I jogged forward, blowing a hole through the next hedge. I tossed pearl after pearl, blasting my own route through the hedge maze until finally, we emerged from the maze.

A trio of armed women ran around the exterior corner, clearly drawn by the explosions. I took out two with a couple of quick shots but tripped on my torn skirt and missed the third with such a poor shot that not even my enhanced weapon could make up for my crappy aim.

Swelling to the size of a panther, Loki launched himself at the remaining impostor. He was on her in two bounds and closed his massive jaws around her neck, ripping out her throat before she could even scream. Blood sprayed *everywhere*, and only my distance from the mauling protected me from the crimson shower.

I flinched, taking a step back, my gut churning at the gruesome scene.

Loki padded back to me, his jaw dripping blood.

I stared at this giant version of him, unable to keep my horror from my voice. "That was incredibly disturbing to watch."

"Kill or be killed," Loki said, sitting in front of me. He licked a paw and began to clean his face. "Perhaps it is time to shed the dress," he suggested. "The disguise is worthless now, and your skirt is only getting in the way."

I watched him for a moment longer but seeing that he had a good point, I pulled an ever-sharp knife from my personal pocket of virtual space and quickly cut through the bodice of my dress. I let the ruined dress fall to the ground and stepped out of the ring of fabric.

Another pair of impostor women rounded the corner of the hedge maze, and I fired off a couple of quick shots, taking them out easily. I was definitely getting used to my role as a super soldier.

Maybe this wouldn't be so hard, after all.

[42]

"Are you ready?" I asked Loki, secretly hoping he would respond with, "I was born ready."

He didn't. He merely lowered his paw and prowled toward me.

I turned and ran in the opposite direction from the scattered dead bodies. The gig was up. They knew I was here, and they had to assume I was here to rescue the imprisoned players. We needed to get Colin and the others out now before the entity had a chance to call in all her reinforcements. If I was caught and incapacitated, there was a good chance that I would be trapped here . . . forever. I didn't think they would kill me, at least not until after I had been body snatched. But I would be as good as dead.

I dashed around the corner of the maze and followed the border hedge back toward the stable. Armed, deadly women closed in from all directions, and I slowed as the lawn gave way to the gravel surrounding the stable. Two steps onto the gravel, I stopped, the circle of enemies tightening around me, at least a dozen laser pistols raised and ready to fire on me.

The stable was ten, maybe fifteen yards away. A quick glance down told me Loki was gone, and I could only hope his absence meant I was close enough to the stable for him to deliver the rings to each and every one of the players within.

"Put down your weapon," one of the women ordered.

I did as she bade, setting my gun on the gravel and kicking it away when instructed to do so. "Looks like you win," I said, raising my hands into the air. A sly smile tugged at my lips, and I lowered my face to the ground to conceal it.

"On your knees," that same woman ordered.

Again, I did as I was told. All I had to do was buy Loki a little more time. I had the impression these women were waiting for someone—their leader, the entity, perhaps?

Not that it really mattered. As soon as Loki returned, I was out of here. And I was never, *ever* coming back.

Loki winked into existence in front of me. "It's done," he said, scanning my captors. "They've all made it out."

My heart swelled so big, I thought it might burst out of my chest. We had done it. We had saved them. It was over.

I made to slip my hand into the pocket of my skirt to retrieve my ring of instant death. And froze when my hand only touched air. My heart skipped a beat—or three.

I wasn't wearing my dress. I had left it in a discarded heap near the back side of the hedge maze, and with it, I had left the last ring of instant death. The ring was in the pocket of the dress, maybe a hundred yards away, but it might as well have been on the other side of the world for all the good it would do me now. My escape hatch was gone, my easy way out now a virtual impossibility.

Picking up on my distress, and likely the reason for it, Loki prowled around me, growing until he was as large as a horse, his razor-sharp claws as long as my forearms. He hissed and swiped at our encircling attackers, pushing them back. I had the impression that he was trying to give me the space I needed to make a break for it.

One of the women responded to Loki's antics by shooting him.

"No!" another yelled.

Loki yowled as the laser blast seared through his foreleg in a spray of silver gigi blood. And then he lunged at the woman who had wounded him, his jaws opening wide, and bit her head clean off.

A moment later, Loki spat out the woman's head as her body dropped to the ground. The rest of our attackers shrank back, giving us even more room.

"Hold your fire," the woman in charge barked. "Mother wants this one alive. She is to be *her* avatar."

Sensing my window of opportunity was closing, I dove for my pistol and, as my fingers closed around the handle, rolled onto my side. I didn't need to put on a ring to escape from the game. All I needed to do was to die.

I turned the gun on myself, aiming at my temple.

There was a loud *zap*, and searing pain exploded in my hand. I dropped the pistol and stared at my hand. It was a bloody mess of flesh and bone, so mangled it barely resembled a hand. It took a moment for my brain to register the full force of the pain. An avalanche of agony overwhelmed my awareness, and I curled into a ball on the ground, cradling my mangled hand against my middle.

There had to be something else in my inventory I could use to end this. To escape from this hell. But I couldn't hold on to the thought long enough to actually formulate a plan. The pain in my ruined hand was all-consuming.

Movement in the circle of hostile women surrounding me drew what little of my attention remained free. Another woman strode through the circle, laser pistol in hand as though she was the one who had fired the shot that had trapped me here. Her expression was imperious, and she wore authority like a favorite cloak.

It took my pain-addled brain a moment to recognize her. I was looking at Lady Catherine de Bourgh, the mistress of Rosings Park. And though Lady Catherine looked like just another of these strange, not-quite-human warrior women, there was not a single doubt in my mind that she was the one in charge. That she was *the entity*.

Lady Catherine stopped two steps in from the perimeter of the circle and tutted me, shaking her head.

Loki paced protectively in front of me, his tail lashing and only a slight limp to his step.

Lady Catherine's lip curled. "And so we meet again," she said, her voice as sharp as surgical steel. "It was unwise of you to release the others . . . but even less wise to return at all. Now that you are here, caught in my net, you must know you are never leaving."

I swallowed roughly, choking on the pain, and shifted my attention from Lady Catherine to my pacing gigi. "Loki? Can you get to my dress?"

"I cannot," he said, not taking his eyes off Lady Catherine. I didn't need him to tell me it was too far away. I had already known, but I figured it was worth a shot.

"Enough of this," Lady Catherine growled and shifted the aim of her pistol, firing on Loki. Three quick laser blasts.

Loki stumbled, and I shrieked, shock numbing my pain. He collapsed, struggling to regain his feet as he rapidly shrunk back down to his normal size.

Holding my ruined hand against my chest, I crawled closer to Loki. His breathing was rapid and shallow, and silver blood seeped from the three wounds puncturing his torso. I pulled him onto my lap, cradling his small, limp body.

Tears streamed down my cheeks as I held my dying gigi and glared at Lady Catherine and the small army of her followers closing in around us once more. This was it. Game over.

"Loki!" A man shouted. I recognized that voice. It was Colin's.

My head whipped around, and I searched for Colin in the gap between two of the warrior women.

Colin ran out from behind the corner of the hedge maze, heading straight for us. "Loki!" he repeated. "Catch!" He tossed something tiny and metallic into the air. My ring of instant death glinted in the sunlight.

I stared, my lips parted in astonishment.

Loki's weight vanished from my lap, and I looked down to see that he really was gone. He appeared mid-air in the direct path of the ring, a mere flash of midnight, gone again in a blink. My gigi reappeared on the gravel in front of me and immediately collapsed.

I scooped his little cat body onto my lap, curling around him protectively even as I peered through the space between the two impostors. I spotted Colin just in time to see him slip a ring onto his finger. His eyes rolled back in his skull, and his knees gave out. He dropped onto the grass, boneless.

He was dead. Gone. Free of this place. This nightmare.

And Loki wasn't moving. He wasn't even breathing. I didn't know if gigis could die a true, final death, but he was sure making a good show of it. Maybe if we could get out of this game, he would be okay, but I had the feeling that so long as I stayed here, he was as good as dead.

I had never felt so alone.

Lady Catherine took a step toward me, and my head snapped up. I scooted backward a foot or two, careful not to jostle Loki too much.

Something fell out of Loki's mouth. The ring of instant death. It landed on my calf before sliding to the gravel in front of me.

Without warning, Lady Catherine dove for the ring.

But I was closer and faster. I snatched the ring off the ground with my good hand and met Lady Catherine's rage-filled eyes as I slipped the ring onto my middle finger one-handed.

In a flash of white, the world disappeared.

[43]

The blinding white light that seemed inherent to all transitions within *Allworld Online* slowly faded, and once again, I found myself standing in the Jane Austen alcove in the Romance section of the Biblioverse.

I suppressed the urge to run for my life, strong as it was. Fiona and her team were watching me, and they would have seen the moment I escaped from *Pride and Prejudice*. The game would already be quarantined, completely cut off from the rest of the virtual world, not just "locked down" as it had been before. Meaning, Lady Catherine—or who- or *what*ever she really was—and her minions were trapped. Nobody would be leaving the game to chase me down, not this time.

I peered around the alcove, searching for Loki's black feline form, but the gigi was nowhere to be seen. Was it possible he had truly died? Surely gigis couldn't be killed permanently, at least, not outside of a programmer deleting their code. Gigis battled in-game alongside their players all the time. Their lives, however virtual, *had* to be as flexible and rebound-able as their players. But if that was the case, then where was Loki?

A nightmare smile appeared hovering above the back of the

alcove's lone armchair. Slowly, the rest of the black cat became visible, perched primly on the back of the armchair, and relief flooded me.

"That was unpleasant," Loki said, slow blinking at me. "Remind me to never do that again."

With a squeal of delight, I scooped up the cat and hugged him tight against my chest. Much to my surprise, Loki didn't struggle to get free. Rather, he gave in to the sudden outpouring of love and purred loudly.

After a long snuggle, I set him down on the seat of the armchair and grinned, hopped up on our victory. I was anxious to see Charlie, as well as Colin and the other players. I wanted to see with my own two eyes that they really were all right.

I glanced over my shoulder at the books arranged in the center of the fireplace mantel and noticed that *Pride and Prejudice* was gone. Good.

I looked down at Loki. "Let's get out of here."

[44]

I sat on the porch swing at my parents' house, Charlie at my side, belly full, and a mug of lavender chamomile tea warming my hands. The world beyond the porch was muted by the hushed stillness of dusk. The *real* world. Maybe the real world didn't have all the bells and whistles—or endless possibilities—of the virtual world, but it was good enough for me.

Though I did miss having Loki around. I couldn't help but wonder what he got up to in *Allworld Online* when I wasn't around. Maybe I would ask him the next time I logged in. *If* I ever logged in again.

A black sedan pulled over to the curb in front of the house, and Charlie and I exchanged a look.

"More reporters?" Charlie mused.

I frowned. "They're not supposed to come here."

They had already tracked me down here and been shooed away by the VCIA, and I had barely been home for half a day after the couple days spent in the hospital. My vitals and brain activity had been monitored extensively to gauge the lingering after-effects of having spent so much continuous time in *Allworld Online*. All signs pointed to me being A-OK. No expected long-term damage to my brain or body. No physical signs at all of what I'd been through.

In a way, it was anticlimactic. A scar on my cheek might have been nice. Something to remind me that I had been through hell and had survived. But all of my scars were on the inside, visible only to me. And I supposed they would be visible to Loki if I were ever brave enough to venture back into the virtual world.

The curbside back door on the sedan opened, and Colin stepped out.

I sat up a little straighter.

Charlie chuckled. "I'll just go in and see if Mom needs any help with the dishes . . ."

I barely heard my brother. My attention was glued to Colin as he walked up the path from the sidewalk to the porch. He was dressed much as he'd been the first time I met him—worn jeans, black T-shirt, black leather coat, scuffed leather boots. His facial hair had grown past the stubble phase and was in short beard territory, and his straight, chin-length dark hair was slightly mussed, as though he'd been running his fingers through it during the ride over.

He stopped at the bottom of the porch stairs and offered me a closed-mouth smile. "I hope it's okay," he said, "me coming here."

Voice caught in my throat, I nodded and chewed on my bottom lip. "Why *are* you here?" I finally managed to ask. He hadn't visited me in the hospital, though I had held out hope that he might show until the moment of my discharge. But now he was here.

Belatedly, my cheeks heated as I registered how my question sounded. "I don't mean you're not welcome," I added in a rush. "It's just that . . ." I shrugged, my gaze dropping to the floor-boards. "I expected to see you sooner. When you didn't show . .

." I glanced up at Colin, meeting his eyes for a fraction of a second.

He bowed his head in mute understanding. "Can I join you?"

Gaze still averted, I nodded to the empty place beside me on the porch swing. "Be my guest."

Out of the corner of my eye, I watched Colin climb the stairs. He crossed the porch and eased down on the swing, leaving a few inches between us. Leaning forward, he propped his elbows on his knees and stared out at the sedan idling at the curb in front of the house. That the car was still running meant he wasn't planning on staying long.

"I wanted to come see you at the hospital," he started, his voice rough. "I was on my way there when I was called back to the office." He sighed and sat back in the swing, his hands gripping his knees. "It escaped."

It took me a moment to catch his meaning. I looked at Colin, my brow furrowing. He didn't mean . . . couldn't mean . . .

"The entity," he said, confirming my worst fear. "It escaped from *Pride and Prejudice* before we could quarantine the game."

Liquid nitrogen suddenly flowed through my veins, and I gulped, attempting to swallow down the panic. I focused on the boards at my feet, on something *real*. I was safe here, in the real world. And yet, I could already feel my hands starting to tremble. "Where is she now?"

I couldn't call her an *it*, not when, to me, she was Lady Catherine de Bourgh. Oh, sure, I knew that wasn't her true identity, if she could even be said to have one. But she would always be Lady Catherine to me.

"We tracked the entity through several games before we lost track of it," he told me. "It seems to have camouflaged itself in code once more, and, well, we can't *see* it. Not like you can."

Sensing where this was going, I shook my head.

"We need—" Colin stopped himself and took a deep breath.

"We *would greatly appreciate* your help in tracking the entity down."

I swallowed roughly, attempting to clear my mouth of the paste that had once been my saliva, then cleared my throat and looked at Colin. "I can't." I looked away, ashamed by the tears welling in my eyes. Ashamed by my cowardice. "I can't do that again. I won't risk my life for a world that isn't even real."

Part of me wondered why they didn't just shut the whole thing down, but even I knew that *Allworld Online* had all but replaced the traditional internet. The World Wide Web was a thing of the past; the future was *Allworld Online*. Shutting it down might very well destroy the world economy. It would never happen.

Colin was quiet for a long moment. "The world might not be real, but the players in it are," he said quietly. "And what about Loki? Is he not real?"

My heart beat faster as my panic mounted at the thought of returning to the virtual world to hunt down Lady Catherine. I squeezed my eyes shut, and tears streamed down my cheeks. I wiped the tears away with a quick swipe of my hand.

"I just—" I opened my eyes and inhaled a shaky breath. "I can't go back in there." I forced myself to look at Colin, hoping that if he saw my fear, he would let it go. "I'm sorry," I whispered.

Colin clenched his jaw, broadcasting his disappointment loud and clear, but nodded as though he understood. "I have to get back," he said, standing. He started for the stairs, but paused, a hand on the post. He peered back at me over his shoulder. "Let me know if you change your mind," he said, reaching into his pocket. "You could save lives." He set a business card on the porch railing. "See you around, Olivia."

Heart lodged in my throat, I nodded once and watched Colin walk down the steps and back to the idling sedan. I waited until the car turned a corner and drove out of sight to stand and retrieve the business card from the railing.

There was no number or other contact information on the card, merely a gamertag. Which meant if I ever wanted to see Colin again, I would have to log back into *Allworld Online*.

[45]

I sat on the stool in front of the vanity in my childhood bedroom, brushing my hair and thinking back on Colin's visit from earlier in the evening. My eyes automatically sought out the business card sitting on the corner of the vanity. A braver person would have said yes. Would have helped. Would have seen him again, and maybe even saved some lives.

But I wasn't brave.

With a sigh, I set the brush down and raised my hands to braid my hair for bed. Motion caught my attention in the mirror, and I looked at the reflection of the bed behind me. A black cat perched on the foot of the mattress.

My parents didn't have a black cat.

I spun on the stool, my heart hammering in my chest. But the bed was empty. There was no black cat. Loki wasn't here. It was a phantom, a trick of the mind from spending so much time in the VR world.

Laughing under my breath, I combed out my incomplete braid and started over. When I was finished, I crawled into bed and situated my pillows just so. It certainly felt good to be laying down in my own bed. Groaning, I turned to the nightstand and stretched out my arm to turn off the lamp.

A black cat sat on the corner of the nightstand.

I froze, unable to blink. Unable to breathe.

The cat slow blinked at me, and then his mouth spread into a nightmare grin. "Hello, Olivia."

September 21, 2026

And now, the mysteries surrounding the video game beta-test-gone-wrong deepen. While the players that had been trapped in the *Pride and Prejudice* game world are all alive and recovering well after their extended stay in the virtual world, the man believed to be responsible for the debacle is not. William St. George, the former CPO of Rockville Softworks who had recently been arrested for the kidnapping of colleague Priya Burman, was found dead in his cell earlier this evening. An inside source reports that a hole appears to have been burned through his chest with a laser, damaging his heart and causing his death. The source of the supposed laser has yet to be identified, as prison surveillance equipment blacked out shortly before the time of death. We'll keep you updated as the story develops.

Thanks for reading! You've reached the end of *Allworld Online: Pride & Prejudice*, but not the end of Olivia's adventures. Join my newsletter for updates on the next installment in *Allworld Online,* coming in 2021, and to receive a FREE novella! Newsletter: https://www.authorlindseysparks.com/sacrifice

MORE BOOKS BY LINDSEY SPARKS

ECHO TRILOGY

Echo in Time

Resonance

Time Anomaly

Dissonance

Ricochet Through Time

KAT DUBOIS CHRONICLES

Ink Witch

Outcast

Underground

Soul Eater

Judgement

Afterlife

ATLANTIS LEGACY

Sacrifice of the Sinners

Legacy of the Lost

Fate of the Fallen

Dreams of the Damned

Song of the Soulless

Blood of the Broken

Rise of the Revenants

ALLWORLD ONLINE

AO: Pride & Prejudice

AO: The Wonderful Wizard of Oz

Vertigo

THE ENDING SERIES

The Ending Beginnings: Omnibus Edition

After The Ending

Into The Fire

Out Of The Ashes

Before The Dawn

World Before

THE ENDING LEGACY

World After

For more information on Lindsey and her books:

www.authorlindseysparks.com

Join Lindsey's mailing list to stay up to date on releases

AND to get a FREE copy of Sacrifice of the Sinners.

www.authorlindseysparks.com/sacrifice

To read Lindsey's books as she writes them, check her out on Patreon:

https://www.patreon.com/lindseysparks

Lindsey Sparks is a bestselling Science Fiction and Fantasy author who lives her life with one foot in a book—so long as that book transports her to a magical world or bends the rules of science. Her novels, from Post-apocalyptic to Time Travel Romance, always offer up a hearty dose of unreality,  along with plenty of history, mystery, adventure, and romance.

When she's not working on her next novel, Lindsey spends her time hanging out with her two little boys, working in her garden, or playing board games with her husband. She lives in the Pacific Northwest with her family and their small pack of cats and dogs.

www.authorlindseysparks.com
Facebook: www.facebook.com/authorlindseysparks
Facebook Reader Group: www.facebook.com/groups/lovelyreaders
Instagram: @authorlindseysparks
Pinterest: www.pinterest.com/authorlindseysparks
Newsletter: www.authorlindseysparks.com/join-newsletter
Patreon: www.patreon.com/lindseysparks